THE MAN FROM BROKEN HILLS

THE MAN FROM BROKEN HILLS

LOUIS L'AMOUR

LITERARY EXPRESS, INC.

THE MAN FROM THE BROKEN HILLS

A *Literary Express Inc., Book*
(a subsidiary of Doubleday Direct, Inc.)
Published in arrangement with
Bantam Books, Inc.
1540 Broadway
New York, NY 10036

PRINTING HISTORY

Bantam paperback edition / October 1975
Louis L'Amour Hardcover Collection / March 1998

If you want to purchase more of these titles, please write to:
The Louis L'Amour Collection
1540 Broadway
New York, NY 10036

ISBN 1-58165-010-8

Published simultaneously in the United States and Canada

PRINTED IN THE UNITED STATES OF AMERICA

To Art Jacobs,
with appreciation—

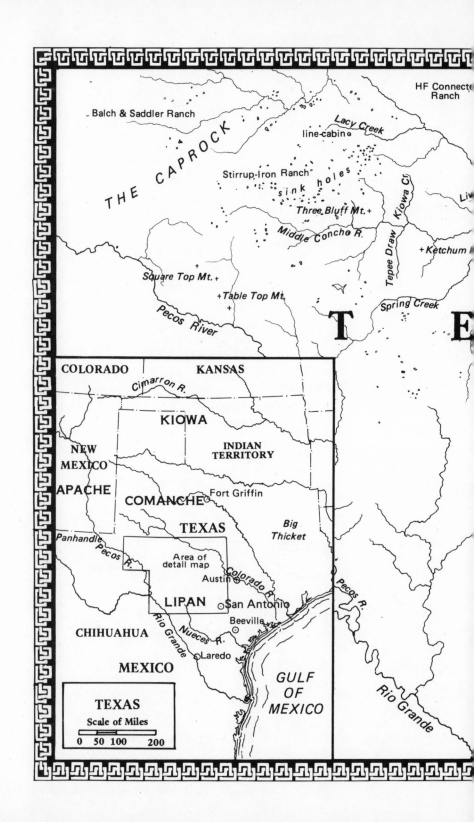

Balch & Saddler Ranch

THE CAPROCK

HF Connected Ranch

line-cabin

Lacy Creek

Stirrup-Iron Ranch

sink holes

Kiowa Cr.

Tepee Draw

Three Bluff Mt. +

+Ketchum

Li

Middle Concho R.

Square Top Mt. +

+Table Top Mt.

Spring Creek

Pecos River

T E

COLORADO   KANSAS

Cimarron R.

KIOWA

NEW
MEXICO

INDIAN
TERRITORY

APACHE

COMANCHE

Fort Griffin

TEXAS

Big
Thicket

Panhandle

Pecos R.

Area of
detail map

Colorado R.

Austin

Pecos R.

LIPAN

San Antonio

Beeville

CHIHUAHUA

Rio Grande

Nueces R.

Laredo

MEXICO

GULF
OF
MEXICO

Rio Grande

TEXAS

Scale of Miles

0   50 100   200

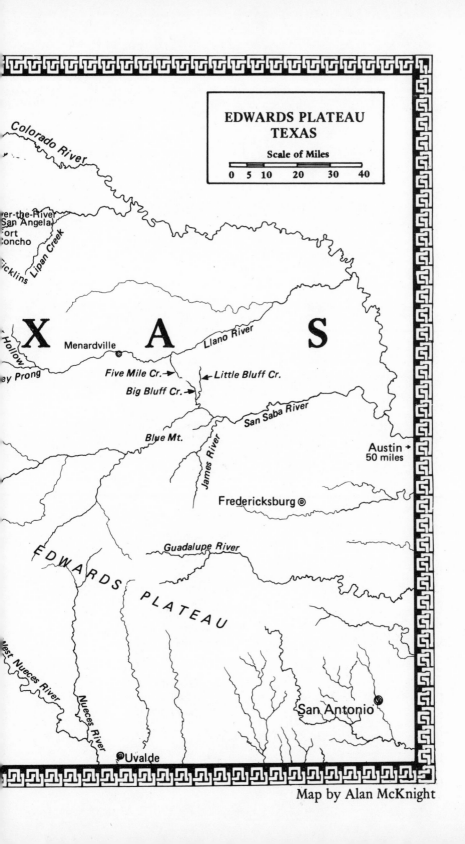

Map by Alan McKnight

ONE

I caught the drift of woodsmoke where the wind walked through the grass.

A welcome sign in wild country . . . or the beginning of trouble.

I was two days out of coffee and one day out of grub, with an empty canteen riding my saddle horn. And I was tired of talking to my horse and getting only a twitch of the ears for answer.

Skylining myself on the rimrock, I looked over the vast sweep of country below, rolling hills with a few dry watercourses and scattered patches of mesquite down one arroyo. In this country, mesquite was nearly always a sign that water was near, for only wild mustangs ate the beans, and if they weren't bothered they'd rarely get more than three miles from water. Mesquite mostly grew from horse droppings, so that green looked almighty good down there.

The smoke was there, pointing a ghost finger at the sky, so I rode the rim looking for a way down. It was forty or fifty feet of sheer rock, and then a steep slope of grass-grown talus, but such rims all had a break somewhere, and I found one used by run-off water and wild animals.

It was steep, but my mustang had run wild until four years old, and for such a horse this was Sunday School stuff. He slid down on his haunches and we reached bottom in our own cloud of dust.

There were three men around the fire, with the smell of coffee and bacon frying. It was a two-bit camp in mighty rough country,

1

with three saddle-broncs and a packhorse standing under a light-ning-struck cottonwood.

"Howdy," I said. "You boys receivin' visitors, or is this a closed meetin'?"

They were all looking me over, but one said, "You're here, mister. 'Light and set."

He was a long-jawed man with a handlebar mustache and a nose that had been in a disagreement. There was a lean, sallow youngster, and a stocky, strong-looking man with a shirt that showed the muscle beneath it.

The horses were good, solid-fleshed animals, all wearing a Spur brand. A pair of leather chaps lay over a rock near the fire, and a rifle nearby.

"Driftin'?" the stocky fellow asked.

"Huntin' a job. I was headed east, figurin' to latch onto the first cow outfit needin' a hand."

"We're Stirrup-Iron," the older one commented, "an' you might hit the boss. We're comin' up to roundup time and we've just bought the Spur outfit. He's liable to need hands who can work rough country."

Stepping down from the saddle I stripped off my rig. There was a trail of water in the creek, about enough to keep the rocks wet. My horse needed no invitation. He just walked over and pushed his nozzle into the deepest pool.

"Seen any cattle over west?" the handlebar mustache asked.

"Here an' there. Some Stirrup-Irons, HF Connected, Circle B... all pretty scattered up there on the cap-rock."

"I'm Hinge," the handlebar said, "Joe Hinge. That long-legged galoot with the straw-colored hair is Danny Rolf. Old Muscles here is Ben Roper.

"The boy there," he added, "is all right. Seein's he ain't dry behind the ears yet an' his feet don't track."

Rolf grinned. "Don't let him fool you, mister. That there ol' man's named Josiah... not Joe. He's one of them there pate-ree-archs right out of the Good Book."

I collected my horse and walked him back onto the grass and drove in the picket pin, my stomach growling over that smell of bacon. These were cowhands who dressed and looked like cow-hands, but I knew they were doing some wondering about me.

My rope was on my saddle and I was wearing fringed shotgun

chaps, a sun-faded blue shirt, army-style, and a flat-brimmed hat
that was almost new but for the bullet hole. I also wore a six-
shooter, just as they did, but mine was tied down.

"Name's Milo Talon," I said, but nobody so much as blinked.

"Set up," Hinge suggested, "we're eatin' light. Just a few biscuits
and the bacon."

"Dip it in the creek," I said, "and I'll eat a blanket."

"Start with his," Ben Roper gestured to Rolf. "He's got enough
wild life in it to provide you with meat."

"Huh! I—!"

"You got comp'ny," I said, "five men, rifles in their hands."

Roper stood up suddenly, and it seemed to me his jaws turned
a shade whiter. He rolled a match in his teeth and I saw the muscles
bulge in his jaws. He wiped his hands down the side of his pants
and let them hang. The kid was up, movin' to one side, and the
oldster just sat there, his fork in his left hand, watching them come.

"Balch an' Saddler," Hinge said quietly. "Our outfit an' them
don't get along. You better stand aside, Talon."

"I'm eatin' at your fire," I said, "and I'll just stay where I am."

They came on up, five very tough men, judging by their looks—
well-mounted and armed.

Hinge looked across the fire at them. "'Light an' set, Balch,"
he offered.

Balch ignored him. He was a big man, rawboned and strong
with a lantern jaw and high cheekbones. He looked straight at me.
"I don't know you."

"That's right," I said.

His face flushed. Here was a man with a short fuse and no
patience. "We don't like strange riders around here," he said flatly.

"I get acquainted real easy," I said.

"Don't waste your time. Just get out."

He was a mighty rough-mannered man. Saddler must be the
square-shouldered, round-faced man with the small eyes, and the
man beside him had a familiar look, like somebody I might have
seen before.

"I never waste time," I said. "I thought I'd try to rustle a job
at the Stirrup-Iron."

Balch stared at me, and for a moment there we locked eyes,
but he turned his away first and that made him mad. "You're a
damn fool if you do," he said.

"I've done a lot of damn fool things in my time," I told him, "but I don't have any corner on it."

He had started to turn his attention to Hinge, but his head swung back. "What's that mean?"

"Read it any way you like," I said, beginning not to like him.

He did not like that and he did not like me, but he was not sure of me, either. He was a tough man, a mean man, but no fool. "I'll make up my mind about that and when I do, you'll have my answer."

"Anytime," I said.

He turned away from me. "Hinge, you're too damn far west. You start back come daybreak and don't you stop this side of Alkali Crossing."

"We've got Stirrup-Iron cattle here," Hinge said. "We will be gathering them."

"Like hell! There's none of your cattle here! None at all!"

"I saw some Stirrup-Irons up on the cap-rock," I said.

Balch started to turn back on me, but Ben Roper broke in before he could speak. "He saw some HF Connected, too," Roper said, "and the major will want to know about them. He will want to know about all of them."

Balch reined his horse around. "Come daybreak, you get out of here. I'll have no Stirrup-Iron hand on my ranch."

"Does that go for the major, too?" Roper asked.

Balch's face flamed with anger and for a moment I thought he would turn back, but he just rode away and we watched them go, then sat down.

"You made an enemy," Hinge commented.

"I'm in company," I replied. "You boys were doing pretty well yourselves."

Hinge chuckled. "Ben, when you mentioned the major I thought he'd bust a gut."

"Who," I asked, "is the major?"

"Major Timberly. He was a Confederate cavalry officer in the late difficulty. Runs him some cattle over east of here and he takes no nonsense from anybody."

"He's a fair man," Hinge added, "a decent man ... and that worries me. Balch an' Saddler aren't decent, not by a damn sight."

"Saddler the fat one?"

"It looks like fat, but he's tough as rubber, and he's mean.

Balch is the voice and the muscle, Saddler is the brain and the meanness. They come in here about three, four years ago with a few head of mangy cattle. They bought a homestead off a man who didn't want to sell, and then they both homesteaded on patches of water some distance off.

"They've crowded the range with cattle, and they push... they push all the time. They crowd Stirrup-Iron riders and Stirrup-Iron cattle, and they crowded the cattle of some other outfits."

"Like Spur?" I suggested.

They all looked at me. "Like Spur... crowded him until he sold his brand to Stirrup-Iron and left the country."

"And the major?"

"They leave him alone. Or they have so far. If they crowd him, he'll crowd back... and hard. The major's hands don't scare like some of the others. He's got a half dozen of his old Confederate cavalrymen riding for him."

"What about Stirrup-Iron?"

Hinge glanced at Roper. "Well... so far it's been kind of a hands-off policy. We avoid trouble. Just the same, come roundup time we'll ride in there after our cattle, calves and all."

We ate up. The bacon was good and the coffee better. I ate four rolls dipped in bacon grease and felt pretty good after my fifth cup of coffee. I kept thinking about that third man. The others had been cowhands, but the third man... I knew him from somewhere.

Most of the last three years I'd been riding the outlaw trail. Not that I was an outlaw. It was just that I liked the backbone of the country, and most of the outfits I'd worked for since leaving the home ranch had been along the outlaw trail. I'd never crossed the law at any point and had no notion of it, but I suspect some of the outlaws thought I was a cattle detective, and more took me for some kind of a lone hand outlaw. It was simply that I had a liking for rough, wild country... the high-up and the far-out.

My brother Barnabas... named for the first of us ever to come across from England... he took to schooling and crossed the ocean to study in England and France. While he learned the words of Rousseau, Voltaire and Spinoza, I was cutting my educational teeth on the plains of the buffalo. While he courted the girls along the old Boul' Miche, I busted broncs on the Cimarron. He went his way and I mine, but we loved each other none the less.

Maybe there was a wildness in me, for I had a love for the

wind in the long grass blowing, or the smell of woodsmoke down some rocky draw. There was a reaching in me for the far plains, and from the first day that I could straddle a bronc it was in me to go off a-seeking.

Ma held me as long as she could, but when she saw what it was that was choking me up with silence she took down a Winchester from the gunrack and handed it to me. Then she taken a six-shooter, holster, belt and all, and she handed them to me.

"Ride, boy. I know it's in you to go. Ride as far as you've a mind to, shoot straight when you must, but lie to no man and let no man doubt your word.

"It is a poor man who has not honor, but before you do a deed, think how you will think back upon it when old age comes. Do nothing that will shame you."

She saw me to the door and when I started to saddle my old roan, she called after me. "No son of mine will go forth upon a horse so old as that. Take the dun... it's a wicked one he is, but he'll go until he drops. Take the dun, boy, and ride well.

"Come back when you're of a mind to, for I'll be here. Age can seam my face as it can the bark of an oak, but it can put no seams in my spirit. Go, boy, but remember you are a Sackett as well as a Talon. The blood may run hot, but it runs strong."

They were words I still remembered.

"We'll ride home in the morning," Hinge said. "We will talk to the major, too."

"Who's your boss? Who runs the Stirrup-Iron?"

Danny Rolf started to speak, but shut up at a look from Roper. It was Hinge who replied. "An old man," he said, "and a kid girl."

"She ain't no kid," Danny said. "She's older'n me."

"A girl-kid," Roper added, "and the old man is blind."

I swore.

"Yeah," Roper said, "you'd better think again, mister. You ain't in this like we are. You can ride on with a clear conscience."

"If a man can ever leave a pair like Balch and Saddler behind and still have a clear conscience. No," I said, "I ate of your salt, and I'll ride for the brand if they'll take me on."

"What's that mean?" Danny asked. "That about the salt?"

"Some folks think if you eat of somebody's bread and salt it leaves you in debt... or something like that," said Hinge.

"That's close enough," I said. "Are you boys quitting?"

There was no friendly look in their eyes. "Quittin'? Who said anything about quittin'?"

"Goin' against a tough outfit for a blind man and a girl," I said, "just doesn't make sense."

"We ain't about to quit," Roper said.

I grinned at them. "I'm glad I ate that salt," I said.

TWO

The ranch house on the Stirrup-Iron was a low-roofed house of cottonwood logs chinked with adobe, its roof of poles covered with sod where grass had sprouted and some flowers grew.

Nearby were three corrals of peeled poles, and a lean-to barn with an anvil at one end, as well as a forge for blacksmithing.

It was a common enough two-by-twice outfit with nothing special about it. Others of its kind could be found in many parts of Texas and other plains states. Only when we rode down the long, gradual slope toward the house did we see a man standing in the yard with a rifle in the hollow of his arm.

He must have agreed with what he saw, for he turned on his heel, seeming to speak toward the house. Then he walked back to the bunkhouse which lay across the hard-packed yard facing the shed.

A thin blonde girl stood on the steps, hair blowing in the wind, shading her eyes to see us.

Joe Hinge said, "Ma'am, I brought you a hand."

"He's welcome, and when you've washed, come up for supper."

She looked after me as we rode to the corral and stripped the gear from our horses.

"Who was that with the rifle?" I asked.

"You'll see," Danny cautioned, "but step light and talk easy. He's a neighbor."

"How many hands do you have?"

"We're them," he explained. "Harley comes over to help, sometimes. He's got him a rawhide outfit over east against the break of the hills."

The bunkhouse, also of logs, was long and narrow with bunks along the sides and a sheet-iron stove at the end. There was a pile of dusty wood near the stove with somebody's socks drying on it, and a fire-blackened coffeepot atop the stove.

Four of the bunks had rumpled bedding and four had no bedding at all, only cowhide for springs, lashed to each side of the bed frame with rawhide strings.

Coats and slickers hung on pegs along the wall, and there were a couple of benches and a table with one slightly short leg. A kerosene lamp stood on the table, and there was another in a bracket on the wall near the stove. There were two beat-up lanterns sitting along the wall.

The floor was scuffed and dusty, not looking like it had been swept in a while, but I'd grown up with Ma watching and knew that wouldn't last. Outside the door there was a washstand with a broken piece of mirror fastened to the log wall with nails, and a roller-towel that had been used forty or fifty hands too long.

Rinsing the basin I washed my hands and combed my hair, looking in the mirror at the man I was: a man with a lean, dark face and sideburns and a mustache. It was the first time I'd seen myself in anything but water for three or four months, but I didn't seem to have changed much. The scar where a bullet had cut my hide near a cheekbone was almost gone.

Danny came out and slicked back his hair with water. A cowlick stuck up near the crown of his head. "The grub's good," he said. "She's a mighty fine cook."

"She does the cooking?"

"Who else?"

I whipped the dust from my clothes with my hat, drew the crease a mite deeper and started toward the house, my eyes sweeping the hills around, picking out the possible places for anyone watching the place. They were few, as the hills were bare and lonely.

There was a picket fence around a small bare yard in front of the house and a few pitiful, straggly flowers. A stone-flagged walk led to the door, and the table inside was spread with a red and white checked cloth. And the dishes were kind of blue enamel and there was a chipped enamel coffeepot.

There was a fine looking beef stew steaming on the table, and an apple pie on the sideboard... dried apples, of course, but it looked good. There was also a pot of beans, some crab-apple jelly and slices of thick white bread looking fresh from the oven.

She was even thinner than I'd thought, and her eyes were bluer. "I am Barby Ann." She gestured to the head of the table. "And this is my father, Henry Rossiter."

He had the frame of a once-big man, and the hands and wrists of one who must have been powerful. Now he was grizzled and old, with a walrus mustache and white hair that was too long. There was no sight to his eyes now, but I'd have known him anywhere.

"Howdy," I said at the introduction, and his head came up. He looked down the table at me, his eyes a blank stare, yet with an intentness that made me uneasy.

"Who said that?" His voice was harsh. "Who spoke?"

"It's a new hand, Father. He just rode in with the boys."

"We had us some words with Balch and Saddler," Hinge explained. "He stood with us."

Oh, he knew, all right! He knew, but he was shrewd enough to ask no more questions... not of me, at least.

"We can use a hand. You ready for war, son?"

"I was born ready," I said, "but I ride peaceful unless crossed."

"You can ride out if you're of a mind to," Rossiter said, "and if you ride west or north you'll ride safe. You ride south or east in this country and your chances of getting through are mighty poor... mighty poor."

Hinge explained what had happened with Balch and Saddler in a slow, casual tone that made enough of it but no more, leaving nobody in doubt.

Barby Ann ate in silence. Twice she looked at me, worried-like, but that was all. Nobody talked much, as it was not the way of ranch folk to talk much at supper. Eating was a serious business and we held to it. Yet at my home there'd been talk. Pa had been a man given to speaking, an educated man with much to say, and all of us had the gift of gab. We talked, but amongst ourselves.

When we were down to coffee and had the pie behind our

belts, Rossiter turned his dead eyes toward Hinge. "There will be trouble?"

"Reckon so. I just figure he aims to keep us this side of the cap-rock, no matter whose cattle run up yonder. Unless we're ready to fight, we just ain't a-goin' to get 'em."

Rossiter turned his eyes in my direction, and he wasn't off-center one whit. "Did you see any Stirrup-Iron cattle?"

"I wasn't keeping count. I'd guess fifteen, maybe twenty head along where I rode. Probably twice that many Spur."

"There will be trouble then. How many hands does he have?"

Hinge was careful. He thought a minute, then shrugged. "No tellin'. He had eight, but I hear he's been hirin', and there was a man with him I'd never seen before."

The boys finished off and headed for the bunkhouse but Danny lingered, sort of waiting for me. I held on, then gave it up and stood.

"You," Rossiter said. "You set back down. You're a new hand and we'd better talk." He turned his head. "Good night, Danny."

"Good night," Danny said grudgingly, and went out.

Barby Ann went to the kitchen, and he said, "What did you say your name was?"

"You know what it is," I said.

"Are you hunting me?"

"No, I was just drifting."

"Seven years... seven years of blindness," Rossiter said. "Barby Ann sees for me. Her an' Hinge. He's a good man, Hinge is."

"I think so."

"I've got nothing. When we've made our gather and drive, there won't be much. Just what I owe the hands, and supplies for a new year... if we can round up what we have and get to the railhead with the herd."

He put his hand to the table, fumbling for his pipe and tobacco. Just when I was about to push it to him, his hand found it. He began loading his pipe.

"I never had anything. It all turned sour on me. This here is my last stand... something for Barby Ann, if I can keep it."

"She'd be better off in some good-sized town. There's nothing here for a girl."

"You think there is in them towns? You know an' I know what's in them towns, and her with nothin' put by. This here is all I got, an' it's little enough. You could take it all away from me right now, but you'd still have a fight on your hands."

"You borrowed trouble, Rossiter. I don't want your outfit. You cheated your friends and you've only got what you asked for."

"Ssh! Not so loud! Barby Ann don't know nothing about them days."

"I'll not tell her."

"Your ma? Is Em still alive?"

"Alive? Em will die when the mountains do. She runs the outfit since Pa died, and she runs it with a tight hand."

"She scared me. I'll admit to that. I was always afraid of your ma, and I wasn't alone. She put fear into many a man. There was steel in that woman...steel."

"There still is." I looked across the table at him. He was still a big old man, but only the shell remained. I remembered him as he was when I was a boy and this man had come to work on the Empty.

He had been big, brawny and too handsome, a good hand with a rope. And he knew stock. We had been short-handed and he did the work of two men. But the trouble was, he was doing the work of three, for at night he'd been slipping away from the ranch and moving cattle to a far corner of the range.

Pa had been laid up with a badly injured leg, and Ma was caring for him, and this big young man had been always willing to help, but all the while he was stealing us blind. Yet he had helped us through a bad time.

He left suddenly, without a word to anyone, and it had been two days before we knew he was gone and almost a week before we knew anything else was wrong. It was Ma who got suspicious. She took to scouting, and I was with her when we found the corral where he'd been holding the stock. By that time he had been gone nearly two weeks.

It was a box canyon with a stream running through it, and Henry, as we knew him then, had laid a fence of cottonwood rails across the opening.

There were indications there had been four men with Henry when he drove the cattle away. We knew the hoof tracks of Henry's horse, and they were all over the place. Ma sent me back to the house after Barnabas and one of our hands, as well as a pack horse.

"Tell your pa we're going after the cattle. It may take us a while."

When we got back, Ma was long gone down the trail, so we taken off after her. Them days, she mostly rode a mule, so her tracks were mighty easy to follow.

We found where the four extra men had camped, while waiting for Henry to tell them to come in and drive the herd. Judging by the tracks, they had five or six hundred head. It was a big steal, but on a place the size of ours—and us short-handed—it hadn't been so difficult. All he'd done was to move a few head over that way each time he rode out, and then gradually bunched them in the canyon.

On the third day we caught up with Ma, and on the fifth day we caught up with them. We'd no cattle to drive, so we'd come along fast. Ma was from Tennessee mountain stock, nigh to six feet tall and rawboned. She was all woman, and where she came from women were women. She could ride as well as any man and use a rifle better than most, and she'd no liking for a thief. Especially one who betrayed a trust like Henry had done.

She wasted no time. We came up on them and Ma never said aye, yes, or no, she just cut loose. She had left her Sharps .50 at home but she had a Spencer .56, a seven-shot repeater, and she let drive. Her first shot emptied a saddle.

Coming down off the hill, we stampeded the herd right into them.

Henry, he lit a shuck out of there. He knew Ma would noose a rope for him and he lit out of there like somebody had lit a brushfire under his tail.

The other two taken off up a canyon and, leaving a hand to gather the stock, we taken out after them. We run them up a box canyon and Ma, she throwed down on them with that Spencer and she told it to them.

"You can throw down those guns an' come out with your hands up, or you can die right there. An' I don't care a mite which it is. Also, you might's well know. I ain't missed a shot since I was close on five year old and I ain't about to start now."

Well, they'd seen that first shot. She was nigh three hundred yards off and in the saddle when she pulled down on that moving rider, and she'd cut his spine in two. They only had their six-shooters and there was Ma with her Spencer, and Barnabas an' me with our Winchesters.

Where they stood, there wasn't shelter for a newborn calf, whilst we were partly covered by the roll of the hill and some brush. They decided to take a chance on the law, so they dropped their guns.

We brought them out and hustled them to the nearest jail and then went to the judge. We were a hundred miles from home then, and nobody knew any of us.

"Cow thieves, eh?" The judge looked from Ma to me. "What do you think we should do with 'em?"

"Hang 'em," Ma said.

He stared at her, shocked. "Ma'am, there's been no trial."

"That's your business," Ma said quietly. "You try them. They were caught in the act with five hundred of my cattle."

"The law must take its course, ma'am," the judge said. "We will hold them for the next session of court. You will have to appear as a witness."

Ma stood up, and she towered above the judge, although he stood as tall as he was able. "I won't have time to ride back here to testify against a couple of cow thieves," she told him. "And the worst one is still runnin'."

She walked right down to the jail and to the marshal. "I want my prisoners."

"Your prisoners? Well, now, ma'am, you—"

"I brought them in, I'll take them back." She took up the keys from his desk and opened the cell doors while the marshal, having no experience to guide him, stood there jawing at her.

She rousted them out of their bunks and, when one started to pull on his boots, she said, "You won't need those," and she shoved him through the door.

"Now, ma'am! You can't do this!" the marshal was protesting. "The judge won't—"

"I'll handle this my own way. I'm the one who made the complaint. I am withdrawing it. I'm going to turn these men loose."

"Turn them loose? But you said yourself they were cow thieves!"

"They are just that, but I haven't the time to go traipsing across the country as a witness, riding a hundred miles back home, then a hundred miles up here and maybe three or four such trips while you bother about points of law. These are my prisoners and I can turn 'em loose if I want."

She herded them down to the horse corral in their long johns, where she picked out two rawboned nags with every bone showing. "How much for them?"

"Ma'am," the dealer shook his head, "I'd not lie to a lady. Those horses got no teeth to speak of, an' both of them are ready for the bone yard."

"I'll give you ten dollars apiece for them, just as they stand."

"Taken," he said quickly, "but I warned you, ma'am."

"You surely did," Ma agreed. Then she turned to the cow thieves, shivering in the chill air. "You boys git up on those horses...*git!*"

They caught mane-holts and climbed aboard. The backbones on those old crow-baits stood up like the tops of a rail fence.

She escorted them out of town to the edge of the Red Desert. We rode a mite further and then she pulled up. "You boys steal other folks' cows, but we ain't a-going to hang you...not this time. What we're goin' to do is give you a runnin' start.

"Now my boys an' me, we got rifles. We ain't goin' to start shootin' until you're three hundred yards off. So my advice is to dust out of here."

"Ma'am," the short one with the red face pleaded, "these horses ain't fit to ride! Let us have our pants, anyway! Or a saddle! These backbones could cut a man in two, an'—"

"Two hundred and fifty yards, boys. And if he talks any more, one hundred yards!"

They taken out.

Ma let them go a good four hundred yards before she fired a shot, and she aimed high. That old Spencer bellowed, and those two gents rode off into the Red Desert barefooted and in their underwear on those raw-backed horses, and I didn't envy them none a-tall.

That was Ma, all right. She was kindly, but firm.

THREE

We drove our cattle home, but Ma never forgave or forgot the man we knew as Henry. He had betrayed a trust, and to Ma that was the worst of sins. Now he was here, across the table from me, blind and only a shell of the fine-looking big man we remembered.

Without a doubt, his hired hands had no idea of the kind of man he had been and still might be. As cowhands they were typical. When they took a man's wages, they rode for the brand, for loyalty was the keynote of their lives. They would suffer, fight and die for their outfit at wages of thirty dollars a month... if they ever got them.

They did not know him, and could be forgiven their ignorance. I did know, so what was I going to do?

It was a question I did not consider. It was Balch who had made my decision for me, back there at our first meeting. For there was something about such a man, prepared to ride roughshod over everybody, that got my back up.

There was range enough for all, and no need to push the others off.

"I'll stick around, Rossiter," I said. "Hinge tells me you're going to round 'em up soon?"

"We are. There are only six ranches in the Basin, if you want to call it that, but we're going to round up our cattle, brand them, and drive to the railhead. If you want to stay, we can use you. We'll need all the hands we can get."

16

*   *   *

There was a checker game going in the bunkhouse when I walked in. There were not enough checkers, so Hinge was using bottle corks—of which there seemed to be an ample supply.

Hinge threw me a quick, probing glance when I came in, but offered no comment. Roper was studying the board and did not look up.

Danny was lying on his back in his bunk with a copy of a beatup magazine in his hands. "You stayin' on?" he asked.

"Looks like it," I said, and opened up my blanket roll and began fixing my bed on the cowhide springs.

Hinge made his move, then said, "You'll take orders from me then, and we'll leave the stock west of here until the last.

"We've got one more hand," he added. "He's away over east tonight, sleepin' in a line-shack." He glanced at me. "You got any objections to ridin' with a Mexican?"

"Hell, no. Not if he does his work. We had four, five of them on my last outfit. They were good hands... among the best."

"This man is good with stock, and a first-class man with a rope. He joined up a couple of weeks back, and his name is Fuentes."

Hinge moved a king, then said, "We start rounding up in the morning. Bring in everything you see. We'll make our big gather on the flat this side of the creek, so you'll just work the breaks and start them down this way.

"There's grub at the line-shack, and you and Fuentes can share the cooking. You'll be working eight to ten miles back in the rough country most of the time."

"How about horses?"

"Fuentes and Danny drove sixteen head up there when he went, and there's a few head of saddle stock running loose on the range."

Hinge paused. "That's wild country back in there, and you'll run into some old mossyhorn steers that haven't been bothered in years. You're likely to find some unworked stuff back there, too, but if you get into thick brush, let Fuentes handle it. He's a brush-popper from way back. Used to ride down in the big thicket country."

At daybreak the hands scattered, but I took my time packing.

Not until I had my blanket roll and gear on a packhorse and my own mount saddled did I go to the house for breakfast.

Henry Rossiter was not in sight, but there was movement in the kitchen. It was Barby Ann.

"You weren't in for breakfast, so I kept something hot."

"Thanks. I was getting my gear ready."

She put food on the table, then poured coffee. She filled two cups.

"You're going to the line-cabin?"

"Is there only one?"

"There were two. Somebody burned down the one that was west of here, burned it down only a few weeks ago."

She paused. "It's very wild. Fuentes killed a bear just a few weeks ago. He's seen several. This one was feeding on a dead calf."

"Probably killed by wolves. Bears don't kill stock as a rule, but they'll eat anything that's dead."

She had curtains in the windows and the house was painfully neat. There must have been at least three more rooms, although this seemed to be the largest.

"You met Mr. Balch?"

That 'mister' surprised me, but I nodded.

"He's got a fine big ranch, he and Mr. Saddler. He brought lumber in from the eastern part of the state to build the house. It has shutters and everything."

It seemed to me I detected a note of admiration, but I could not be sure. Women-folks set store by houses and such. Especially houses with fixings.

She should see our house up in Colorado, I thought. It was the biggest I'd ever seen, but Pa had been a builder by trade and he designed it himself—and did most of the work himself. With Ma helping.

"Roger says—"

"Roger?" I interrupted.

"Roger Balch. He's Mr. Balch's son. He says they are bringing in breeding stock from back east, and they will have the finest ranch anywhere around."

Her tone irritated me. Whose side was she on, anyway? "Maybe if you're so friendly you should tell him to leave your father's hands alone, and to let us gather our cattle where they happen to be."

"Roger says there's none of our cattle up there. His pa won't have anybody coming around his place. I've told father that, and I've told Joe, but they won't listen."

"Ma'am, it's none of my business yet, but from the way your Mr. Balch acted, I'd say your pa and Joe Hinge were in the right. Balch acted like a man who'd ride roughshod over everything or anybody."

"That isn't true! Roger says that will all change when he tells his father about—"

She stopped.

"About you and him? Don't count on it, ma'am. Don't count on it at all. I've known such men here and there, and your Mr. Balch doesn't shape up like anyone I'd want any dealings with. And if he has any plans for that son of his, they won't include you."

She went white, then red. I never saw a woman so angry. She stood up, and her eyes were even bigger when she was mad. And for a moment I thought she'd slap me.

"Ma'am, I meant nothing against you. I simply meant that Balch wouldn't want his son tying up with anybody he could ride over. If he wants somebody for his son, it will be somebody big enough to ride over him. The man respects nothing but money and power."

Riding away from there I figured I'd talked out of turn, and I'd been guilty of hasty judgment. Maybe I'd guessed wrong on Balch, but he seemed like he didn't care two whoops for anything, and had I not been there to more or less even things up he might have been a whole lot rougher.

I wondered if Hinge and the boys knew that Barby Ann was seeing Roger.

Somehow, I had an idea they knew nothing about it, nothing at all.

Riding over the country, I could see they'd had a dry year, but this was good graze, and they had some bottoms here and there where a man could cut hay.

Riding over country I was going to have to work, I took my time, topping out on every rise to get the lay of the land. I wanted to see how the drainage lay, and locate the likely spots for water. Fuentes would fill me in, but there was nothing like seeing the land itself. Terrain has a pattern and, once the pattern is familiar, finding one's way about is much easier.

As I went east, the hills grew steeper and more rugged. Turning in the saddle I could see the cap-rock far off against the sky. What lay behind me was what was loosely called the Basin, and far off I could see the tiny cluster of buildings that was Stirrup-Iron headquarters.

It was midafternoon before I sighted the line-shack. It lay cupped in a hand of hills with a patch of mesquite a few yards off and a pole corral near the cabin.

A rider's trail came down off the hill into the trail to the cabin—a trail that looked fresh. In the corral were a number of horses, yet not more than a half dozen, one of them still damp from the saddle.

The cabin was of logs that must have been carted some distance, for there were no trees around. They had been laid in place with the bark on, and now, years later, the bark was falling off. There was a washstand at the door and a clean white towel hanging from a peg.

Tying my horses to the corral bars, and with my Winchester in my right hand and my saddlebags and blanket roll in the left, I walked up to the cabin.

Nothing stirred. A faint thread of smoke pointed at the sky. I tapped on the door with the muzzle of my rifle, then pushed it open.

A lean Mexican with a sardonic expression was laying on his back on a bunk, with a six-shooter in his hand. "*Buenos días, amigo*... I hope," he said smiling.

I grinned at him. "I hope, too. I'm in no mood for a fight. Hinge sent me up to watch you work. He told me he had a no-account Mexican up here who wouldn't do any more work than he could help."

Fuentes smiled, rolling a thin cigar in his fine white teeth. "Of all he might say, that would not be it. I was sent to gather cattle. Occasionally, I gather them, and occasionally I lie down to contemplate where the cattle might be—as well as the sins of men. More often I just look for cattle to gather. I am trying to figure out," he swung his boots to the floor, "the number of miles to catch each cow. Then if I figure the wages they pay me, the expense of keeping horses for me to do the work, I should be able to figure out whether it is good business to catch cows."

He paused, brushing the ash from his cigar to the floor. "Moreover, some of these steers are *big*, very, very big, and very, very mean. So I lie down to contemplate how to get those steers out of the canyons."

"No problem," I said, "no problem at all. You send back to the ranch for one of those screw jacks. If they don't have one there, go to town. If you go to town you can always have a drink and talk to the señoritas.

"You get one of those screw jacks... You know, the kind they lift buildings with when they wish to move them? All right. You get one of those. Better yet, get several. You go back of the east rim of the country, and you stick them under the edge and you start turning. You turn and turn and turn, and when you get the country tilted high enough, the cattle will just tumble out of the canyons. And you wait here with a big net and you bag them as they fall out. It is very simple."

He picked up his gunbelt. "I am Tony Fuentes."

"And I am Milo Talon, once of Colorado, now of anywhere I hang my hat."

"I am of California."

"Heard of it. Ain't that the land they stacked up to keep the ocean from comin' in over the desert?"

Fuentes pointed toward the coals of a dying fire, and the blackened pot. "There are beans. There are also a couple of sage hens under the coals, and they should be ready to eat. Can you make coffee?"

"I'll give it a try."

Fuentes stood up. He was about five-ten and had the easy movement of a bullwhip. "Did they tell you anything down there? About Balch?"

"Met him... along with Hinge and some others. I didn't take to him."

We ate, and he filled me in on the country. The water was mostly alkali or verging on it. The country looked flat, but was ripped open by deep canyons in unexpected places. Some of these canyons had grassy meadows, some thickets of mesquite. There was also a lot of rough, rocky, broken country.

"There are cattle back in those canyons that are ten years old and never been branded. There's even a few buffalo."

"About Balch," I said.

"A bad one...and some other bad ones with him."

"I'm listening."

"Jory Benton, Klaus, Ingerman and Knuckle Vansen. They get forty a month. His regular hands get thirty, and Balch has passed the word that any of his hands who prove themselves will also get forty."

"Prove themselves?"

Fuentes shrugged. "Rough stuff against anybody who gets in the way...like us."

"And the major?"

"Not yet. Saddler doesn't think they are strong enough. Besides, there are other considerations. At least, that is what I think, but I am only a Mexican who rides a horse."

"Come daylight you can show me. Want to tackle some of the big stuff?"

"Why not?"

The mosquitos were getting bad so we moved indoors. Besides, it was cooling off. At the door I turned to look around.

It was a nice little hollow, undistinguished but nice. The sun was setting behind us, leaving a faint brushing of pink along the clouds. Somewhere an owl hooted.

The cabin floor was hard-packed but it had been swept. The fireplace was obviously little used. It too was neatly swept, with a fire laid. No doubt it was pleasant to cook outside.

"Balch has a son? Roger, I think his name is?"

Fuentes's features became bland. "I think so. I see him here and there."

"Big man?"

"No...not big. Small. But very strong, very quick...and how do you say it? Cruel."

Fuentes sat silent, considering the subject. "He is very good with his hands. Very good. He likes to punish. The first time I see him is in Fort Griffin. He has beaten a woman there, a woman of the dance halls. He has beaten her badly, and her man comes after Balch...a big man, ver' strong.

"Roger Balch moves in very fast. He bobs his head to get in close and then he hits short and hard to the belly. He beats that big man, but finally they pull him off, and in Fort Griffin they do not stop a fight for nothing. It was bad, señor, bad."

Fuentes took out another of the cigars and lighted it. He waved the match out with a gesture. "You have reason for asking, amigo? Some particular reason?"

"Oh... not exactly. Heard some mention of him."

Fuentes drew on his cigar. "He rides... wherever he will. Rides very much. And he seeks trouble. I think he tries to show himself better than anyone else. He likes to fight big men, to beat them."

It was something to remember. Balch bobbed his head, threw short punches from in close. Probably he had done some boxing, learned how to fight big men, and that would give him an advantage. For most men knew only about fighting what they had learned by applying it. So a man who knew something of boxing would have little trouble.

It was a thing to remember.

FOUR

We rode into the broken hills before the sun rose, across thin, scant pasture drawn tight over cracked white rock. It was high country with no edge but the sky until we rode into the canyons, but here and there were bones, bleached by wind and sun, grass growing through the rib cages where once had been beating hearts. Among other bones, some burned-out wagons.

"Some pioneer," I said, "played out his string."

Rusted rims of wagon wheels, the solid oak of a hub, scattered bolts and charred wood. It was not much for a man to leave behind.

Fuentes indicated the bones. "You and me, amigo. . .sometime."

"I'm like the Irishman, Fuentes. If I knew where I was going to die, I'd never go near the place."

"To die is nothing. One is here, one is no longer here. It is only that at the end one must be able to say 'I was a man.'"

We rode on. "To live with honor, amigo. That is what matters. I am a vaquero. They expect little of me, but I expect much of myself.

"What is it a man wants? A few meals when he is hungry and, at least once in his lifetime, a woman who loves him. And, of course, some good horses to ride."

"You have forgotten two things: a rope that does not break, and a gun that does not hang when one starts to draw."

He chuckled. "You ask too much, amigo. With such a rope and such a gun a man might live forever!"

24

We began to see cattle. I swung out toward four or five that were feeding nearby and started them drifting. They would not go far, but they would move easier when we came back with more cattle. Ours was to be a slow job and a dusty one, to roust out these cattle and start them toward the flat country.

This was rough, broken country, and the mesquite thickets were mixed with prickly pear, some of the largest I'd ever seen. I wished for a leather jacket, or one of heavy canvas. Fuentes had a tight buckskin jacket that was some help to him. We plunged into the brush, rousting out the cattle. Some of the old mossyhorn steers were as quiet as cougars in the thick brush, moving like ghosts.

When we got them out of the brush, they'd circle and make a dash to get back. We both rode good cutting horses, but they had to work. We kept the cattle moving.

Sweat trickled down my back and chest, under my shirt, and my skin itched from the dust. When we paused there were the black flies. I'd worked cattle all my life, but this was some of the roughest.

Often the draws were empty. We would follow them to where they ended and find nothing. In others there were little gatherings of cattle, four or five, sometimes more. By noon we had started fifty or sixty head down toward the flat with only a little young stuff.

The sun was past the midmark when Fuentes topped out on a rise and waved his sombrero at me. It was a magnificent hat, that one. I envied the Mexicans their sombreros.

When I joined him, he said, pointing with his hat, "There is a spring down there, and some shade."

We walked our horses along the slope and into a pocket of hills. Two huge old cottonwoods grew there, and some willows. Further downstream there was much mesquite.

It was a mere trickle of water from the rocks, and a small pool where the horses could drink. A stream that ran a mere seventy yards before vanishing into the ground.

We stepped down and loosened the girths a little, and let the horses drink. Then we drank, ourselves. Surprisingly, the water was cold and sweet, and not brackish like most of the springs and water holes.

Fuentes lay down on the grassy slope in the shade, his hat over his eyes. After a few minutes, he sat up suddenly and lit the stub of one of his cigars. "You see something, amigo?"

"There isn't much young stuff, if that is what you mean."

"It is what I mean. There should be calves. There should be yearlings. We've seen nothing under two years old, almost nothing under three."

"Maybe," I said, too seriously, "these cattle go over to Balch and Saddler to drop their calves. Or maybe these cows just don't have calves."

"It is a thing," Fuentes agreed. He looked at the glowing end of his cigar. "I will be unhappy, señor, if we find that Balch's cows have twins."

Fuentes went to the spring for another drink. It was very hot, even there in the shade. "Amigo, I am suddenly hungry. I am hungry for beef. There's a nice fat steer that carries a Balch and Saddler brand. Now if we—"

"No."

"No?"

"It might be just what they want, Tony, so they could say we were rustling their beef. You mark that steer in your mind—and all the steers with doubtful brands."

"And then?"

"At the roundup. We'll peel a hide at the roundup. Right in front of witnesses. We'll be sure there are witnesses, sort of accidental-like on purpose, so when we take that hide off we'll have a lot of people watching."

Fuentes stared at me. "You would skin that steer right in front of Balch? You'd do that?"

"You or me . . . one to skin, one to watch so nobody stops him."

"He will kill you, amigo. He is good with a gun, this Balch. I know him. He has men who are good with guns, but none so good as him. They do not know this, but I know it. He will not shoot unless he must. He will let others do his shooting, but if he must—"

"He'll either shoot or ride," I said quietly, "because once we peel a hide wearing his brand, and they see it has been worked over, he'll either leave or have his neck stretched."

"He is a hard man, amigo. He does not believe anybody would dare, nor will he let them dare."

I got to my feet and put on my hat. "I'm a mighty narrow-minded man. These folks hired me to ride in their roundup. They hired me to round up their cattle...all their cattle."

We split up again, and each went into the canyons. We saw nobody, nor did we see tracks except those of cattle. Twice we came upon buffalo—once a group of five, the other time a lone bull. He was in no mood to be disturbed so I circled and went my way, leaving him pawing the earth and rumbling in his huge chest.

Once I put a loop over the horns of a big steer who promptly charged. My horse was quick, but tired, and just barely dodged the charge. And then we raced for a tree with the steer after us, and we did a flat-out turn around the tree and I snubbed him tight.

He snorted and blew, tugged and crashed one horn against the tree, but it was sturdy and held its place. Wild-eyed, he peered up at me, undoubtedly thinking of all he would do if he got free. I walked my horse into the shade and wondered why we had come so far without additional horses, when Fuentes came through the brush riding a short coupled bay, with black mane and tail and leading a roan.

"Meant to get the horses before nooning," he said. "I got to worrying about those brands."

We moved into the slight shade of some mesquite clumps and I switched my saddle. "I'll take your horse back." He pointed. "There's a corral...an old one...over there."

"Water?"

"Sí...good water. It is an old place. A Comanchero place, I think."

He glanced at the steer. "Ah? So you have the old devil? Three times I have chased that one!"

"I wish you'd caught him. He nearly got me."

Fuentes chuckled. "Remember the bones, amigo! Nobody lives forever!"

I stared after him as he rode away, leading my horse. "Nobody lives forever," he said, "and nobody does...but I want to!"

The horse was a good one, and he put in a hard afternoon. By the time Fuentes came along, he was played out.

Now he was leading a big old ox, heavy-muscled and slow. "Amigo, this is Ben Franklin Ox. He is old and slow, but very wise. We will tie him together with your wild one, then we will see what happens!"

A good neck-ox—which Ben Franklin Ox certainly was—could be worth his weight in gold to an outfit with wild steers to bring out of the brush, and Ben Franklin knew his job. We tied them together and left them to work it out. Of course, unless the wild one died, Ben would bring him in a few days from now, right to the home corral at the ranch. If the steer died, we'd have to track them down and release Ben.

We fell into bed that night too worn-out to talk, almost too tired to eat. Yet at daybreak, I was outside washing in ice-cold water when Fuentes came out, rubbing his eyes.

"How many head, do you think?"

"Hundred... more probably, along with what we've got on the trail."

"Let's take them in."

He got no argument from me. Fuentes was a good enough cook, better than me, but the food Barby Ann put out was better. We'd ride in, deliver our stock, catch a fast meal and start back.

"The old corral?" He squatted on his heels and drew a map in the dust. "It is here? You see? I will cook something, you take our horses and bring back mounts for us. Better bring our own horses, too, so we can leave them at the ranch."

Saddling up, I lit out, leading his horse. It was only a few miles, and I did not relish leaving the dun out there so far from home. Ma gave me that dun, and it was a fine horse who understood my ways.

The way he had shown was closer than the way we had gone while rounding up steers, so it was no more than a half hour before I topped out on a rise in thick brush and glimpsed the corral not more than half a mile off. Suddenly, I pulled up, standing in my stirrups.

It looked to me like somebody...

No, I must be mistaken. Nobody would be at the corral. After all...

Yet I rode cautiously, and came down into the clearing smelling dust... My own? Or had somebody been there? The horses had their heads up, looking over the corral bars toward the east, where the old trail led off toward the once-distant settlements. I thought I had seen somebody, but had I? Was it just a trick of the eyes? Of the imagination?

Slipping the thong from my pistol, I walked on up to the corral and glanced toward the old cabin. Keeping a horse between me and it, I stripped my gear, roped a fresh horse and then called the dun to me.

As I worked, my eyes swept the ground. Tracks...fresh tracks. A shod horse, and well-shod at that.

Saddling the fresh horse, an almost white buckskin with black mane and tail and four black legs, I listened and looked, without seeming to.

Nothing.

Turning my horse into the corral, I checked the trough through which the spring had been guided to be sure there was water.

There was...but there was something else, too. There were a couple of green threads caught in the slivers at the edge of the trough—the sort of thing that might happen if a man bent over to drink from the pipe and his neckerchief caught on the slivers.

I took them in my hand, then tucked them away in my shirt pocket.

Somebody had been at the corral. Somebody had drunk here, but why had they not come by the line-shack? In cattle country, even an enemy would be welcomed at mealtime, and many a cattleman in sheep country had eaten at sheep wagons. In a country where meals and food might be many miles apart, enmity often vanished at the side of the table.

Balch had not hesitated to come to our fire, nor would his men be likely to. Yet somebody had come here and had ridden swiftly away, somebody who had deliberately avoided our line-shack, which everybody in the country was sure to know.

Leading my horse and that of Fuentes, as well as a fresh horse for him, I started back.

Fuentes had suggested that Roger Balch was a trouble hunter, so it was unlikely that he would hesitate to stop by. Nor Balch, either, for that matter.

Saddler? I had an idea Saddler spent little time out on the range. What of that other man? The one who seemed somehow familiar?

Irritably, I rode back. There was a lot going on that I did not like. One thing I had done before leaving the corral, and that was to look to see how the tracks had pointed, and they had gone east, a man riding a horse with a nice, even stride...a horse more carefully shod than many a western horse I'd seen.

"Balch leaves the major alone?" I asked suddenly.

Fuentes glanced at me. "Of course. You do not think—" He broke off and then he said, "Balch may have other ideas. You see, the major has a daughter."

"A daughter?" The thought made no connection and Fuentes saw it, smiling tolerantly.

"The major has a daughter, and the largest outfit anywhere around. And Balch has a son."

"Then—?"

"Of course... And why not?"

Why not, indeed. But where did that leave Barby Ann?

FIVE

As we moved back what cattle we had, our work was cut out for us. Most of the stock had kind of settled down, but there were two or three hardheaded old mossyhorns who would keep cutting back and trying to head for the breaks, and the worst of all was a lean old cow with one horn growing across, in front of her skull, and one perfectly set for hooking, and she knew it.

We'd had unusually good luck. Time and again I've combed the breaks for cattle on one outfit or another and come up with nothing, or only a few head. Of course, this was the beginning, and it would get tougher as we went along, and the cattle more wary.

Right now, most of them hadn't decided what was happening. Hopefully, by the time they did they'd be at the ranch and mixing with the growing herd on the flat.

It was sundown before we got in. Danny and Ben Roper were down on the flat with about sixty head. I scanned their gather and then looked over at Fuentes, who had cut in close to me. "Same thing here," I commented. "No young stuff."

Joe Hinge was in front of the bunkhouse with a man I hadn't seen before, a lean, hungry-looking man with no six-shooter in sight but a rifle in his hand. He had careful blue eyes and an easy way about him.

"Talon, this here's Bert Harley. He's a neighbor of ours, helps out once in a while."

"Pleased," he said, bobbing his head a little. Seemed to me

31

there was a kind of a stop in his eye movement when Hinge said my name, but it could have been imagination.

"He'll help with the night herding. And we'll need all the help we can get."

Harley strolled over to the corral and flipped out a loop to catch up a horse. I poured water into the tin basin and rolled up my sleeves.

"Looked that bunch over?" I said to Hinge.

"You mean the size of it? You an' Tony must've worked your tails off."

"Look at 'em."

"I got to see the Old Man. What is it, Milo? What's wrong?"

"No young stuff."

Hinge had taken a couple of steps toward the house. Now he turned back. His eyes were haunted as he looked toward the cattle.

"Talon, we just got to find them. Those folks need ever' cent they can get. That girl... Barby Ann... she'll have nothing when the old man dies. Not unless we can make it for her. You know what that means? A girl like her? Alone and with nothing?"

"It's no accident," I told him, washing my hands. I splashed water on my face and looked hopefully at the roller towel. I was in luck... this one hadn't been up more than two days and I found a clean spot. "I've worked a lot of country and never seen so few calves. Somebody's been doing a mighty sly job of rustling."

"Balch!" Hinge's face tightened with anger. "That—!"

"Take another look at it," I said. "We've got no evidence. You brace Balch with something like that and you'll be shootin' the next minute. I'll admit he's an unpleasant sort of character, but we don't know nothing."

I paused. "Joe, do you know of anybody who might have been over our way today? A man on a nice-moving, easy-stepping horse with a long, even stride... almost new shoes."

He frowned, thinking. "None of our boys were over that way, and the only horses I know of that move like that belong to the major.

"You see somebody?" He looked at me. "It might have been the major's girl. She rides all over the country. You're liable to run into her anywhere. That girl doesn't care where she is as long as she's in the saddle."

"Be careful what you say about Balch," I warned. "I don't think Barby Ann would like it."

"What?" He had started off again. "What's that?"

"She's been talking to Roger. I think she's sweet on him."

"Oh, my God!" Hinge spat. "Of all the damn fool—!" He turned on me again. "That's nonsense! She wouldn't even—"

"She told me herself. She's serious about him, and she thinks he is."

He swore. Slowly, violently, impressively. His voice was low, bitter and exasperated.

"He's bad," Hinge said slowly, "a really bad man. His pa is rough, hard as nails, and he'll ride roughshod over everybody, but that son of his... he does it out of sheer meanness."

He walked on up to the house and I stood there. Maybe I should have kept my mouth shut, but that girl was walking into serious trouble. If Roger was thinking of the major's daughter...

But what did I know? And the one thing I did know was that there was no figuring out what went on in a woman's mind. Or a man's either, for that matter. I could handle horses, cattle, and men with guns, but when it came to human emotions I was a poor excuse for a prophet.

A girl like her, growing up in a place like this, would meet few men, and fewer still that would cause her to start dreaming. Roger Balch, whom I'd not met, was obviously young, not too far from her own age, and he was a rancher's son... Class had more to do with such things than most folks wanted to admit.

Fuentes and me, figuring to start back as soon as we could, were first at the table. First, that is, except for Harley. He was going to be riding night-herd on the stuff we had gathered in, so he was eating early.

"You boys made you a good day of it," Harley said when we sat down. "That's a mighty lonely country over there... or so I hear."

"You haven't been over there?"

"Off the track for me. My place is south of here. When a man's batching it, and workin' his own place, he doesn't have much time to get around."

"You runnin' cows?"

"A few scrubs. I'll get me some good stock someday. Takes a man a while to get started."

He wasn't joking about that. I had seen a number of men start from nothing and build ranches, and it was anything but easy. If a man had good water, and if there was plenty of open range, he had a chance. I'd seen many of them start, and a few who lasted.

"If I was going to try it," I commented, "I'd try Wyoming or Colorado. The winters are hard but there's good grass and plenty of water. That is, in the mountain country."

"Heard of it," Harley admitted, "but this here's where I'll stay. I like a wide open country where I can see for miles... But a man does what he can."

"Had a friend who favored Utah," Ben Roper commented. "There's country there no white man has ever seen. Or so he told me."

"Them Blues," Harley began, then cut himself off short, "them Mormons... I hear they're a folk likes to keep among their own kind."

"Good folks," I said. "I've traveled among 'em, and if you mind your ways you'll have no trouble."

We talked idly, and ate. Barby Ann was a good cook, and Roger Balch was missing a bet if that was what he wanted. I had an idea his father was thinking about an alliance. The major was the one man who made Balch and Saddler hold their fire, but if they could marry him into the family...

Harley rode off to begin his night watch on the cattle, and we finished our supper, taking our time. We'd decided to start back that night, and not wait for morning.

Joe Hinge hadn't a word to say, all through supper, but when it was over he followed me outside. "Ben tells me you're a gunfighter."

"I've ridden shotgun a few times, but I wouldn't call myself a gunfighter."

"Balch has some tough men working for him."

I shrugged. "I'm a cowhand, Joe, just a cowhand. I'm a drifter who's just passin' through. I'm not hunting any kind of trouble."

"I could use a man who was good with a gun and didn't mind usin' it."

"I'm not your man. I'll fight if I'm pushed, but a man would have to push pretty hard."

We stood there in the dark. "You an' Fuentes gettin' along?"

"He's a first-class hand," I said, "and a better cook than me. Why shouldn't I like him?" I paused, then asked, "Harley stayin' here or his place?"

"Back an' forth. He's got stock to take care of. Lives away back in the breaks of the hills. I don't wonder he likes to work around... Lonely place."

"You've been there?"

"No, but Danny was once. He rode over there after Harley one time. Had himself a time locatin' him. But that's Danny. He's a fair hand but he couldn't find a church steeple in a cornfield."

It was moonlight when we started back, loaded up with grub for a good long stay. Fuentes was an easy-riding man, and working with him was as I liked it, no strain.

And for the next four days we worked ourselves to a frazzle and had little to show for it. Where there had been cattle a few days ago, now there were none. Fuentes was a brush-popper who knew his business, and riding the brush was both an art and a science. None of your big, wide loops would work here. You saw a steer, and then you didn't. If you got him in the open at all, it was in a clearing your horse could cross in three or four jumps. And if you got a rope on him, you had to send it in like a bullet, and just wide enough to take him. In among the ironwoods, prickly pear and mesquite, you had no chance to build a loop... it was like casting for fish, only your fish weighed from a thousand to fifteen hundred pounds—and some of them would run heavier.

Fuentes could do it. And he had done it, and carried the scars of a lifetime in the brush. It was a business that left scars. You wore heavy leather chaps, a canvas or leather jacket and you had tapaderos on your stirrups so a branch wouldn't run through your stirrup and dump you or stab your horse.

We worked hard, and in four days we rounded up just nine head, and it didn't make sense.

"There's tracks, Tony," I said, "lots of tracks. It doesn't figure."

We were eating.

He put his fork down, staring out the door, thinking. "There is one I am thinking of," he said, "a little red heifer. Maybe two years old, very pretty, but very wise for one so young. Every day I saw her, every day she eluded me, every day she was back, but since we have come back, I do not see her."

"Maybe she found herself somebody else to chase her," I said, amused. "They all do sooner or later."

He took up his fork again. "I think maybe you have said something, amigo. I think tomorrow we will not hunt cows."

"No?"

"We will hunt... maybe a little red heifer. Maybe we find her... maybe we find something else. I think we will take our rifles."

We went out at daybreak, and I rode the bay with the black mane and tail. It was a cool, pleasant morning, and we ate a quick breakfast. Fuentes led the way toward our hidden spring, and as he neared it he began casting back and forth, suddenly to draw rein and point: "See? Her track. Two days... maybe three days old."

She had drunk at the pool below the spring, and then had moved off, browsing, as cattle will, along with several others. We followed them out of the hollow and up on the high country beyond, yet it was almost noon before there was a change.

"Amigo? Look!"

I had seen it. Suddenly the wandering ceased and the little red heifer took on direction. She was going straight along now, hurrying occasionally, and she was with several others whose browsing had been interrupted. The reason was immediately obvious:

The track of a horse!

Now more cattle, brought in from the north, more cattle being driven east toward the hills. Another rider.

"If they see us," I suggested, "they will see we follow a trail. Let us spread out, as if searching for strays, but let us keep within sight of one another."

"*Bueno*, amigo." He cut off from me, occasionally standing in his stirrups as if looking. But we kept on, first one and then another cutting the trail of the small herd... at least thirty head now... perhaps more.

It was no wonder we had found no cattle. Somebody was deliberately driving them away from us.

Occasionally they let the cattle drift while they rounded up more, until at the end of what was obviously several days' work they had made a gather of at least a hundred head.

"They drive them far," Fuentes said, "but I am puzzled. If they wish to steal them, why not drive south, no?"

A thought came to me. "Maybe they do not plan to steal them, Fuentes. Maybe they just hope to keep us from sellin' them. If we don't get them to the roundup, they won't be sold."

"And if they are not?"

"Then Rossiter won't have as much money as he may need. Maybe then he will lose the ranch, and maybe then somebody will buy it who knows there are more cattle than Rossiter thinks he has."

"It is a thought, amigo, a very likely thought, and it is another way of stealing, no? Señor Rossiter believes he has few cattle left, he is in trouble, he sells for little, when there are truly many cattle."

"There's one thing wrong, I think. Aside from your little red heifer, I didn't see the tracks of much young stuff. These are steers, some cows... their hoofs are a little sharper... but very few young ones."

We made dry camp in the hollow atop a ridge, a sheltered hollow that allowed us to have a fire after the darkness came, by using buffalo chips for fuel. It was a high ridge, with a good view, and after we had eaten we left the coffeepot on the coals and went out on the ridge to look over the country. Above was a vast field of stars, but we scarcely saw them. We looked for another kind of light... a fire.

"You know this country best," I said. "Where do the ranches lie from here?"

He thought about that for an instant. "We are too far east, amigo. This is wild country where no man rides, only the Comanches or the Kiowa sometimes, and for them we must be wary.

"Back there lies the major's place... It is the closest. Away to the horizon yonder is where Balch and Saddler are."

"And Harley?"

"He has no ranch, amigo, only a homestead, I think, a very small place. He is there." He pointed at a place nearer, yet still some distance off.

"Tony?" I pointed. "Look there!"

It was—and not more than a mile away—a fire. A campfire in wild country!

SIX

This country was wild and lonely, and there was reason for it. East of us, the ranches were pushing west from Austin and San Antonio; and west of us, a few venturesome ranchers were trying to settle in the Panhandle country. But this area where we were was a hunting ground and traveling route of the Kiowas and the Comanches who raided into Mexico.

It was Apache country, too, mostly Lipans, I believed, but I was no expert on this area of Texas. Most of what I knew was campfire talk... An army patrol had been massacred south of us two years before, and a freighter trying a new route toward Horsehead Crossing had been attacked, losing two men and all of his stock.

A rider for one of the Panhandle outfits had cut loose to go on his own and had tried settling down in this country. He lasted through one hardworking spring, fighting sleet, dust storms and late frost. The country killed his crops and the Indians got his cattle. When he tried riding out, leaving in disgust, they got him.

His cabin was somewhere south and east of us. Everybody had heard of it, but nobody knew exactly where it was. There were also rumors of some big caves in the country, but those we had yet to see.

Neither Fuentes nor me had any great itch to ride any closer to that campfire, although we were curious. If it was Kiowas, it was a good chance to lose hair, and the same for Lipans or Comanches. Anyway, we could ride down there tomorrow and, if they had pulled out, as seemed likely, we could put almost as much together by studying the remains of camp as if we actually saw it alive from close up.

A greenhorn might have tried slipping up on that camp. And if he was a good man at outguessing Indians, he might get close and get away... but he might not, either.

It never seemed wise to me to take unnecessary chances, and Fuentes was of the same mind. We were way past that kid stage of daring somebody, or doing something to show how big and brave we were.

That was for youngsters not dry behind the ears. We moved when we thought it right to move, and we fought when the chips were down, but we never went around hunting trouble.

After studying that fire we went back and turned in, letting our horses keep watch for us.

We'd been lyin' there a while when I spoke out. "Tony, there's something wrong about this."

"*Sí?*" His voice was sleepy, yet amused. "Somebody stealing cows, no?"

"Maybe... All we've got is some idea that cows have been moved, and the cows that were moved are a mixed lot. On the other hand, the cattle that are missing are young stuff.

"The old stock somebody might try to steal. But the young stuff? It's mostly too young to sell with profit, which means that whoever has the young stuff intends to hold it a while... And of course the young stuff hasn't been branded."

Fuentes said nothing and he was probably asleep, but it kept me awake a while, thinking about it. If all they wanted was young stuff, why had they broken the pattern and stolen older stock?

At daybreak we rolled out and had coffee over a buffalo-chip fire. We ate a little jerky and biscuit and then crawled into the saddle and left out of there. We taken a roundabout route and cut down into the bottom where we'd seen the cattle.

There was quite a bit of timber down there, and some rough, broken country. We saw no cattle at first, then a scattering of stuff, most of it wearing Stirrup-Iron brands. There was a sprinkling of

Spur stuff, too, and we started them drifting toward home...knowing a few of them might keep going, but that we'd have to round up and push most of them.

We taken our time, scouting around as if hunting strays, but working closer to where the campfire had been. It was nigh onto two hours after sunrise when we came up on the camp.

It was deserted. A thin feather of smoke stood above the coals, which had been built with care not to let the fire get away. Two people had been in the camp, and they'd had two packhorses. One of the men carried a rifle with a couple of prongs on the butt plate that would kind of fit over the shoulder at the armpit. I'd seen another such gun some years back, and some fancy boys had them. I never cared for them myself, but it was easy to see that was his kind of gun, because wherever he put it down he left that mark in the ground.

Fuentes saw them too. "We'll know him when we see him," he commented, dryly. "It isn't likely there's more than one like that in the country."

Two men, and they had camped here at least two days and possibly longer. There were other signs of camping, too, so the place had been used more than once. We saw a big old brindle steer with a white nose that would weight eighteen hundred easy. There were a couple of others with him, one an almost white longhorn cow with a splash of red along one hip.

Fuentes was starting to haze them back when I had an idea. "Tony, let's leave them."

"What?"

"Let's leave them and see what happens. You'd know that brindle steer or white cow anywhere, so let's just see where they show up."

He nodded. "*Bueno*, I think that's a good idea."

The truth was that we'd know every head we saw that day. A man working cattle develops a memory for them—and the crowd they run with, so when we started back we had more than twenty head for our ride. It took some doing, like always, but it helped that they were headed back to their home range...even though their range was nowhere as good as what we were leaving.

Riding gives a man time to think—and to look. A man riding wild country has busy eyes if he hopes to stay alive, but a cowhand has them naturally. He learns to spot trouble before he comes close

to it, and his eyes can pick out a bogged steer or one with
screwworms. A good horse will smell screwworms when a man
can't see the steer for the brush, and he will locate cattle where a
man can't see them.

It was hot, dusty riding, and the black flies hung about us in
a swarm. We picked up two three-year-old steers on the drive
back. They just saw our cattle and joined up, as cattle will, and
Fuentes and me, knowing they would be spooky, kept clear of
them.

We were almost back to the line-shack when we saw a rider.

"Ah!" Fuentes grinned. "Now you will see her!"

"Her?"

He gestured at the rider. "The major's daughter. Be careful,
señor. Sometimes she thinks she is the major."

She came riding toward us on as pretty a gray gelding as you
ever saw, riding sidesaddle on something I'd never seen before, a
black patent-leather saddle. She wore a kind of riding habit in
checkered black and white—a fine check—and a black hat, black
polished boots and a white blouse.

She gave me a quick glance that missed nothing, I'd guess,
and then nodded to Fuentes. "How are you, Tony?" She glanced
at the cattle. "Any T Bar T stuff in there?"

"No, señorita, only Stirrup-Iron and Spur."

"Mind if I have a look?"

"Of course not, señorita."

"Just don't spook those two speckled three-year-olds," I suggested. "They're edgy."

She threw me a glance that would have cut a wide swath at
haying time. "I've seen cattle before!"

She rode around our gather, studying them, and mostly they
paid her no mind. Then she cut in close to those steers and they
taken one quick look at the sun shining off that patent-leather
sidesaddle and they taken off, and it took some hot fast work by
Tony an' me to hold our bunch together.

I pulled in close to her. "Ma'am, you go tell your papa to wipe
behind your ears before you come out on the grass again, will you?"

Her face went white, and she took a cut at my face with her
quirt. It was one of those woven horsehair-handled quirts in green
and red, a pretty thing. But when she cut at my face with it, I just
threw up my hand, caught the quirt and jerked it out of her hand.

She had a temper, that one did. She lost hold of the quirt, but she didn't stop. She grabbed for her rifle in its scabbard, and I pushed my horse alongside hers and put my hand over the butt of the gun so she couldn't draw it.

"Just take it easy," I said coolly. "You wouldn't shoot a man over something like this, would you?"

"Who the hell said I wouldn't?" she flared.

"You'd better also tell your papa to wash your mouth out with soap," I said. "That's no word for a lady to use."

She was sashaying around, trying to get away from me, but that little bay I was riding knew its business and was staying right close to her gray gelding. For three or four minutes we kicked up dust, sidling around on the prairie until she saw it was no use.

Maybe she cooled down a little. I don't rightly know, but she called over to Fuentes, who was sitting his saddle watching. "Fuentes, come and get this man away from me."

Tony walked his horse over and said, "I do not want you to shoot him, señorita. He is my compadre."

"I'll say this for you," I said. "You may have the devil of a temper, but you sure are pretty."

Her eyes narrowed a little. "The major will have you hung for this," she told me, "if the boys don't get to you sooner."

"Why don't you fight your own battles?" I asked. "You're a big girl now. No need to call on your papa to help you, *or* the big boys at the ranch."

"Stop calling him my papa!" she said angrily. "He's 'the Major!'"

"Oh, I'm sorry," I said, "I didn't know he was still in the army."

"He's not in the army!"

"Then he isn't a major, is he? I mean, he's a used-to-be major, maybe?"

She didn't know what to say to that. Defensively, she said, "He's the major! And he was a major . . . in the Civil War!"

"Well, good for him. I knew a couple of them, up north. There was one used to clerk in a hotel where I stayed, and then I punched cows with a colonel up Wyoming way. Nice fellas, both of them."

My face was smooth, my voice bland. Suddenly she said, "I don't think I like you!"

"Yes, ma'am," I said politely, "I gathered that. When a girl comes after me with a quirt...well, I sort of get the feeling she doesn't care for me. I'd say that wasn't really the romantic approach."

"Romance?" Her tone was withering. "With *you?*"

"Oh, no, ma'am! *Please!* Don't talk about romance with me! I'm just a drifting cowboy! Why, I'd never even think of romance with a daughter of the major!"

I paused. "Anyway, I never start courting a girl the first time I see her. Maybe the second time. Of course, that depends on the girl.

"You—," I canted my head on one side. "Well, maybe the third time...or the fourth. Yes, I think so. The fourth time."

She swung her horse around, glaring at me. "You! You're impossible! Just wait! Just you wait!"

She dashed away, spurring her horse. Fuentes pushed his sombrero back on his head and looked woeful. "I think you are in big trouble, amigo. This one...she does not like you, I think."

"I think, too," I said. "Let's get on with the cattle."

The two three-year-olds were gone, and neither of us were of a mind to follow or try to recover them. Besides, they'd be skittish now, and we'd be lucky to even get close.

We drifted along behind our cattle. Several times I thought I heard movement in the brush, as though the young ones were following along, but soon we were out on the open plain and they did not appear.

So she was the major's daughter? The one Roger Balch was supposed to be trying to round up...or so the talk went. Well, he could have her.

Still, she was pretty. Even when she was mad, she was pretty— very pretty. I chuckled. And she had been mad.

We bunched the cattle in a corral and bedded down for the night.

"Those steers," I suggested, "maybe they'll come up during the night."

Fuentes shrugged, and then he said, "It is Friday tomorrow."

"There's one most ever week," I said.

"On Saturday there is a, what you call it, social at the schoolhouse."

"A box social?" I asked skeptically.

"*Sí*...and I think of these cattle that they need to be with the herd. They will be restless and they might get away...somehow. It is in my mind that we should drive them in."

"Well," I agreed thoughtfully, "I do think they should be with their kinfolk. Of course, while we're over yonder we might's well stop by and see how they run that social affair."

"*Bueno*," Fuentes agreed seriously. "And you will see a dozen, maybe two dozen head of the finest looking girls in Texas."

"And that's pretty fine lookin' by any man's standards," I agreed. "You been to these box socials before? Here, I mean?"

"Often...whenever there is one."

"Who makes the best box?"

He shrugged. "Ann Timberly...the major's daughter."

"Next best?"

"Maybe Dake Wilson's daughter...maybe China Benn."

"China Benn? That's a girl?"

He kissed his fingers. "Ah! And such a girl!"

"She and Ann Timberly friends?"

"*Friends?* But no, señor! The major's daughter does not like her! Not one little bit! China is too...too..." he made gestures to indicate a rather astonishing figure.

"Good!" I said. "I know whose box I'm bidding for."

Fuentes just looked at me and shook his head. "You are a fool, a very great fool, but I think I shall enjoy this social."

He paused. "China Benn is beautiful. She is also the girl Kurt Floyd likes."

"If she's as pretty as you say, there must be a lot of men who like her."

His smile was tolerant of my ignorance. "Not as long as she is Kurt's girl." We were making camp in the lee of a low hill, a little way from the corral. We were hoping those steers would come up during the night, and they might...if we weren't too close. "Floyd is *mucho grande*, amigo. How you say? He is *big!* He is also strong. He does not fight with a gun, like a gentleman, but with his fists. We Texans do not like to fight with fists. It is what we call 'dog-fighting,' you see?"

"You're a Texan? I thought you were from California?"

He shrugged. "When I am in Texas, I am a Texan. On the other side of the border I am a Mexican. It is political, you see?"

"All right, I see your point. Has this Floyd ever really beaten anyone?"

"There was One-Thumb Tom, there was George Simpson . . . a hard fight, that one. There was Bunky Green . . . only two punches, I think."

"You will introduce me to China?"

"Of a certainty. Then I shall stand back and watch. It will be so sad . . . you are so young! To see one so young demolished. Well, so be it."

"If you were a true friend," I suggested, "you'd offer to fight him while I get away with the girl."

"Of course. And I am a true friend. Up until I introduce you to China Benn . . . Then I shall be an observer, amigo, a spectator, an interested spectator, if you will, but a spectator only. Any man who endeavors to court China Benn in the presence of Kurt Floyd needs only sympathy."

"In the morning then," I said, "we will drive these steers to the home ranch. We will bathe, wash behind the ears, brush the dust from our boots and join the rush to . . . where is this fandango, anyway?"

He chuckled. "At Rock Springs Schoolhouse. And Rock Springs Schoolhouse is on the Balch and Saddler range, and Kurt Floyd is the Balch and Saddler blacksmith. And remember this, amigo. You will get no sympathy from the major's daughter. She detests China Benn."

"I remember now. You told me that before. Now I wonder how I ever forgot!"

SEVEN

Henry Rossiter went with Barby Ann in a buckboard with Ben Roper and Danny— Fuentes and me riding a-horseback alongside.

The schoolhouse was built on a low knoll with the spring from which it took its name about twenty-five yards off. There must have been a dozen rigs around the place, mostly buckboards, but there was one Dearborn wagon, a surrey and an army ambulance among them.

As for riding stock, there looked to be forty or fifty horses under saddle. I wouldn't have believed there were that many people in the country but, as I was to discover, it was just like other western communities and some of the folks had been riding all day to get there. Parties, dances and box dinners were rare enough to draw a crowd at any time.

Saddler was just pulling up. On the seat beside him was a thin, tired-looking woman whom I discovered was his wife. Also beside him, a lean but heavy-shouldered man was dismounting. "Klaus," Fuentes whispered. "He gets forty a month."

When opportunity offered, I glanced at him. He was no one I knew, but he was wearing a gun and unless I was mistaken, had another under his coat but tucked behind his belt.

Somebody was tuning up a fiddle, and there was a smell of coffee on the air.

Suddenly, somebody said, "Here comes the major!"

46

He came in a surrey, spanking new, polished and elegant, surrounded by six riders. In the surrey itself were Ann, beautifully but modestly gowned, and the man who had to be the major... tall, square-shouldered, immaculate in every sense.

He stepped down, then helped his daughter to the ground. With them was another couple, equally well-dressed, but whose faces I could not see in the dim light. I knew none of the riders with them, but they were well set-up, square-shouldered men with the look of the cavalry about them.

Standing back in the shadows as I was, Ann Timberly could not see me as she went in, and I was just as pleased. I'd dug out an expensively tailored black broadcloth suit I had, and was wearing my Sunday-go-to-meetin' boots, polished and fine. I also wore a white shirt and a black string tie.

Ann was beautiful. No getting around it, she was beautiful and composed, and as she swept into the schoolhouse you had no doubt that Somebody had arrived. Her manner, I decided, would have been neither more nor less had she been entering the finest home in Charleston, Richmond or Philadelphia.

Yet she was only in the door when somebody let out a whoop in the near distance and there was a rush of hoofs. A buckboard wheeled up, coming in at a dead run and skidding to a halt with horses rearing. And as the buckboard halted, a man leaped from a horse and caught the driver as she dropped from her seat.

The man caught her and swung her around before putting her down, but immediately, and without looking back at either man or rig, she strode for the door.

I caught a glimpse of dark auburn hair, of green, somewhat slanted eyes, a few freckles over a lovely nose, and I heard somebody inside say, "Here's China!"

She swept into the schoolhouse, only a step behind Ann Timberly, and I followed, pushing among the crowd, taking my time. Somebody, I noticed, was caring for her team, but the big man who had lifted her from the buckboard was right behind me.

As he started to push me aside, I said over my shoulder, "Take it easy. She'll still be there when you get there."

He looked down at me. Now I am two inches over six feet and weigh usually about an even one-ninety, although my weight is often judged to be less, but beside this man I was a shadow. He was at least four or five inches taller, and he weighed a good fifty pounds more. And he was not used to anybody standing in his way.

He looked again, and started to push me aside. I was half-facing him now and as he stepped quickly forward, my instep lifted under his moving ankle and lifted the leg high. Off-balance, he tottered and started to fall. It needed only a slight move toward him to keep him off-balance. He fell with a thud, and instantly I bent over him. "Sorry. Can I help you?"

He stared up at me, uncertain as to just what had happened, but I was looking very serious and apologetic, so he accepted my hand and I helped him up. "Slipped," he muttered. "I must've slipped."

"We all do that occasionally," I said, "if we've had one too many."

"Now, see here!" he broke in. "I haven't been—"

But I slipped away into the crowd and walked down the length of the room. As I reached the end I turned and found myself looking into the eyes of China Benn.

She was across the room but she was looking at me, suddenly, seriously, as if wondering what manner of man I was.

Fuentes moved over beside me. "What happened, amigo?"

"He was shoving too hard," I said, "and I guess he slipped."

Fuentes took out a cigar. His eyes were bright with amusement. "You live dangerously, amigo. Is it wise?"

On a long table at the end of the room were stacked the box lunches the girls had packed, their names carefully hidden. It was simple enough. A box would be held up by an auctioneer and the bidding would begin, the box going to the highest bidder. And the buyer of the box would then eat dinner with the girl who prepared it.

Naturally, there was a good deal of conniving going on. Some of the girls always succeeded in tipping off the men they wished to buy their boxes as to just which ones they were. Knowing this, other cowhands, ranchers or storekeepers from the town would sometimes deliberately bid up a box to raise more money... the proceeds always going for some worthy cause... or simply to worry the man who wanted the box.

There was also a good deal of pride in having one's box bring a high price.

Fuentes whispered. "The biggest bids will be for the major's daughter or China Benn, although there's a plump blonde over by the door who'll do pretty well... And some of the older women have the best dinners."

The room was crowded. The desks and chairs had been taken out and stored in the barn for the evening, and the benches pulled back along the walls. A number of the men usually spent most of the evening outside, just talking. There were a good many youngsters of all ages running around underfoot, probably having more fun than any of us.

The girls seated themselves on the benches, some of them surrounded by friends.

Barby Ann came in, looking frail, pale and lovely. She looked quickly around. For Roger Balch, no doubt.

A small, pretty girl came in, a girl with large dark eyes wearing a somewhat faded but painfully neat gingham dress. She was, I realized after a second look, really not that pretty. Some might have thought she was quite plain, yet there was something about her, some inner spark of strength that appealed.

"Who is that?" I asked Fuentes.

He shrugged. "I never saw her before. Seems to be alone."

Looking around, my eyes met those of Ann Timberly. Deliberately, she turned her back on me. I chuckled, feeling suddenly better.

Everybody here knew everybody else, apparently. At least, most of them knew each other. Only a few knew me.

Balch came in suddenly, with Saddler and his wife beside him, and a slender, wolfish man whom I knew instantly. Why had not the name struck me when it was first mentioned by Fuentes?

Ingerman... one of Balch's men, and a gunman. Did he know me? I doubted it, although I had seen him in Pioche and again in Silver City.

Ingerman was no working cowhand. He could do the work, and would, but only when he was drawing fighting wages. Balch and Saddler evidently meant business.

It needed only a few minutes of standing around and watching to see that the belles of the evening were Ann Timberly and China Benn, and if there was to be high bidding for boxes they would be the chief rivals. As for me, I was out for fun, as well as to show Ann Timberly that there were other girls about.

Fuentes had drifted off with some Mexican girls he knew, and Ben Roper was having a drink with some friends. So I was alone, just standing there, looking the crowd over, and I could see some of them looking me over, too.

After all, I was a stranger. The black suit I wore was tailored, and I was somewhat better turned out than most of the men around me. I'd had a liking, picked up from my father and carried on by brother Barnabas, for the better things of life, and so I indulged myself whenever my finances would allow. Though the mere fact of being a stranger at such a time was enough to attract attention.

The music began, and for the first two dances I merely watched. Both China Benn and Ann Timberly danced beautifully, but when on the third dance I decided to take part, I asked Barby Ann. She danced well enough, but her attention was elsewhere. She kept turning her head and looking about, and obviously she was alert for the coming of Roger Balch.

He came in suddenly, flanked by two men whom I judged from descriptions to be Jory Benton and Knuckle Vansen, two of Balch and Saddler's fighting men. They came in, led by Balch, who was a well-built man of not over five feet five, which was only an inch or so below the average. He also wore a dark suit, a gray shirt, black tie and he wore black gloves, which he did not remove. He also wore two guns, which though done occasionally, was far from customary. It was something I'd never seen at a dance.

He stopped, feet wide apart, his fists resting on his hips.

"That is Roger Balch?" I asked.

"Yes." I could sense that she wanted the dance to be over. It was not flattering, but I minded not at all, and knew how she felt.

"Why two guns?" I asked mildly.

She stiffened defensively. "He always wears them. He has enemies."

"He does? I hope those aren't for your father. He does not even carry a gun anymore, and he doesn't hire gunfighters."

She looked up at me suddenly. "What about you? I have heard you are a gunfighter?"

Now where had she heard *that?* "I've never hired out as a fighting man," I replied.

Something else had her attention. She looked up at me again. "What did you mean when you said my father did not wear a gun anymore? You spoke as if you had known him before."

"I merely assumed that before he lost his eyesight he had carried one. Most men do."

Fortunately, the music ended before she could ask any more questions, and I left her at the edge of the floor, near where her father sat. I was turning away when I was stopped. It was Roger Balch.

"You the man riding the MT horse?"

"I am."

"You want to come to work for Balch and Saddler?"

"I am working for Stirrup-Iron."

"I know that. I asked if you wanted to work for us. We pay fighting wages."

"Sorry. I like it where I am." I smiled. "And I am not a fighter. Just a cowhand."

Before he could say more, I strolled away from him and suddenly found myself face to face with Ann Timberly. She was all prepared for me to ask her to dance, and was ready to say no. It showed in every line of her. I looked at her, smiled, but I walked by her to China Benn.

"Miss Benn? I am Milo Talon. May I have this dance?"

She was a striking girl, vibrant and beautiful. Her eyes met mine and she was set to refuse. Then suddenly her manner changed. "Of course." She glanced over her shoulder. "Do you mind, Kurt?"

I got only a glance at the startled eyes of the big man, and then the music was playing. And China Benn could dance.

She could really dance, and the musicians knew it. Suddenly the tempo changed to a Spanish dance, but I'd spent some time below the border in Sonora and Chihuahua, and liked dancing Spanish style. In a moment we had the floor to ourselves... and she was good.

I caught one flashing glimpse of Ann Timberly, her lips tightly pressed with what I hoped was anger or irritation. When the dance ended, there was a round of applause and China looked up at me. "You dance beautifully, Mr. Talon. I did not think anyone here but Tony Fuentes could dance Mexican style so well."

"I used to ride down Sonora way."

"Well," she said "evidently you did more than ride. Let's do it again later, shall we?"

Leaving her, I glanced across the room and met the eyes of

the girl in the faded gingham dress. Turning in midstride, I walked over to her. "Would you dance? I am Milo Talon."

"I know who you are," she said quietly, rising with just a touch of awkwardness. "Thank you for asking me. I was afraid no one would."

"You're a stranger?"

"I live here, but I've never come to a dance before, and I can't stay much longer."

"No? That's too bad."

"I . . . I have to get back. I am not supposed to be away."

"Where do you live?"

She ignored the question. "I just had to come! I wanted to see people, to hear the music!"

"Then I am glad you came."

She danced stiffly, holding herself with care, each step a little too careful. I did not think she had danced very much.

"Did you come with your father?"

She looked at me quickly, as if to wonder if there might be some knowledge in the question. " No . . . I came alone."

Every other girl here had come with someone, if not a man friend, then with her family or other girls, and there were no houses close by. "You'd better find somebody to take you home," I suggested. "It's very dark out there tonight."

She smiled. "I ride every night . . . alone. I like the night. It is friendly to those who understand it."

I was surprised, and looked at her again. "You knew my name," I said then. "Not many here know it."

"I know more about you than any of them," she said quietly, "and if they knew who you really were they'd be astonished, all of them."

Suddenly, her manner changed. "Sometimes they seem so stupid to me! They are so pompous! So impressed with themselves! The major! He's really a nice man, I think, if he would drop that foolish title! He doesn't need it. Nor does she."

"Ann?"

She turned sharply and looked at me. "You know her?"

"We've met. I am afraid the meeting was not friendly."

She smiled, a little maliciously, yet I did not think there was any malice in her. "If they only knew who you were! Why, the

Empty is larger than all their ranches! You run more cattle on your ranch than Balch and Saddler and the major combined!"

Now I was startled. "Now how did you know that? Who are you, anyway?"

"I am not going to tell you." She paused, and the music ended with us on the other side of the floor from where she had been. "It would mean nothing to you, anyway. I mean, you would not know the name."

"You aren't married?"

There was just a moment of hesitation. "No," she said then, "I am not." Then bitterly she said, "Nor likely to be."

EIGHT

Fuentes drifted around the room. "Didn't know you knew our dances," he said. Then he said, more quietly, "Don't get too far away. There may be trouble."

Across the room, I saw Ben Roper walk over to stand near Danny Rolf. They were only a few steps from where Rossiter sat with Barby Ann. So far, Roger Balch had not approached her.

"What is it?"

Fuentes shrugged. "I don't know what nor where, but I've got a feeling."

My eyes swept the room. I knew nothing about Danny, but was not worried about either Fuentes or Roper. They would stand.

"On the boxes," I asked. "How do the bids usually run?"

"Ten dollars is mighty high. Mostly they start at a dollar, run up to three or five dollars. A five dollar bid will usually be high. I've only seen one go to ten... and that's a lot of money.

"Nobody but Roger Balch can afford a price like that, or maybe the major."

"What about Balch himself?"

Fuentes smiled. "You joke, amigo. Balch would not spend dollars on such a thing. He'll bid for a box, more than likely, but he will not go over three dollars."

"How about Ann Timberly's box?"

He glanced at me. "You are reckless, amigo. But it will bring three, probably as much as five."

"And China Benn?"

54

"The same."

"Tony?"

"*Si?*"

"The little one, the strange one. She came alone. She must go early, and she knows some things about me that nobody else knows...nobody here, at least."

He glanced at her, then at me. "I have said it. I do not know her, nor did I see her come. She knows something about you? Maybe she comes from where you do?"

"No...I know she does not. At least, she is no one I have ever known or known of. And there are no girls within fifty miles of our home ranch whom I do not know."

He chuckled. "I would place a bet upon that. You have a ranch, then?"

"We do...my mother, my brother and I."

"Yet you are here?"

"There's a promised land somewhere beyond the mountain. I was born to look for it."

"I, also. But we will never find it, amigo."

"I hope not. I was born for the trail, not for the journey's end." I paused. "We were born to discover and to build, you and I, for the others who will come after us. They will live in a richer, sweeter land, but we will have made the trails. We go where the Indian goes, and the buffalo. We will ride far lands where the only companions are wind and rain and sun."

"You talk like a poet."

I smiled wryly. "Yes, and work like a dog, often enough, but it's the poetry that keeps us going. It's my blessing or my curse, according to the way you believe, to live with awareness.

"All of them," I gestured at the room, "are living poetry, living drama, living for the future, only they do not know it, they do not think of it that way. Most of them heard stories when they were youngsters, stories told by men who had been over the mountain or had dreamed of it, and those who did not hear the stories read them in books.

"I talked to an old gunfighter once who told me he'd been a farm boy in Iowa when one day a man on a fine black horse rode into the yard. A man wearing buckskins and a wide hat. The man had a rifle and a pistol, and he wanted only to stop long enough to water his horse.

"The gunfighter talked him into staying for supper and spending the night. And he listened to the stories the man told of Indians and buffalo, but mostly it was the land itself, the far mountains and the plains, with long grass blowing in the wind."

Fuentes nodded. "It was so with me also. My father would come down from the hills and tell us of the bears he saw, or the lions. He would ride in dusty and tired, his hands stiff from the rope or the branding iron, from twenty hours of work in a single day, but he had the smell of horses and woodsmoke about him. And one day he did not come back."

"You and me, Fuentes. Some day we will not come back."

"With him it was Apaches. When his ammunition was gone, he fought them with a knife. Years later I lived among them and they told me of him. They were singing songs of him, and how he died. It is the way of the Indian to respect a brave man."

"We talk very seriously, Fuentes. I think I will bid for a box."

"I, also. But be careful, my friend, and do not get too far away. I have a bad feeling about tonight."

Folks were beginning to come in from outside and gather on benches and chairs where they could see the small platform from which the boxes would be offered. We could see them all there, in neat piles. some of them decorated with paper bows, some tied with carefully hoarded colored string, and you can bet most of the boxes were intended for somebody special.

It was Ann Timberly's box I wanted, but she didn't want me to have it, and probably wouldn't talk to me if I got it. But there's more than one way of doing things, and I had my own ideas.

China Benn... now there was a girl! But if I bid for her box I might tangle with Kurt Floyd, and on a night when the whole outfit might have trouble there was no time for private arguments. Anyway, I knew what I was going to do.

The bidding started. And from the first box it was animated. The first one to go was a buxom ranch-woman of forty-odd, her box going to an oldster, a onetime cowboy with legs like parentheses, his thin shoulders slighty stooped, but a wry twinkle in his eyes. He bought the box for a dollar and fifty cents. A second box went a moment later for two dollars, a third for seventy-five cents.

Often, other men deliberately avoided bidding, so that a certain man might buy a box at a price within his grasp. Others just as deliberately built up the price to tease some ambitious would-be lover, or somebody who'd be joshed about it later.

The auctioneer knew all the bidders, and usually knew which boxes they wanted, although there was much bidding just for amusement.

I watched, enjoying it, until suddenly a box I was sure was Ann Timberly's box was put up. From the comments by the auctioneer I was doubly sure, so when he asked for bids, I bid twenty-five cents.

Ann stiffened as if struck, and for a moment there wasn't a sound. Then somebody countered with a bid of fifty cents and the moment was past, but our eyes met across the room. Her face was white, her chin lifted proudly, but the anger in her eyes was a joy to see. I should have been ashamed of myself, but I was remembering how she had tried to hit me with a quirt, and her arrogance.

The box went to Roger Balch for five dollars and fifty cents.

China Benn's box went up, and somebody opened the bidding at a dollar. I countered with two dollars, and saw Ann turn to look at me. I did not bid again, and China's box finally went to Kurt Floyd for four dollars, largely because nobody wanted to bid against him and run into trouble. I'd have done it, but I had other ideas.

There was that quiet little girl in the faded gingham dress. I had a notion nobody might bid for her box, and I could see she had that notion, too. She was edging a bit toward the door, wishing she had not even come, afraid of being embarrassed and having to eat her dinner alone. No doubt it took a lot of nerve to come alone, and it began to look like her nerve had just about petered out.

Her box came up. I knew it was hers by the frightened way she reacted and the sudden move she made toward the door. Nobody knew her, and that counted against her, and also the fact that so many of the cowpunchers present, despite their loud talk, were really very shy about meeting a new girl.

Finally the auctioneer, seeing there would be no bidding, opened the bid with one of his own. He bid fifty cents and I came up with a bid of a dollar.

I saw her eyes turn to me, and she stopped moving toward the door. And then something happened.

Jory Benton bid two dollars.

Jory was young, good-looking in a kind of a flashy, shallow

sort of way, and he was tough. I knew a little about him. He'd stolen a few head of stock here and there, had carried a gun in a couple of cattle wars. He wanted to be considered a bad man, but was nowhere nearly as tough as Ingerman, for example. That girl was nowhere and no way the type who should be with him, and being alone, he'd surely want to take her home. And there was nobody to tell him no.

And she knew it.

"Two-fifty," I said, casually.

Fuentes had drifted away, now he started back toward me, stopping a few feet away.

Jory had had a few drinks, but I was not sure if it was that, or if he really wanted the girl, or whether it was a deliberate matter of policy by Balch and Saddler, who were watching.

"Three dollars!" Jory said instantly.

"Three-fifty," I replied.

Jory laughed and said "Four dollars!"

The room was silent. Suddenly everybody knew something was happening. The girl's face was white and strained. Whoever she was, wherever she came from, she was no fool. She knew what was happening, and she could see it meant trouble.

"Five dollars," I said, and saw Danny Rolf turn away from the girl he was with and face toward the front of the room.

Jory laughed suddenly. He glanced right and left. "Let's get this over with," he said loudly. "*Ten* dollars!"

Even at forty dollars a month fighting wages, that was a strong bid, and he had no idea it would go any further.

"Fifteen dollars," I said quietly.

Jory's face tightened and for the first time he glanced at me. He was a little scared. I did not know how much money he had, but doubted whether he had more than that in his pocket, at least not much more.

"Sixteen dollars!" he said, but from his manner I figured he had about reached the end of it.

Suddenly from behind me there was a whisper. It was Ben Roper. "I got ten bucks you can have."

Keeping my manner as casual as possible, I said, "Seventeen."

Roger Balch pushed through the crowd behind Jory, and I saw him taking some coins from his pocket. He whispered something to Benton and Jory put a hand back for money.

He glanced quickly at what was in his hand. "Twenty dollars!" he said triumphantly.

"Twenty-one," I replied.

For a moment there was silence. The auctioneer cleared his throat. He looked hot and worried. He glanced at Roger Balch, then at me.

"Twenty-two," Jory said, but with less assurance. Roger had his feet apart staring at me. I suppose he was trying to bluff me.

"Twenty-three," I said casually. Deliberately, I put my hand in my pocket and took out several gold pieces. I wanted them to realize they were going to have to spend to win. At least, I'd know how badly they wanted to win, or if it was just an attempt to assert themselves.

Jory saw the gold pieces. They were twenty-dollar pieces and I had a handful of them. What I held in my hand was a good year's pay for a cowhand, and they could see it.

"Twenty-three dollars has been bid! *Twenty-three!* Twenty-three once! Twenty-three twice! Twenty-three three times!"

He paused, but Roger Balch was turning away and Jory was just standing there.

"Going... going... *gone!* Sold to the gentleman from Stirrup-Iron!"

The big groups broke up and scattered around the room, gathering into smaller groups. I crossed to the auctioneer to get my box.

Jory Benton was staring hard at me. "I'd like to know where you got all that money," he said belligerently.

I took the box with my left hand, smiling at him. "I worked for it, Jory. I worked hard."

With the box in hand, I crossed to the girl in the gingham dress. "This is yours, isn't it?"

"Yes." She looked up at me. "Why did you do that? All that money?"

"I wanted your box," I said.

"You don't even know me."

"I know you a little... And I know a good deal about Jory Benton, and I know you came alone."

"Thank you." We found a bench corner and sat down together. "I shouldn't have come," she said then, "but... but I was lonely! I can't stay much longer."

"We'll eat then," I said, "and I'll ride you home."

She was genuinely frightened. "Oh, no! You mustn't! I can't let you do that!"

"Are you married?"

She looked startled. "Oh, no! But I just *can't!* You must understand."

"All right... part way, then? Just to be sure you're safely on the way?"

"All right." She was reluctant.

"I've told you my name. Milo Talon."

"Mine is Clarisa... call me Lisa." She mentioned no other name and I didn't insist. If she did not tell me, she had her own reasons.

Her box dinner was simple, but good. There were some doughnuts that were about as good as any I'd ever eaten, and Ma made the best, yet my eyes kept straying across the room to where Ann Timberly sat.

Fuentes crossed to me with Ben Roper. I introduced them, and Fuentes said, "I think we ride together tonight, *sí?*"

"I've got to ride along with Lisa," I said, "but only partway."

"We'll follow," Ben said, "an' you watch your step. Roger Balch didn't like his man bein' beat. He just didn't want to spend that much to win."

They drifted off a ways, and after a bit Danny Rolf joined them. The Balch and Saddler riders were bunching a little too.

Dancing started again, and I danced with Lisa, then left her talking to Ben and crossed the room to Ann.

She turned as I came up and was about to refuse my suggestion of a dance when she suddenly changed her mind.

She danced beautifully, and I did all right. I'd danced more in better places than most cowhands have a chance to, and I could get around pretty good out there, even without a horse. Mostly cowhands don't dance too well, but they don't mind and neither do the girls. The cowhands can always hold the girl while she dances.

Everybody was having a good time. I kept my eyes open, but nowhere did I see a badge. If there was law anywhere about, it wasn't at this dance, which was something to remember.

"Who is she?" Ann asked suddenly.

"Lisa? She's a nice girl."

"Have you known her long?"

"Never saw her before."

"Well! She evidently makes quite an impression!"

"She didn't cuss me out," I said.

Ann looked up at me suddenly. "I am sorry about that. But you made me very angry!"

"So I figured. And when you get angry, you really get angry."

"That was mean, what you did."

"What?"

"Bidding a quarter for my box. That was just awful."

I grinned at her. "You had it coming."

"That girl... Lisa. How did you know which box was hers?"

"Saw her bring it in, and then when they were putting it up for bidding, she started to leave. She was afraid nobody would bid on it. I could see she was scared and embarrassed."

"So you bid on it?"

"Why not? You've got lots of friends. So has China."

"Oh... China. She's the most popular girl around here. All the boys want her box, and most of the older men, too. I don't see what they see in her."

"You do, too," I said, grinning at her, "and so do I. She's got a lot of everything, and she's got it where it matters." Suddenly I wondered. I had been so preoccupied with the bidding and the conversation that followed.

"The man who got your box," I said, "was the lucky one."

She ignored that, then commented, "Roger Balch usually gets what he wants." Then she added, with a touch of bitterness. "Nobody was bidding against him... at least, not for long."

"You cuss at people. How can you expect them to."

"I wouldn't want you to bid against him," she said seriously. "He's very mean and vengeful. If you won over him he would hate you."

"I've been hated before."

Suddenly, I thought of Lisa. She would be wanting to go, and she would be very apt to go alone.

Fortunately, the music stopped and at that moment Fuentes was at my elbow. "If you want Jory Benton to take that girl home, say so."

"I don't," I said. Then I said to Ann, "Maybe we'll be riding the same country again. And anyway, wherever I ride, I'll be looking for you."

"She went out," said Fuentes. "Jory followed."

She was tightening her cinch and Jory was standing by, leaning against a post. What he had been saying, I did not know. But as I walked up, he straightened.

"Just wait a minute," I said to her. "I'll get my horse."

"You don't need to bother," Benton said. "I was just telling the lady. I am taking her home."

"Sorry," I smiled. "I bought the box, don't you remember?"

"I remember, but that was inside. We were inside then. This here's different."

"Is it?"

There was a faint stir in the shadows nearby. My friends or his? Or bystanders?

"You got to go through me to take her," Benton said belligerently.

"Of course," I said, and knocked him down.

He wasn't ready for it. He wasn't ready for that at all. He might have been trying to pick a fight, or maybe just running a bluff, but I'd long ago discovered that waiting on the other man could get you hurt.

My hand had been up, sort of adjusting my tie, so I just took a short step to the left and forward and threw my right from where it was. The distance was short. He had no chance to react. He hit the ground hard.

"Better get up in the saddle, Lisa. I'd help you but I'd rather not turn my back."

Benton sat up slowly, shaking his head. It took a moment for him to realize what had happened to him. Then he got up quickly, staggered a little, still feeling the effects of the blow.

"I'll kill you for that!" he said hoarsely.

"Please don't try. If you go for a gun, I'll beat you to it, and if you shoot, I'll shoot straighter."

"Does that go for me, too?" It was Ingerman.

"If you ask anybody from the Roost to the Hole, Ingerman, they'll tell you I'm always ready."

He had been poised and ready, but now there was a sudden stillness in him. From Robber's Roost to the Hole-in-the-Wall,

Brown's Hole or Jackson's Hole... all hideouts on the Outlaw Trail. Not many here knew what I had said, but Ingerman did, and suddenly he was wary... Who was I?

Yet there was still a need to keep him from losing face.

"We've nothing to fight about, Ingerman. Maybe the time will come, but not here, not about this."

Ingerman was no crazy, wild-eyed kid with a gun. He was ice-cold. He was a money fighter, and there was no money in this. And from the way I spoke, I was trouble. Nobody had told him to kill me... not so far.

"Just wanted to know where we stood," he said quietly. "Don't push your luck."

"I'm a careful man, Ingerman. Jory, here, was about to get himself hurt. I was trying to keep him from it."

There was a crowd around now, and two of them were Danny Rolf and Fuentes. Just the other side of Ingerman was Ben Roper.

"Mount up, Talon," he said. "We're all goin' home."

Ingerman heard the voice behind him, and he knew Ben Roper by sight and instinct. He turned away, and Jory Benton followed.

The night was cool and clear, there were many stars, and the wind whispered in the sagebrush. We started riding, and I had no idea where we were going.

NINE

At first we did not talk. Behind us Ben Roper, Fuentes and Danny Rolf were riding, and I wished to listen. Nor did Lisa wish to talk, so we rode to the soft sound of our horses' hoofs, the creak of our saddles and the occasional jingle of a spur.

When we had several miles behind us, I left Lisa for a moment and rode back to the others. "This may be a long ride. No use for you boys to follow on."

"Who is she, Milo?" Ben asked.

"She hasn't told me. She came alone, and I somehow don't think her people knew she was gone...I don't understand the situation."

We were talking low, and Lisa, some distance off, could not overhear us.

"You watch your step," Danny warned. "It don't sound right to me."

When they took off and I rode back to her, we started on without comment. The country was growing increasingly rugged, with many patches of timber and brush that grew thicker as we rode.

"You came a long way," I commented, at last.

The trail, only a vague one, seldom used, dipped down into a narrow draw that led to a creek bottom sheltered by giant oaks and pecans. At a stream, Lisa drew up to let her horse drink.

"You have come far enough. I want to thank you very much,

both for riding with me and for buying my box. And I hope there is no trouble with that man."

"There would be trouble anyway. He rides for Balch and Saddler."

"And you for Stirrup-Iron?"

"Yes."

Her horse lifted his head, water dripping from his muzzle. My own was drinking also.

"Do not be quick to judge," she said quietly, "I do not know either Balch or Saddler, but I know they are hard men. Yet I think they are honest men."

I was surprised, yet I said, "I haven't formed an opinion. Somebody is stealing cattle, however."

"Yes, I think so. I do not think it is Balch and Saddler, nor do I think it is Stirrup-Iron."

Again I was surprised. "You mean somebody thinks *we* are stealing?"

"Of course. Did you think you were the only ones who could be suspicious? Be careful, Mr. Talon, be very careful. It is not as simple as you think."

"You are sure I should not ride further with you?"

"No... please don't. I haven't far to go."

Reluctantly, I turned my horse. "Adios, then." And I rode away. She did not move, and I could still see the dark patch in the silver of the water until I went into the arroyo. When I topped out on the rise, I drew up and thought I heard the pound of hoofs fading away, the hoofs of a running horse.

I glanced at the stars. I must be southeast of the ranch, some distance away. Taking a course by the stars I started across country, dipping down into several deep draws and skirting patches of brush and timber.

Just as I rounded one patch of brush, maybe three or four acres of it, I saw my horse's head come up. "Easy, boy!" I said softly. "Easy, now!"

I drew up, listening. Something was moving out there, a rustle of hooves in the grass, a vague sound of movement, a rattle of horns. "Easy, boy!" I whispered.

At my voice and my hand on its neck, my horse lost some of his tension, and I shucked my Winchester from its scabbard and waited. Somebody out there was moving cattle, and in ranch country honest men do not move cattle by night... not often, anyway.

They were no more than a hundred yards off, but I could not make them out, moving them southeast. I waited and the sound dwindled. A small bunch, I was sure. Not more than thirty or forty head at most. To move in on them now would just result in getting somebody killed, and that somebody could be me—a thought I viewed with no great pleasure. And the trail would still be here tomorrow.

A thought came to me then... Why ride all the way back to the ranch? True, I had my work to do, and there was a lot of it, but if I could find out where those missing cattle were going, it would make up for the time lost. So when I started on I was hunting a camp, and I found it, a small place alongside a stream, probably the same stream, or a branch of it, where I'd left Lisa. The place was thick with huge old oaks and pecans, and fortunately the night was cool without being cold. I'd no blanket roll with me, nothing but my slicker and a saddle blanket. But I found a place with plenty of leaves and I bunched up more of them, then spread my slicker on the leaves and put the saddle blanket over my shoulders.

I put my Winchester down beside me, muzzle toward my feet, and my six-shooter I took from its holster and laid it at hand. I made no fire, as I had no idea how far off those cattle had been taken or whether the rider might come back by.

It was a cold, miserable night. But there had been many of those, and it was not the first time I'd slept out with nothing but a slicker and a saddle blanket... Nor would it be the last.

Daybreak came and I got up.

Usually I carried some coffee in my saddlebags but I had none now. Going to a box supper a man usually figures there'll be coffee, and there had been. A lot of good it did me now!

At the creek I washed my face in cold water and dried it on my shirt. Then I put the shirt back on, took a long drink from the stream, watered my horse, and mounted up.

The trail was there, and I picked it up, noticed the general way it led, and rode off to the south of it. After a bit, I cut back north as if hunting for strays, and crossed the trail again.

It was getting almost to noontime when the trail led around the roll of a hill into a gap beyond which I could see more oaks and pecans, with some willows and a few cottonwoods. That gap was green, pleasant to see, and promised water. Both my horse and I were thirsty, with no drink since daybreak, but I didn't like the looks of that gap... It just looked too good, and I'm a skeptical man.

So I kept back in the brush and reined my horse around to the north. And I worked my way up the slope, with frequent stops to listen and look, until finally I saw a place where there were trees and brush atop the hill. The trees were scrub oak and didn't look like much, but they could cover a man's approach.

Shucking my rifle, I worked up the slope, weaving in and out among the trees until I reached the top of the hill.

Beyond was a valley, a pretty little place, all hid away like that, with a couple of pole corrals for horses, and a lean-to, and maybe a hundred head of young stuff. I stepped down from the saddle and hunkered up against a busted-down oak tree and gave study to what lay below.

There was no smoke... no movement beyond the cattle, and there were no horses in the corrals. The valley was well-watered and the graze was good... but not adequate for a hundred head for very long. The cattle were in good shape, but I had a hunch this was just a holding place until they could be moved on.

To where? A good question.

The day was warm. I was tired and so was my horse. Moreover, I was hungry. There might be food down there, but I wasn't going to tip my hand by leaving tracks all over the place. Whoever hid those cattle here thought his hideout was unknown and secure, so I'd better leave it thataway.

I gave study to the cattle. Mostly three-year-olds or younger.

All of which brought me back to a thought I'd had before. Whoever was stealing cattle was not stealing them for a quick sale, but to hold and fatten. Give stock like this two to three years, even four, and they'd fatten into real money. And the chances were good that most—if not all—of this stock was unbranded.

I swore softly. I had work to do and they'd be wondering what happened to me. Moreover, my boss had been a thief himself... how did I know he wasn't a thief now? That's the trouble with a bad reputation; folks are always likely to be suspicious.

A thought came to me and I studied the hills around the valley with care. If this was a holding station these cattle would have to be moved, as others had probably been moved before them. So where did they go?

A couple of places in the hills that surrounded the valley gave me some ideas, so I led my horse back a ways, mounted up and rode down the slope, still holding to cover and alert for any movement. The man who drove those cattle was probably long gone, but I couldn't be sure.

Keeping far out, I skirted around the hills. It took me better than an hour to get around to the other side of the valley. But, sure enough, what I was looking for was there.

A trail, probably weeks old, made by sixty to seventy head, a trail pointing off to the southeast. Obviously it was a ride of a day or more—perhaps several days—to their destination.

No use thinking of that. I had to get back. I swung my horse suddenly and at the same instant heard the sharp *whap* of a bullet past my skull.

My spurs touched the flanks of my horse, and he was off with a bound. A good cutting-horse, he was trained to go from a standing start into a sharp burst of speed, and it was well he did, for I heard the sound of another bullet and then I was dodging behind a clump of mesquite. Circling quickly about the end, I turned at right angles and rode straightaway, knowing the rifleman would expect me to appear at the other end. Before he could adjust his aim, I was behind another clump and my horse was running flat-out.

One more shot sounded, and then I was down into an arroyo. The arroyo headed straight back for the hills where I wanted to go, and from where I'd come when trailing the cattle, but I had an idea the hidden marksman knew more about that arroyo than I did. So I watched for a way up, glimpsed a steep game trail, and put my horse up the trail and over the rim and into the rocks.

Slowing down, I studied the country. Somebody had shot from cover, somebody who missed killing me only by the sudden move I'd made. Somebody who could shoot!

My way led west and north, but mostly west. I rode north, putting distance between myself and the man who had been shooting, and utilizing every bit of cover I could.

It was almost midnight when I finally walked my weary horse into the yard at the line-cabin.

A low voice spoke from the door of the dark cabin. "Where did she live, amigo? On the moon?"

Tired as I was, I chuckled. "I stumbled on some cattle moving at night. Made me sort of curious."

"I've coffee on the fire."

Fuentes struck a match and lit the coal-oil lamp. He put the chimney back in place. At the fireplace he dug a pot of beans from the coals and went to the cupboard for biscuits.

"You have something extra, amigo," he said, looking very serious. "How many were they?"

"Who?"

"The men who shot at you."

I had picked up the coffeepot and a cup, but now I stopped, half turning toward him. "Now how the hell would you know that?"

Fuentes shrugged a shoulder. "I do not think, amigo, that you would put bulletholes in your own hat... So I think somebody has been shooting."

I removed my hat. There was a bullet through the crown on the left side. That one had been close... very, very close!

As briefly as possible, I explained the events of the day and of the previous night, my trailing of the cattle, finding the herd of young stuff and turning away from the trail.

He chewed on a dead cigar and listened. Finally, he said, "How far away would you say? I mean, how far off was he when he shot?"

I had not thought of that, but recalling the terrain and what cover there had been, I said, "Not less than three hundred yards."

"My advice, amigo, is do not wear that shirt again, not for a long time. You rode one of the Stirrup-Iron horses, so we will turn it loose. At three hundred yards he might not have recognized you. He might not even know you. So do not ride that horse again, and do not wear that shirt. You have others? If not, you may have one of mine, although I am afraid it would be tight, very tight."

That made sense, a lot of sense, for nobody could be more vulnerable than a working cowhand, riding after cattle in wild country, his mind intent on his business... And punching cows is a business that requires attention. When a roped steer hits the end of that rope, if your fingers are in the way, you have one or two less fingers. A quick turn around the horn with your rope at the wrong moment... I knew a lot of cowhands who had lost pieces of their fingers.

Of course, there was every chance that whoever shot at me

had known exactly who he was shooting at. If he did, there was no help for it. If he did not, we could hope to confuse him. I'd no desire to have a good shooter rim-rocking me as I went about my business.

Long before daybreak we were in the saddle. It was rough country, and some of those big old steers were elusive as ghosts. We'd glimpse them in the brush, but when we got there they'd be gone.

Shortly after sunup, the wind started to blow, and the sand stung our eyes. The cattle went into the thickest brush, and we worked hard rousting them out. A long, brutal day, and at the end of it we had but three head, seven- or eight-year-olds no more friendly than as many Bengal tigers. They'd stalk you along the bars and hook, if you came too close.

"Seen Ol' Brindle today," Fuentes commented, as we walked our horses toward the cabin. "I was hoping he was dead."

"Old Brindle?"

"Sí...a big one, amigo, maybe eighteen hundred pounds. About nine years old, I think, and horns like needles...and long...like so." He held out his arms to show me. "He killed a horse for me last year, treed me and kept me up a tree until long after sundown. Then, when I got away, he picked up my trail and came after me. Very bad, amigo...You watch! Very bad! I think he killed somebody."

"Stirrup-Iron?"

"Spur," Fuentes said, "and he hates me...All men. You be careful, amigo. He will kill. He will hunt you. He was born hating, born to kill. He is like a Cape buffalo, amigo, and a bad one."

I'd seen them before. Maybe not as evil as this one, but the longhorn was a wild animal, bred in the thickets and the lonely places, fearing nothing on earth. To those who have seen only domestic cattle, he was unbelievable...and no more to be compared to them than a Bengal tiger to a house cat.

We ate, and we fell into our bunks and slept like dead men, for morning was only hours away, and our muscles were heavy with weariness.

As if we had not troubles enough, with men stealing our cattle, with a mysterious girl who belonged we knew not where—nor to whom—and now this...a killer steer.

TEN

Ben Roper came by the line-cabin bringing six head of horses to turn into our corral. "Figured you'd need 'em," he said. "How's the coffee?"

"Help yourself," I said.

We walked inside where it was out of the wind. Fuentes looked up from a job of mending a riata. "You findin' any cows?"

"Young stuff seems to have left the country," Ben said, and I told him what I'd found. "Southeast, you say?" He frowned, filling his cup. "That's rough country. Kiowa country."

He looked at my hat. "That wasn't no Kiowa," he commented. "If it had of been, he'd a-kept comin'. Chances are, there'd have been more of them."

"The tracks I saw were shod horses."

"This here's a white man," Ben decided. "One that doesn't want to be seen."

"Brindle's around," Fuentes commented.

"Leave him be," Ben said. "Joe told me to tell you that, if Brindle showed up. He ain't worth a ruined horse or a busted leg."

"I'd like to put a rope on him," I said. "Be something to tie on to."

"You leave him alone. Be like ropin' a grizzly."

"We used to do that in California," Fuentes said. "Five or six of us. Put two or three ropes on him, snag him to a tree and then let him fight a bull. Makes quite a scrap."

71

"You leave Brindle alone," Ben got up. He glanced over at me. "You want to trail those cattle?"

"When there's time. I've got a feeling they aren't far off, and that the thief is somebody around here."

"Balch?"

I shrugged. "I don't know anything about Balch other than he's hard to get along with, and seems to want to have the range all to himself."

Ben Roper got up. "Got to get back. We're pullin' 'em in. But like you say, it's mostly old stuff."

He rode off toward the home ranch and Fuentes and me crawled into the saddle. Both of us had our Winchesters, because even if they were in the way sometimes, you'd better have one in case of Kiowas.

We cut off due south into a wide plain, bunches of mesquite here and there, with enough catclaw and prickly pear to keep it interesting. We found a few head, all pretty wild. "They've been hustled," I told Fuentes. "Somebody has been down here hunting calves."

Several times we saw tracks . . . cow-pony tracks, a shod horse. We rounded up eight or ten head and started them back toward the ranch, adding a couple more, who joined the drive of their own free will. I'd cut off into some rocks to see if any cattle were holed up in the breaks along the foot of a cliff, and suddenly come into a little hollow, wind-sheltered from three sides by the cliff and partly sheltered by mesquite on the other. It was a nice, cozy little spot, and like all other such spots, somebody else thought so, too.

There was a seep . . . nothing very much . . . and the ashes of old fires. When I saw the ashes, I pulled up and stopped my horse where he was, not wishful of leaving more tracks. From the saddle, I could see that somebody had left a pile of wood back under the overhang of a rock, where it would stay dry. So whoever had been here expected to come back.

"Makin' himself to home," Fuentes said, grinning at me.

We drove on. I rousted an old steer out of the brush, and a couple of range cows in surprisingly good shape. We corraled the cattle and it was shading up to dark when we rode up to the cabin.

There was a saddled horse tied to the corral bars, and a light in the cabin.

Fuentes glanced at the brand. Balch and Saddler. We both stepped down. "I'll have a look," I said. "Be right back to care for my horse."

"Watch yourself."

It was Ingerman. He had a fire going and had made fresh coffee. He looked up from under light eyebrows whitened even more by the sun. His old gray hat was pushed back, and he had a cup in his hand.

"You sure stay out late," he said. "Figured you'd developed cat eyes to see in the dark."

"We're shorthanded," I said. "Everybody works hard."

He tried a swallow. "Better have some. I make a good cup of coffee."

Taking a cup from the shelf, I filled it. He watched me, a hard humor in his eyes. "Milo Talon," he said. "Taken me a while to place you."

I tried the coffee. "It is good. You want a job as cook? We can't pay much but the company's good."

"You got a name along the Trail," he commented, looking into his cup. "They tell me you're pretty handy."

"Just enough," I said. "I don't hunt trouble."

"But you've handled some boys who did." He took another swallow. "Sure you don't want to work for us?" He looked at me, his eyes hard and measuring. "You may not know it, but there's some boys noosing a rope for the Stirrup-Iron riders."

"Be a long time using it," I said, casually. "What they upset about?"

"Losing cows... Losing too many cows."

Fuentes came in the door and looked at Ingerman, then at me. "He makes a good cup of coffee," I said. "Have some."

"Losing cattle," I said. "All young stuff?"

Ingerman nodded. "Somebody wants to get rich three or four years from now. Balch figures it's Rossiter."

"It isn't," I told him. "We're losing stock, too. I don't think there's anything on the place younger than three years. What did you come over for, Ingerman?"

"First, because I remembered you. Want you riding with us."

He grinned at me. "I could kill you if I had to, but you're good. You'd probably get some lead into me and I'd rather not have it. We'll pay you more than you'll get here, and you'll have better horses to ride."

He wiped the back of his hand across his mouth. "And you'll be on the right side when the hanging starts."

"How about Fuentes?"

"Roger Balch doesn't take to Mexicans. Never seen any harm in them, myself."

"Forget it. I ride for Stirrup-Iron. You might tell Balch he should have a talk with me before he starts swinging that loop of his. If hanging starts and the shooting begins, we'll take Balch and Saddler first, but there need be no shooting. Something's going on here, but it isn't us, and I don't think it's your outfit."

"Then who is it?"

I shrugged. "Somebody else."

He emptied his cup. "You been told." Then he added, "You watch your step. Jory Benton wants your hide."

"His knife isn't big enough to take it," I said. "If he says that again, you tell him to go to Laredo."

"Laredo? That where you bury your dead?"

"No," I replied, "that's where I tell men to go whom I don't want to bury. It's a nice town, and he'd like it."

When he had gone, Fuentes sliced some bacon into a pan. "What do you think, amigo?"

"I think somebody steals their cows, somebody steals our cows, and somebody plans on the two of us killing each other off. I think somebody wants both outfits, and all the range. And in the meantime he's gathering stock for his ranch to have when the shootin's done."

Fuentes left me in the morning to work a small valley north of us by himself. The wind had died down and I took a cold bath in the water tank, then shaved and dressed, and all the while I knew I was stalling. For my mind kept returning to the trail, and mixed with it were thoughts of Lisa.

Who was she? Where did she live, and with whom? I was not in love with her, but she offered a puzzle that kept gnawing away at my mind. Maybe there was more of Barnabas in me than I had thought. He was the scholar of the family, but we shared some traits in common.

Which brought me around to thinking of myself and just where I was headed. Barnabas seemed to *know*. He had gone to school in Europe, living part of the time with relatives we had in France. I'd been content with wild country and lonely trails, but I kept asking myself if that was going to be enough.

Just being a good cowhand took a hell of a lot of man. It also took a lot out of a man, and I was too restless to stay put. As a cowhand I wasn't as good as either Fuentes or Ben Roper. They knew things by instinct that I'd never learn, and the best thing I had going for me was uncommon strength, endurance and some savvy about stock. And most of all, the willingness to get in there and work.

Maybe the thing wrong with me was that back there in Colorado we had the Empty... the MT outfit that had more cattle, more water and better grass than any of the outfits since.

This was good country, and I liked it. But two weeks of riding would put me right back on land that belonged to me, and that made a difference in my thinking.

Rossiter knew who I was, and so did Lisa, whoever she was, but I didn't want anybody else to know. Henry Rossiter wasn't apt to talk, and somehow I didn't think Lisa would either.

Just for luck I threw a saddle on a buckskin, tied him to the corral and then, taking my rifle, I walked up on the highest knoll around.

A man can ride a lot of country without really knowing it until he gets up high and gets a good picture of how it lays. There are always some areas that will fool him by their position in relation to others. I'd noticed that when I was a youngster back at the Empty, and recalled how surprised I'd been when I first saw an accurate map of the ranch layout.

What I was looking for now was cattle. If I could see a few head I could save a lot of riding, and I'd combed too many likely spots to be confident. Also, I had some thinking to do.

There were too many things that made me uneasy. In the first place, blind or not, Henry Rossiter had stolen cattle before and might be doing it again, with help.

In the second place there was that girl Lisa. Where did she belong? Who was she? Nobody at the dance and box social seemed to have any idea of who she was, and strangers didn't stay strangers very long in the western lands.

Suddenly I caught a flicker of movement and saw a big steer come up out of a draw, followed by several others. I watched, waiting until six had appeared. The big steer was in the lead, and they were a good half mile away. They paused to sniff the air, then moved on into a hollow I remembered visiting a few days before. There was grass there, but no water.

Walking back to the corral I stepped into the saddle. The weather was changing. The air was still, yet great black thunder-heads were looming up along the horizon. Rain? It seemed doubt-ful. Too often in this west Texas country I'd seen the clouds pile up and just hang there, sometimes with lightning, but not a drop of rain.

Riding out of the hollow, I cut across the slope of the hill toward the brush where I'd seen the cattle. Now there's some stock that will drive easy enough. You get them headed the right way and maybe one or two will try to cut out, but generally speaking that bunch will walk right along. There's others you couldn't herd for sour apples. No matter which way you try to head them, they decide that isn't the way they want to go. With luck this bunch would be of the first kind.

The closer I got, the more I began to wonder about that big steer who'd been leading them. Even at that distance he'd looked mighty big... too big.

Brindle? Maybe... and if so I wanted no part of him. When an outfit is in a rush to gather cattle, there's no need to cripple a horse or a man trying to get one mean steer. He isn't worth the trouble, and no doubt that was why Ol' Brindle had gotten along so far... he was just too mean to handle.

I wanted no part of him.

So I eased down into that tree-filled draw where I'd seen those cattle go, and right away spotted several of them. I sat my horse a bit, studying the layout. There was no sign of the big steer. Once I thought I detected a spot of color back in the brush, but sunlight on a tree trunk seen through the brush might look like a steer. They'd seen me, but I was bothering them none at all, and they paid me no mind. Finally, I walked my horse kind of angling toward them with an idea of taking them up the draw and onto the plain behind it.

An old, half-white range cow started away from me, and that buckskin I was riding knew what he was about. He already knew what I had in mind, and we started that cow toward the draw. We came up on another and another, and they started off, pretty as could be. They got right to the mouth of the draw before one of them suddenly cut left, and another right, and the seven head we had by that time scattered, going everywhere but up the draw where I wanted them to go.

My buckskin took out after the first one and we cut her back toward the draw. Slowly we began to round them up again, but they had no notion of going up that draw at all. Well, there was another down the creek a ways, and there was a chance I could ease them up on the plain without them knowing it, so I commenced pushing them down-creek, ever so easy.

I'd made a couple of hundred yards with them when something spooked that old half-white cow and she cut out, running, and the others after her. Before I finally got them rounded up again, my buckskin was worn to a frazzle and so was my patience, but I did get them together and headed for the plain.

There was a place where the creek bed narrowed down between some bluffs, with maybe fifty yards between them—with a lot of deadfalls and brush in there, some of it blackened by an old fire. Off to one side there were several big old cottonwoods, one pecan and a lot of willow brush mixed with catclaw and wait-a-bit. I was right abreast of it when I happened to glance right, and there was Ol' Brindle.

He was standing in thick brush, his head down a little, looking right at me. It had been said he weighed maybe eighteen hundred, but whoever said that hadn't seen him lately. He was bigger . . . and standing there in that brush he looked as big as an elephant and meaner than anything you ever did see.

I don't know what possessed me but I said, "Hi, fella!" And his head came up like he'd been stuck with a needle. He glared at me, showing the whites of his eyes, and those horns of his were needle-sharp.

If he charged me in among those deadfalls, that dry creek bed and the brush, I'd have no more chance than a hen at a hoboes' picnic. But he didn't. He just stood there glaring at me, and I turned my head to watch my stock. And for the second time I got the break of my life. As I turned my head there was a flash, a sharp concussion, and the echoes of a shot racketing away against the bluffs.

I hit the ground hard, automatically kicking free of the stirrups as I fell. I hit the ground, rolled over, and then felt a blinding pain in my skull. For a moment I thought that steer had rushed me. I could hear the pound of my horse's hooves as he raced away, and then I just faded out.

When I opened my eyes again, I thought I was sure enough crazy. A few drops of rain were falling, and something was snuffling around me. I heard a snort as it smelled blood, and out of the tail of my eye I saw a hoof within inches of my side, part white, and a big, scarred hoof.

Ol' Brindle was standing right over me. He pushed at my side with his nose—curiously, I thought—but the drops of rain continued to fall and he rumbled down low in his chest, and then went away from me. I heard his steps, heard him pause, probably to look back, and then he went on. I let the air out of my lungs then.

I'd been shot.

Shot by somebody lying up on those bluffs and not more than a hundred yards off, I figured.

How long ago I did not know.

I lay perfectly still. It might have been minutes, it might have been a half hour to an hour. I tried to think how long it would have taken those rain clouds to get from the horizon to me, but my skull throbbed heavily and my mouth was dry.

He might be still up there, waiting to see if I was alive. He probably hadn't come any closer because of Ol' Brindle. He must have seen him right away, and the chances were the big steer was still not far off. If I got up and started to move, I might get shot. If not that, Ol' Brindle might charge me, and in my shape I'd play hell getting away from him. And I still didn't even know how badly I was hurt.

Now the rain was falling faster. I lay very still, only half aware, only half conscious. Again I must have faded out, for when my eyes opened again I was soaked to the skin and the rain was pouring down upon me.

With an effort, I pushed myself up from the ground. My skull was bursting and my side hurt, but I raised myself enough to see all around and I saw nothing but muddy ground, a trickle of water in the once dry creek bed, and the wet trees and dripping leaves.

Under the big cottonwoods the rain was a little less. I pulled myself to one and sat with my back against the trunk and looked around.

Nearby, another cottonwood had fallen, and under it lay a great trough of bark that had fallen from the underside. Another piece of loosened bark, all of six or seven feet long, lay atop the trunk.

My hat was gone, back near the creek bed, I supposed. My fingers touched my wet hair. There was something of a cut on my scalp, but I did not think it was from a bullet. More likely my head had hit something when I fell from my horse, and I was suffering from concussion.

The only wound I could find was on my hip where I'd been creased just below my belt. When hit, my body must have jerked and my horse swerved, so I fell, hitting my head when landing. That I'd lost blood there was no doubt, for the dark stain of it covered my pants on that side. Often a flesh wound would bleed more profusely than something really serious.

Desperately, I wanted a drink, and the few drops I could catch in my opened mouth helped not at all. Yet it was too far to the creek and I wanted only to rest and be still.

This was the second time somebody had tried to kill me. Jory Benton? Somehow, I doubted that. This must be the same man who had fired at me before, and who was now stalking me to kill.

He might return.

Obviously, he was a man who liked to make sure of his work. He had fired from cover, from ambush, no doubt. He had also shown the ability to hit what he shot at. Yet in each case I'd lucked out through no effort of my own. How many times could I be lucky?

The rain fell steadily. Somewhere off to the south, thunder rumbled. Occasionally, there was a flash of lightning. I could hear the creek now. It was running a fair head of water.

My hand reached to feel for my pistol. It was there. My belt, I remembered, had only two empty loops.

My horse was gone.

This place where I now was couldn't be more than a mile, maybe a mile and a half from our line-cabin. I'd guessed the big steer that led this bunch had been a half mile off, but after reaching the bottom I'd worked along it a ways, rounding up stock, and then I'd tried to get them out of the creek bottom...not more than a mile and a half. Yet I was in no shape for walking, and wasn't wishful of being caught in the open by a man with a rifle. And he might still be around.

Crawling to that dead cottonwood tree, I got those two lengths of bark. I lay down in one and pulled the other over me and I just lay there. After a while, I went to sleep.

Those two slabs of bark kept me off the ground and covered me, just like a hollow tree. Only I remember one of the last thoughts I had before I dropped off was that it was mighty like a coffin.

When that thought came to me, I almost got up and out, but I simply was too weak, too tired, and my head ached too much.

If anybody came looking for me now, I was helpless. A man had only to walk up and shoot me full of holes.

ELEVEN

Fitfully, I slept. I awakened, slept again, and awakened. When I tried to turn over, water leaked in from the sides where the two slabs of bark met, so turning over was an ordeal.

Finally, after an endless night of rain, day came. A day of rain.

My eyes opened to a dripping world. My head throbbed heavily and my side was sore, my muscles cramped. For a long time I simply lay still, listening to the rain on the bark, hearing the running of the creek. To hear it now one would never believe that yesterday it had lain dry and empty.

The line-cabin... I must get back to the line-cabin.

Pushing off the top slab of bark, I struggled to sit up, made it, and rolled over to my knees on the muddy ground. I pushed myself up, got to my feet, tottered, and fell against the trunk of a tree.

For a moment I clung there, trying to get the cramps from my legs. I felt for my pistol... It was in place.

A drink. I desperately needed a drink. Tottering on my injured leg, I got to the creek, lay down on the sand and drank. I drank and drank. Getting up, I saw my hat. It lay on the rain-heavy branches of a clump of mesquite near the stream. I retrieved it and shook some water from it, then put it on.

Clinging to a branch of a tree, I looked carefully around. The clouds were lowering and gray; the trees and the brush dripped with water. All was dark and gloomy, yet I saw no movement, no stir of life. No wild animal would be about on such a day, and probably no man.

I'd lost blood, and was therefore weak, yet I would get no better here. And the nearest chance was the line-cabin. It was near, but terribly far in my present condition. Most of all, I dreaded the thought of that open plain I must cross for most of the distance to it. Once I stepped out on that plain, I was a target for any rifleman who might lie in comfortable shelter and take his own time to make the shot good.

Still clinging to the branch, I reached down and picked a length of dead branch long enough for a staff from the ground. Taking a deep breath, I started toward the bank. Only then did I realize what faced me. The banks I must climb to get away from the creek bed were in all places steep, and the few places that offered a route a man might take were slippery with mud.

When I had gone some fifty-odd feet, I paused to gasp for breath, to ease the pain of my hip and stiffened leg, and to study what lay before me.

There was no way I was going to get up that bank by walking. I must get down and crawl.

Onward I limped. At the foot of the bank I dug in with my stick and hobbled up a step, then two. Trying a third, my foot slipped under me and I came down hard in the mud, gasping with the agony of a suddenly wrenched leg. After a long time of lying in the mud, I pushed myself up, but it was no use. I sank down again and crawled on my hands and knees.

At last I topped out on the edge of the plain. A little scattered brush, and then the open grassland, level as a floor. Beyond it loomed the low hills, and just over those hills, the line-cabin.

A dry place, a warm fire, hot food... a cup of coffee. At that moment, no paradise I could imagine needed anymore than that.

For a time I stood still, muddy and wet, looking carefully around. But again I saw nothing. No horseman, no cattle, no Brindle. No doubt Ol' Brindle was in some snug thicket, laying out the rain. At least, I hoped he was.

A step with my good left leg, then hitching my right forward with the aid of the staff, and then the good leg again. It was slow, and it was painful. My leg not only hurt, but the wound at my hip was bleeding again. The ache in my skull had subsided to a dull, heavy pounding to which I had grown accustomed.

Twice I fell. Each time I struggled up. Several times I stood still for a long time trying to wish myself across the plain. But wishing did no good, so I plodded on.

At last I reached the trail up the hill, and this was not steep. At the crest I looked down at the line-cabin. Two horses were in the corral... No cattle in the corral beyond. No smoke from the cabin.

Where then was Fuentes?

There was a flat rock near a mesquite bush. I lowered myself down, stretching my stiff leg out carefully. From that point I could see the cabin. Everything I wanted was inside, yet I did not want to die to get it.

Fuentes should be there with a fire going. But suppose he was not, and somebody else was? Suppose the unknown marksman who had twice tried to kill me was down there instead?

He might believe me dead, but he might also realize that if I was not dead, and needed a horse, that I would surely come to this place where horses awaited me. I had struggled too much, suffered too much to want to walk through that door into a belly full of lead.

For a long time I watched the windows. At this distance I could see little, but hoped I would catch movement past them. I saw nothing.

Struggling to my feet, I hobbled slowly down the path to the cabin. Approaching it, I slipped the thong from the hammer, leaned my staff against the building and drew my gun.

With my left hand, ever so gently, I lifted the door latch. With the toe of my stiff leg, I pushed the door open.

"*Milo!*"

Swiftly, I turned. The stable! I'd forgotten! My pistol came around, the hammer eared back.

The only thing that saved her was my years of training—never to shoot unless I could see what I was shooting.

It was Ann Timberly!

Cold sweat broke out on my forehead, and slowly I lowered my gun muzzle, easing the hammer down ever so gently.

"What in God's world are you doing *here?*" I demanded, irritated by the fact that I might easily have shot her.

"I found your horse, and I remembered your saddle. I tried to backtrack him, but the rain washed out the trail, so I brought him here. I was just unsaddling when I saw you."

She helped me inside and I slumped down on my bunk, holstering my gun. She stared at me, shaking her head. "What in the world has happened to you?"

Explanations could be long, I made it short. "Somebody shot me. I fell and got this," I touched my head. "And that was yesterday... I think."

"I'll get a fire started." She turned quickly to the fireplace. "You need some food."

"Get my rifle first."

"What?"

"It's still on my horse, isn't it? My rifle and the saddlebags. Somebody wants to kill me, Ann, and I want that rifle."

She wasted no time talking, and in a moment she was back with the rifle and the saddlebags. I had another fifty rounds of ammunition in that saddlebag.

She was quick and she was efficient. Rich girl she might be, but she'd grown up on a ranch and she knew what to do. In no time she had a fire going, coffee on, and was telling me to get out of my wet clothes.

"And into what?" I asked wryly.

She whipped the blanket from Fuentes' bed. "Into that," she said, "and if you're bashful, I'm not."

It was a problem getting out of my shirt, which was soaked and clung to my back. She helped me.

"Well," she said critically, "you've got nice shoulders, anyway. Where'd you pick up all that muscle?"

"Wrestling steers, swinging an ax," I said. "I've worked."

Fortunately, she could get a look at my hip just by me loosening my belt and turning down the edge of my pants, which were stiff with blood. It was a nasty-looking wound, an ugly big bruise around the top of my hipbone and a gash you could lay a finger in.

"You'd better start for home," I said, as she dressed the wound. "The major will be worried."

"He stopped worrying about me a long time ago. I can ride a horse and shoot, and he stopped arguing with me when I was sixteen."

I didn't like her being there, nonetheless. Folks will talk, given provocation or none, and a woman's good name was of first importance. Argument did no good at all. She was a stubborn girl, with her own notions about things, and I could see the major must have his problems.

Still, she could ride and she could shoot, and it was a big, wide-open country where a woman was safer than almost anything else a body could mention.

Wrapped in Fuentes's blanket, I relaxed on the bed while she fixed us a meal with what she could find. Meanwhile, we talked about the situation.

"There's nobody I can think of who'd want to shoot me," I commented, "unless it was whoever was driving those stolen cattle. I figure he must've seen me on his trail."

"Possibly," she agreed, but she did not seem too sure.

"Do you think Balch and Saddler are stealing cattle?"

She hesitated over that, then shook her head. "I don't know. Neither does Pa. We've lost...we've lost a good many but not like you have. Balch claims they've lost young stuff, too. It doesn't make any kind of sense."

She turned to look at me. "There's been talk about you, Milo. I thought I'd better tell you. People are saying no cowboy has the kind of money you spent at the box social."

I shrugged. "I saved some money ridin' shotgun for Wells Fargo, then I hit a pocket of stuff placer-mining up in northern New Mexico."

"Most cowhands would have spent it."

I shrugged. "Maybe. I'm not much of a drinker. I carry a gun, and a good many folks know I've ridden shotgun. Besides, I've covered the Outlaw Trail, Canada to Mexico. A man riding that kind of country has to be careful."

"Is this what you're going to do the rest of your life? Just ride up and down the country?"

Smiling, I shook my head. "No, one day I'll settle down to ranching. Maybe I will. Barnabas says I was born for it, liking stock and the country and all."

I paused. "You'd like Barnabas," I added. "He's traveled in Europe, and he reads. He thinks a lot, too. He's planning to import some breeding stock from Europe, mix it with longhorns. The way he figures, the day of the longhorn is short. They'll do well in rough graze like this, but they walk too much and don't carry enough beef. Although," I added, "I've seen some mighty fat longhorns, given the graze."

It was mighty pleasant, sitting there talking to Ann, but somewhere along the line I just dozed off. I'd lost blood, I was feeling sick and I was tired from my struggle through the mud while ailing.

When I awakened again, the cabin was still, and only coals lay on the hearth. Ann was asleep on Fuentes' bed.

Hearing a stir, I raised up on an elbow and saw Fuentes sitting up. He grinned at me and put a finger to his lips. He'd been sleeping on the floor with his blanket-roll gear.

He went out, and I heard him washing beside the door. He automatically threw the water from the pan where it would usually help settle dust, although on this morning after the rain there was none. Then he came in. And moving silently, except for the tinkle of those big Spanish spurs he wore, he made coffee, stirred up the fire and added fuel.

Favoring my bad hip, I sat up.

Ann had put my rifle on the bed beside me—and my sixshooter, too. She'd forgotten to bar the door, and that was probably because she hadn't intended going to sleep.

She awakened suddenly. She stared at Fuentes and, when he bowed slightly, she smiled. "I must have fallen asleep. I am ashamed. Anyone could have come in."

"You were tired, señorita. It was best that you slept. But the major will be worried."

"Yes," she admitted, "this is the first time I've been gone all night."

She looked delightful, and in a matter of minutes she had washed, done something to her hair, and had taken over the cooking from Fuentes.

"I rode to talk to Hinge," he explained. "When I told him you were missing, he was very angry. He was worried, too. I had ridden to look, but your tracks were gone under the rain."

We ate and talked, then Ann was gone. My fever seemed to have disappeared during the night, although I still felt kind of used up. It gave me a cold twinge when I thought of both of us asleep and somebody out there who wanted to kill me. Yet Ann could not long have been asleep before Fuentes rode in.

Joe Hinge rode in. "Get well," he told me after we'd talked

some. "We're goin' to need you. We got the west range to ride, an' that's where Balch says we can't go."

"Give me three, four days," I said.

"Take you longer than that," he said, "you surely look peaked." He changed the subject abruptly. "Both times you were shot at you were southeast of here?"

At my nod, he took off his hat and scratched his head thoughtfully. "You know, some things a body can figure. There's no way it could be Balch or Saddler...Roger, maybe. Jory Benton was riding away off north of here, and so was Knuckles Vansen."

He paused. "It's mighty easy for somebody to think that way out on the plains. Nobody would ever figure who shot you, but look at it. All the men we know of got jobs. They have to be somewhere. You locate those who were where they were supposed to be and you've trimmed down the list."

Hinge continued. "I can account for most of Balch's hands, and the major's as well. I know where ours were."

"Harley?" I asked.

"Him? He wouldn't shoot nobody. He's got no cause to. Anyway, he never goes anywhere but our place and home. He'd have been home when you were shot at and that's a good distance off."

"Is he friendly to Balch? I'm only asking because I don't know him."

"Balch?" said Hinge. "Hell, no! They had words a while back over a horse, but Harley, he keeps to hisself. Doesn't want any truck with anybody. Does his job, draws his money and keeps that place of his."

The thing that worried me was there was no logical suspect except the unknown cattle thief, and there was a good chance he— or they—would be unknown around here. Chances are, it was somebody laying up in the hills, taking cattle when nobody was around.

Hinge rode off with Fuentes, and I laid back on the bed. They had to get back, and I couldn't yet ride.

I could see the sunlight through the open door, and bees buzzing around the house. And somewhere, I could hear a mockingbird singing.

It was almighty quiet and pleasant, and it was a good time to think.

One by one I began thinking over every aspect of the problem.

First, Barnabas used to say, you've got to state your problem.
A problem clearly stated is often a problem already half solved.

Somebody wanted me dead.

Who? And why?

TWELVE

All my thinking got me nowhere at all. Somebody wished me dead—that was all I knew. I almost dozed off along there, just thinking about it, and then suddenly I was wide awake and scared.

I was alone. I was wounded and in bed.

And somewhere out yonder was a man with a rifle who was hunting me!

That was enough to wake anybody up.

To my way of thinking, he either figured me dead or still down there in that bottom somewhere. But suppose I was wrong? Suppose even now he was up there in the brush somewhere waiting a chance to get a shot at me?

Supposing he had watched Fuentes, Hinge and Roper ride away? Supposing he had seen Ann leave earlier?

Then he surely knew I was alone.

What he couldn't know was that, though I was weak from loss of blood and in no shape to straddle a horse, I was still able and willing to shoot.

Nobody lives long low-rating an enemy. You've got to give the other fellow credit for having as much savvy as you have, and maybe a little more.

Suppose he knew I was here, and was waiting for me to drift off to sleep, like I had almost done? Suppose—another thought came—just suppose he didn't have any plan of coming in on me, but just decided to wait up on the knoll, just waiting for me to come out?

Yet, me being sick and in bed, he couldn't expect me to come out and give him a target. Unless something drove me out.

Fire!

That was foolish. I was just imagining things. No doubt, whoever it was who'd shot at me was miles away with his stolen cattle. He had wounded me, put me out of action, and I wouldn't be trailing him for a while. If I was the kind who scared easy, he might figure I'd never try.

What sleep had been coming over me had disappeared. I was wide awake now, and scared. The trouble was, I was in no shape to move quick, in no shape for a running battle—or for a battle of any kind.

I could get out of the cabin. If I was lucky, I could get into the brush. But I knew what brush fighting meant. A man has to be ready to move, and if he moves too slow he's dead. He has to be alert, too, and I was kind of foggy. I could think, all right, but could I think fast enough? React with enough speed?

The door stood open, for the air was fresh and clear. There were two windows, one on each side of the cabin, but only that one door. And the windows were high as a man's shoulder. A body could hoist himself up and crawl through one, but there was no easy way to do it and no way that wouldn't, for a minute or so, leave a man helpless. And going through a window would be sure to break what scab had started healing over my wound.

Yet I was only easily visible from one window. The bed was close against the wall and hard to see except from the door or one window.

It was very still. I strained my ears for the slightest sound, and heard nothing.

One hand was on my Winchester, but I withdrew it and slid my Colt from its scabbard. I needed a gun I could move quickly, easily, to cover any point.

Minutes passed... Nothing.

Whoever was out there... if anybody *was* out there... might be waiting for me to move.

So I would not move.

Yet I was being almighty foolish. I was getting scary as a girl alone in a house. I'd no reason to believe anybody would be coming after me here—except for my imagination.

The trouble was, I was a sitting duck and I didn't like the idea.

No sound, no movement.

My horse was in the corral. If I heard a sound, it would probably be that horse, yet I heard nothing.

1 dozed. Scared as I was—and worried—I dozed. That was what weakness would do for a man.

What snapped me out of it was a noise. It was a very small noise and maybe it was just inside my own head. Gun in hand, I rolled up on one elbow and tried to look out the open door, but I could see nothing but the gradually drying earth beyond the door, a distant hillside and a corner of the corral.

What had I heard? Had it been a step? No...A step had a different sound. A horse bumping a trough, or something? No.

It had been a small sound, a kind of *plink*. It might have been anything. The handle of the coffeepot lay against the side of the pot, and it might have been raised a little, and just finally settling down against the side of the pot as the lessening of heat cooled the metal.

It might have been that, but I didn't believe it was. I lay back on the bed, staring up at the ceiling. Somebody wanted me dead...The problem was still there. If I could figure out who, I might know why, and even figure how he—or they—would try to kill me.

Here I was, worried and all on edge just at the idea that somebody might be out there.

The sound...What had it been? Carefully, I mentally sorted familiar sounds and tried to discover what it was I'd heard. In any event, I hadn't heard it again.

It had been a very small sound, anyway.

Yet I could not relax. My muscles were tense, my nerves on edge. Something was wrong...Something was about to happen. I forced myself to lie still, telling myself I was being silly. I could see out the door and all was quiet, and the one horse I could now see was browsing quietly on some wisps of hay left about the corral. What I needed was rest...just rest. I had to calm down and relax.

I turned on my side, facing the wall.

For a moment I lay absolutely still, petrified into immobility.

For as I turned on my side to face the wall, I found myself staring into the muzzle of a gun pushed through a crack where the chinking between the logs had been picked out. I stared, and then I came off the bunk with a lunge that sent a shock of agony through my wounded hip. I fell sprawling on the floor, the blast of the shot ringing in my ears. There was smoke in the room and the smell of singed wood and wool, and then I was on my feet, gun in hand, hopping toward the door.

Outside my horse had his head up, ears pricked, looking off to my right. I turned around the door post, gun poised... and saw nothing.

I could feel the blood running down my side from my reopened wound, but I waited, clinging to the doorjamb with my left hand, my right gripping the gun, poised for a shot.

Nothing...

For several minutes I waited, and then I turned myself around and fell into a chair, back to the wall, looking at my bunk.

Somebody had picked the dried clay from the cracks between the logs, using a stick or a knife blade, perhaps, and then had thrust the muzzle through. Had I remained lying where I'd been, I would now be dead, for that bullet would have taken me right through the skull.

Again I got up, peering from the windows, but there was nothing to see.

That faint, first sound I had heard was probably the dried mud falling to the ground, striking against a rock or something.

Whoever had tried to kill me had been in this cabin. Whoever had tried had known exactly where the bed was, exactly where my head would be lying on the pillow. He had known exactly the spot at which to pick away the plaster.

Whoever it was wanted to kill *me*. Not just a cowhand who happened to trail a horse thief, but *me*, a particular person.

It might be one of the Balch and Saddler outfit. For there was no doubt that my presence among the Stirrup-Iron riders stiffened their backs, and my death would weaken them considerably.

I limped along the wall. I looked out... nothing, nobody. Now I must be very careful. I dared not trust myself anywhere without being careful.

Impatiently, I looked around. I had to get out of here. The cabin was a trap. As long as I was here, I was available to the planning of the would-be killer, and I had to get out. Yet how to escape with him out there? And he would be, I was sure, somewhere right outside, awaiting a chance.

In my present condition, moving swiftly was out of the question. I would have to get to the corral, get a saddle and bridle on a horse, get the corral bars down and mount up, then ride out. And during every movement I would be sitting there like a duck in a shooting gallery, waiting for the shot.

After a moment, I took a chunk of wood from the fireplace and placed it in front of the hole in the wall. Then I lay down again, heaving a great sigh of relief.

I *was* tired. I lay back, exhausted. All my life I'd been a loner, but at that minute I wanted desperately for somebody to come. Somebody... anybody... Just somebody who could watch while I slept, if only for a few minutes.

I strained my ears for the slightest sound, and heard only the birds, the slight movements of my horse. I closed my eyes...

Suddenly they opened wide.

If I slept I would die.

Rolling over, I sat up. Fumbling with a cup and the coffeepot, I poured coffee. It was no longer hot, for the untended fire had gone down. I tasted the lukewarm coffee, something I'd never liked, then knelt before the fire and coaxed some flame from the coals with slivers of wood.

Would no one friendly ever come?

Hopefully, I continued to listen for the sound of a rider, and heard nothing. I could fix myself something to eat. That would keep me awake and busy. Again I pushed myself up off the bed, my hands trembling with weakness. At the cupboard, I got out a tin plate, a knife, fork and spoon.

In a covered kettle, I found some cold broth Ann had fixed for me, and I moved the kettle to the fire, stirring the broth a little as it grew warm. Again I looked from the windows, careful not to show my head.

What I needed more than anything was rest, yet to rest might be to die. Had I my usual speed of movement and agility, I would have gone outside and tried to hunt down whoever was trying to kill me, but my movements were too slow, I was too tired, and too weak.

Suddenly, I heard hoofbeats. A rider was approaching. Gun in hand, I moved cautiously toward the door, and peered beyond it. A moment later the rider appeared.

It was Barby Ann.

She rode right up to the door and swung down, trailing her reins.

She walked right in, then stopped, seeing me and the gun in my hand. "What's the matter?"

"Somebody took a shot at me. A little while back. Right through a crack in the wall."

When I showed her, she frowned. "Did you see him?"

"No," I said, "but it's likely the same one who tried to kill me twice before, and he'll try again. You'd better not stay."

"Joe Hinge said you were hurt. You'd better get back into bed."

"*That* bed?"

"You've covered the hole, so why not? He can't shoot through that wall. You need some rest."

"Look," I said, "would you stay here for an hour or so? I do need the rest, need it the worst way. If you'll stay, I'll try to sleep."

"Of course I'll stay. Go to bed."

She turned her back on me and walked outside the door, leading her horse to the corral trough for water.

Sitting on the edge of the bunk, I watched her go. She had a neat, if too thin figure, and she carried herself proudly. It was in me to ask her about Roger Balch, but it would not do. After all, it was none of my business. I was only a cowhand working for her father.

She tied her horse to the gate, then turned to come back to the line-cabin.

Inside the door, she looked at me, sitting there. "You'd better lay down," she said. "I can't stay too long."

Easing back on the bunk, I stretched out with a great sigh of relief. Slowly, I felt the tension ease from my muscles. I let go then, letting myself sink into the bed, just giving myself up to the utter exhaustion I felt.

The last I remembered was her sitting by the door staring out into the afternoon.

It was shadowed and still when I opened my eyes, but even before they opened I heard the low murmur of voices—of more than one voice. Danny Rolf and Fuentes were in the room. There was no sign of Barby Ann.

Fuentes heard me move. "You sleep," he said, chuckling. "You sleep ver' hard, amigo."

"Where's Barby Ann?"

"She rode back when we came. Or rather, when Danny got here. Then I came in. You've really slept. It is two hours since I came."

I lay still for a few minutes, then sat up. "You wish to eat? I have some stew... very good... and some tortillas. You like tortillas?"

"Sure. Ate them for months, down Mexico way."

"Not me," Danny said. "I'll take hot biscuits!"

Fuentes waved at the fireplace. "There it is. Make them."

Danny grinned. "I'll eat tortillas." He looked over at me. "Barby Ann said you'd been shot at?"

Indicating the chunk of stove wood I'd laid over the crack, I told them about it. Fuentes listened, but had no comment to offer.

"I'll not ride with you!" Danny said. "He might shoot the wrong man."

"Finding any cattle?" I asked.

"We rounded up sixteen head today, mostly older stuff. We got one two-year-old heifer, almost the color of Ol' Brindle."

"Seen him?"

"He's around. We saw his tracks along the bottom. He stays to the brush during the day, feeds mostly at night, I think."

We talked of horses, cattle and range conditions, of women and cards and roping styles, of riders we had known, mean steers and unruly cows. And after a while, I slept again, pursued through an endless dream by a faceless creature, neither man nor woman, who wished to kill me.

I awakened suddenly in a cold sweat. Danny and Fuentes were asleep, but the night was still and the door was open to the cool breeze.

A horse moved near the corner of the corral, and I started to turn over. Then like a dash of icy water I knew. *That was no horse!*

I'd started to turn over and I did, right off the bed and onto the floor. And for the second time that day a bullet smashed into the bed where I'd just been.

Fuentes came off the floor with a gun in his hand. Rolf rolled over against the wall, grabbing around in the darkness for his rifle.

I lay flat on the floor, my side hurting like the very devil, with a bruised elbow that made me want to swear, but I didn't. This was one time when a single cuss word might get a man killed.

All was still, and then there was a pound of hoofs from some distance off, a horse running, and then the night was still.

"If I was you," Danny said, "I'd quit."

"Maybe that is it," Fuentes said. "Maybe they want you to quit. Maybe they want all of us to quit, starting with you."

He struck a match and lighted the lamp, then replaced the chimney. I pointed to the rolled-up blanket I'd been using for a pillow. There was a neat bullethole there, neat and round and perfect, despite the fuzzy material.

"He doesn't want me to quit," I said, "he wants me dead."

THIRTEEN

Headquarters ranch lay warm in the sunlight when I came down the slope, walking my horse. Fuentes and Danny rode with me, because three men can watch the country easier than one, and I was almighty tired when we reached the bunkhouse.

Barby Ann came out on the porch. "What's the matter, boys?"

Danny went up to the porch and told her, while Fuentes saw that I got safely inside. "You will be better off here, I think." The Mexican squatted on his heels near the door. "Joe will be here, and Ben Roper."

"I'm better," I said. "The fever's gone, all right, and now I'm only tired from the walk. Give me a couple of days and I'll be working again."

"You staying on?"

"Somebody shot at me. I'd like to find him and see if he'll shoot at me face to face. If I ride away now, I'd never know."

For two days I rested at the ranch. On the second day I walked outside into the sunlight, and when chow time came I went up to the house rather than have food brought to me. Nothing in me was cut out for laying abed, and I was itching to get into a saddle again. I'd been thinking, and I had some ideas.

There was nobody in the ranch house except Barby Ann. When I got to the table, she came from the kitchen. "I was just coming down to see how you felt."

"I felt too good to have you walking all the way down there."

She brought two cups and the coffeepot, then went back for

some other food. She was still in the kitchen when I heard somebody coming. I slid the thong off my six-shooter. It was probably
Rossiter, but after a man has been shot at a few times, he gets
jumpy.

Suddenly Rossiter loomed in the doorway, stopping abruptly.
"Barby? Barby Ann? Is that you?"

"It's me," I said. "It's Milo Talon."

"Oh?" He put out a hand, feeling for a chair. I jumped up and
took his hand and led him to a place near me at the table. "Talon?
Are you the one who's been having trouble?"

"I've been shot at, if that's what you mean."

"Who? Who did it? Was it some of the Balch crowd?"

Barby Ann came in from the kitchen, looking quickly from her
father to me. "Pa? You want coffee?"

"Please."

Barby Ann hesitated. "Pa? Milo's been shot. He was wounded."

"Wounded? You don't say! Are you all right, boy? Can you
ride?"

"I'll be back at work in a couple of days," I said cautiously.
Something in his manner irritated me, but I was not sure what it
was. And I had to remember that, due to my own discomfort, I
was more easily irritated.

We drank coffee and talked while Barby Ann got something
on the table. "Hope this won't make you leave us, son. Barby Ann
and me, well, we'd like to have you stay."

"I'll finish the roundup. Then I'll be drifting, I think."

"Hear you bid for some girl's box at the social. Paid a good
sum for it." He paused. "Who was she?"

"As a matter of fact, I don't know. She never told me her whole
name, and she wouldn't let me ride all the way home with her."

Rossiter frowned, drumming on the table with his fingers.
"Can't imagine that. Everybody around here knows everybody."
He turned his head toward Barby Ann. "Isn't that so, honey?"

"They didn't know her, Pa. I heard talk. Nobody had any idea
who she was or where she came from. She was...well, kind of
pretty, too."

After a while he turned and went into the next room. I sat
over my coffee, half dozing. Yet my mind kept going back to those
shots. Whoever had dug that hole between the logs in the cabin
wall had known where to dig. Yet that might not be surprising, for

line-cabins were often used by any passing cowboy who might stop overnight. The chances were good that every rider within fifty miles of the North Concho knew the place.

"How's the gather?" I asked Barby Ann.

"Good . . . We've nearly four hundred head down there now."

"Seen Roger lately?"

She flushed, and her lips tightened. "That's none of your business!"

"You're right. It isn't." I got up slowly, carefully, from the table. "Just making conversation. I think I'll go lay down."

"You do that." She spoke a little sharply. No doubt what I'd said had irritated her, and she was right. I'd no business asking a personal question, yet I couldn't help but wonder if Henry Rossiter knew his daughter was meeting Roger Balch.

For those two days I rested, slept, and rested. My appetite returned, and it became easier to walk around. On the third day, I got Danny to saddle up for me, as I still hesitated to swing a saddle on a horse for fear of opening the wound. I rode down to where the herd was gathered.

Harley was there, rifle in hand. It was a very good rifle, and well cared for.

"Nice bunch," I commented.

"They'll do," he said shortly. "Should have enough to drive."

He moved off to check a big cow that was showing an inclination to move toward the hills. The grazing was good, and they were close to water and showed little inclination to wander off. I could see another rider, Danny Rolf, I believed, on the other side.

It felt good to be back in the saddle, and I was riding my own horse with his easy way of moving. Harley seemed in no mood to talk, so I drifted on around the herd and into the edge of the hills. Yet I rode with care.

As I turned away from the herd to start back toward the ranch, I saw Joe Hinge coming down the slope from the west with a mixed lot of cattle. As they neared me, I drew up and helped guide them toward the main herd. With one or two exceptions they were Spur branded.

Joe pulled up near me, removing his hat to mop his brow. Despite the coolness of the air, he was sweating. And I didn't wonder. "How're you feelin'?" he asked me.

"So, so. Give me another day."

"Sure... But I can use you." He glanced at me. "You up to working out west?"

"Anytime," I said casually.

I decided against saying anything about a hunch I had.

"Good... But watch your step."

After a bit I rode back toward the bunkhouse, and unsaddled my horse when I got there. Doing the casual things that a man does all the time gives him time to think, and I was doing some thinking then.

Somebody wanted me dead... Why?

Another day I slept, loafed, and was irritable with myself for not being back on the job. The following morning I saddled up the bay with the black mane and tail, a short-coupled horse—and a good horse from which to rope.

The line-cabin was empty but there was a note written on a slab of wood with charcoal: WATCH OUT FOR BRINDLE.

Well, I would. I'd no notion of tangling with that one if it could be avoided.

All day I worked the bench and a couple of long, shallow arroyos, and rounded up eight head, then struck a dozen atop the mesa and started them back down toward the ranch.

At noon I was near the line-cabin and rode in to swap horses. Fuentes had just come in. We both switched our saddles, mine to a steel-dust that I'd never ridden, and then we went inside for coffee.

Fuentes was quiet. Suddenly he broke his silence. "Balch... He rode this way. Two, three times I see him. He keeps out of sight."

"Balch himself? Alone?"

"Sí."

That was something to study about, for this was in an area where few of his cattle would be found. Those of his we did find we were drifting back down to the holding ground, just like the others. For they could all be separated during the roundup, as was usual.

Puzzles didn't suit me. I'd hired on to handle stock, and I was ready to do just that, but I'd no idea of getting myself killed when I didn't even know what was going on. Balch was a man likely to ride roughshod over anything that got in his way, and Saddler was no better. Roger Balch had a problem with himself, trying to prove to everybody what a tough man he was. The major seemed able to take care of himself. And as for Henry Rossiter...what could a blind man do?

Rossiter had some loyal hands, and Joe Hinge was a good cattleman.

"Take it easy," Fuentes suggested. "You look tired."

I shrugged. "What the hell? Should I leave it all for you to do?"

When we went outside, Fuentes warned me. "Don't tie onto anything with the steel-dust. That's one of the fastest horses on the place, and a good cutting horse—but skittish on a rope."

We split up and I turned off toward the southeast, riding right where I'd gotten into trouble. Which shows how much I've got in the way of brains. Yet the pickings were good. I found a half dozen head in the first few minutes, broke them out and started them back. I cut wider and brought in several more, then moved the lot down on the better grass en route to the ranch.

Circling back, I looked for signs. No horse tracks anywhere. Suddenly, I came upon several head of cattle, and had turned them, when I heard a crackling in the brush. The steel-dust started nervously and rolled his eyes. Sure enough, it was Ol' Brindle standing there with his head up, looking at me.

I'd no bones to pick with him. In fact, he'd probably saved my bacon there a while back. So I just waved a hand and worked away from him. When I turned to look back, he was still there. He had his head up and he was watching me.

The truth of the matter was that I had a warm feeling for the old boy. He was tough and mean, and someday he might kill a cowhand, even me. But he was wild and free and full of fight, and I liked that. And he had ruled the roost there in his own corner of the country for a long time.

There never was a fiercer animal than a big longhorn who had run wild in the plains or the brush. They'd tackle anything that walked, even a grizzly. Nonetheless, I think most of the riders in that part of the country wanted to get a rope on him. It was a challenge to see him there. A challenge, because you knew when you dabbed a loop on Ol' Brindle you had tied onto a cyclone, and you'd have to win or get smashed up or killed. You give a cowhand a rope and, sooner or later, he'll dab it on anything that's running loose. He'd rope wolves, coyotes, mountain lions and bears...And I knew of one even roped an eagle.

But as far as I was concerned, Ol' Brindle could make his own way and he'd get no trouble from me...unless he started it.

Which he might.

Topping out on a rise, I pulled up short. Down in the hollow before me, a man with his back to me had roped a steer and was kneeling on its side.

His horse looked up at us, ears pricked, but the stranger was too busy with what he was doing to know we were there.

Branding? I saw no fire.

Slowly I walked my horse down the hillside, shucking my Winchester as I went.

The steer was dead. The man had cut its throat, and now he was cutting a piece of hide from the hip. And I knew that steer. It was one of those we'd pushed out of the brush the first day I was back.

"Is this a one-man party," I said, "or can anybody get in?"

He turned swiftly, his hand dropping to his gun.

It was Balch.

FOURTEEN

His face flushed even redder, then seemed to pale slightly. "Look," he said, "this isn't what you think."

"Take your hand off your gun and we'll talk about it," I said mildly. And very carefully he let go of his gun and lowered his hand.

"Seems to me," I said, "that you've killed one of our steers, on our range. I've seen men hung for less."

The stiffness and harshness had gone out of him. He measured me carefully. "Talon, this looks bad, mighty bad. The worst of it is, it *is* your steer, and he's wearing my brand."

"Your brand?" I was startled. To tell the truth, I'd seen that steer around and hadn't noted the brand, something a cowhand does naturally as he rides about his business. But this one had been pushed in among other cattle, and somehow I hadn't noticed.

"*Our* steer? Wearing *your* brand?" I repeated.

"Talon, this brand's two or three years old. And you can believe it or not, but I'm no rustler. I want every cow critter I can latch on to, but *honestly* latch on to. I'd steal from no man."

He paused. "Rossiter may believe different, an' you boys, too, but it's a fact. I never stole a beef from any man except for range eating... which we all do when we're out from home."

He continued. "A couple of years back I saw this steer following one of your cows. Now that'll happen now and again, when a calf loses its ma early and just takes after some cow that happens to be

103

close by. But I paid it no mind until something else showed up a while back. Then I started to get curious, almighty curious."

Balch held out the patch of hide he had cut from the steer's hip. When a brand has been reworked, with another brand burned over it, it may look all right from the outside, but a look at the back side of the hide shows plainly what has been done.

"Been altered, all right," I agreed. "Ours to yours. There's evidence for a hanging, Balch."

He nodded. "Talon, I'll take an oath I didn't do it, and I'll speak for my boys, too. I'll admit, I've hired on some rough men lately, but the boys I had two years ago—and most of them are still with me—were honest as the day is long."

Balch paused again. "And why should I check the brand on a steer that reads to be mine? Talon, there's something goin' on here. I don't know what it is, or why, but somebody has been misbranding stock. Somebody has branded your cattle to look like mine, and they've done it the other way, too."

Now I didn't like Balch. He was a rough, hard-shouldered man who'd walk right over you if he could, but right now I believed him.

"Looks like somebody might be trying to stir up trouble," I said. "Maybe somebody wants us to fight."

"I thought of that."

"Maybe somebody wants to fall heir to all this range and what cattle are left, somebody who figures he's got a lot of time."

"Maybe... But who?"

Oddly, at that moment I thought of Lisa. I did not like mysteries or puzzles, not when they concerned my life or my work. And now we had two.

Might they be solved the same way?

After all, who *was* Lisa? Where was her family? Where was her home?

You'd think, in a big, wide-open land like this, that people wouldn't know each other. But a ranch community is tightly knit and everybody knows everything about each other... or thinks they do. A stranger is spotted at once, and nobody's quite satisfied until the stranger has been fitted into a place in the scheme of things. Yet nobody knew anything about Lisa.

Which meant two things, at least. Lisa was new to the country, and she lived in some remote place.

Who else was there?

The major... obviously out of the question. He had all he wanted, lived exactly like he wanted, was the most important man in the area, both in his own mind and that of others.

"Take some thinking," I said, after a bit. "Balch, let's keep this under our hats. If you come up with any ideas, let me know."

Suddenly, on an inspiration, I told him how I'd been shot. Of somebody hunting me down.

"Why you?" he was puzzled.

"Some of our boys thought it was your outfit. It seems some of the folks around have heard I was good with a gun, and they figure your boys would like to have me out of it."

"No... I doubt that." He looked up at me. "Talon, my boys aren't afraid of you... or anybody else. They've offered to brace you, bring matters to a showdown, and I've put my thumb down on it. Talon, if somebody shot at you, it was not one of our bunch."

"All right," I agreed. "You keep your lot and I'll try to keep ours. Meanwhile, let's say nothing and see what develops. When it begins to appear that we aren't going to fight, whoever it is may try something more drastic."

Balch held up his hand. "All right, Talon. I'll ride with that."

He rode out of the hollow and, not being a wasteful man, I stepped down and cut myself a few steaks before turning back to the cabin.

Now I had to talk to Joe Hinge. Fortunately, none of the Stirrup-Iron outfit were trouble hunters. There must be no trouble with Balch and Saddler.

All the way back to the new corral that had been put together in the brush while I was laid up, I thought about the situation. But I came no closer to seeing an answer.

Joe Hinge, Roper, Fuentes and Harley had done some work. Using a wide clearing in some brush, they had fenced in the few openings and had them an easy corral for holding stock, until it could be drifted down to the ranch. It was a rawhide job, but it was all we needed. There were a dozen places the cows might get out if they knew it, but we'd not leave them in there long enough for them to make any discoveries, or even to realize they were penned.

Fuentes showed up with some cattle and we bunched them, and got them into the corral. When we had the bars up on the crude gate, I told him about Balch.

"Say nothing... not to anybody," I said. "You'll see that steer, anyway, and you should know. Something stinks to high heaven, and I want to know what it is."

He rolled his cigar in his white teeth and gave me an amused look. "You do not think I am a thief, eh? You do not think I steal cows?"

"Well," I said, "I don't know about that. I'm just bettin' you wouldn't steal the cows of a man you worked for." I grinned. "To tell you the truth, I don't think you'd steal any cows. And I don't want you to shoot anybody without reason."

He looked at the end of his cigar. "I think, amigo, you be careful. I think something happen soon. I think maybe these thieves, I think they find out what you know. They try to kill you."

"They've already tried," I said.

We rode back to the cabin and stripped our horses of their gear and went to the line-cabin and washed up. I was putting on my shirt when a horse came over the rise, coming fast.

It was ridden by Ann.

Fuentes was standing by the doorjamb with a Winchester. She gave him a quick look. "You all forted up? What's happened?"

"Nothing," I said. "We just don't want it to happen to us."

"Pa wants to see you," she said to me. "You're invited for dinner."

"Sorry," I said. "I've got nothing but my range outfit with me."

"That's all right." She glanced at Tony. "Sorry, he wants to talk to Milo... confidentially."

Fuentes shrugged. "Both of us could not be away, but if he goes, keep him all night. He is not strong, señorita. He works but he is still weak. I see it."

"Who's weak?" I blustered. "I can down you anytime!"

He grinned at me. "Perhaps, amigo. Perhaps. But I think the night air on a long ride, I think it not good for you, eh?"

I knew what he was getting at, and he had a point. But I wasn't the only one. "Night air isn't good for you, either," I said. "I'm scared to leave you alone. The boogers might get you."

"Me?" He looked surprised.

"Even you. Boogers get funny ideas. They might think you know as much about them as I do."

"Will you two stop the nonsense?" Ann said impatiently. "You talk like a couple of children."

"He is always the joker, this one," Fuentes said. "Only sometimes does he make the sense."

Luckily, I had a clean shirt in the line-cabin. It took me no time to get into it, and I'd just washed and combed my hair, so we lit out. Fortunately, she wanted to get to the ranch and she was in a hurry. We rode fast and I liked that, because a fast-riding man makes a poor target.

What I'd expected I was not sure, but what I found was certainly unexpected. The major's house was big, white and elegant, with white columns across the front, four of them, and a balcony between the two on each side of the door. There was a porch swing and some chairs, a table, and three steps up to the porch.

For a moment, I hesitated. "Are you sure he wants me in there? And not out at the bunkhouse?"

"I am sure."

We walked in, and the major looked around from the big chair in which he sat, removing his glasses as he did so.

"Come in, come in, son!" He got to his feet. "Sorry I had to send Ann for you, but she had a horse saddled."

"It was a pleasure, sir."

He looked at me again, a puzzled measuring look. He gestured toward a chair opposite his. "Something to drink? A whiskey, perhaps?"

"Sherry, sir. I'd prefer it...unless you have Madeira."

He looked at me again, then spoke to the elderly Chinese who came in at that moment. "Fong, brandy for me, and Madeira for this gentleman." He glanced at me again. "Any particular kind?"

"Boal or Rainwater...either will do."

Major Timberly knocked the ashes from his dead pipe and sucked on it thoughtfully. Several times he glanced at me from under his thick brows. Then he began to pack his pipe with tobacco. "I don't quite place you, young man."

"No?"

"You are working cattle for a neighbor, and from what I hear you are known as a man who is good with a gun. Yet you have the manners of a gentleman."

I smiled at him. "Sir, manners do not care who wears them, no more than clothes. Manners can be acquired, clothes can be bought."

"Yes, yes, of course. But there is a certain style, sir, a certain style. One knows a gentleman, sir."

"I've not noticed that it matters to the cattle, sir, if a man has a good horse and knows how to swing a rope. I don't believe they have any preference as to whether a man is a gentleman or not... And in these days all manner of men come west."

"Yes, yes, of course." Major Timberly lit his pipe. "I understand you've been shot at?"

"More than that, sir. I've been hit."

"And you've no idea who did it?"

"Not at present, sir."

"Talon, I need men. Especially, I need a man who is good with a gun. It looks to me like this country is headed for a war... I don't know why, or how, or when... I don't know who will begin it, but I want to win." He puffed strongly on the pipe. "Furthermore, I intend to win."

"What do you hope to gain, sir?"

"Peace... Security. For a little while, at least."

"Of course, sir. They are things we never have for long, do we, sir?" I paused. "If you are wanting to hire me as a warrior, don't waste your time. I am a cowhand, that's all."

"Is that why Rossiter hired you?" the major spoke sharply, his irritation showing.

"I suspect I was hired because Joe Hinge said he needed a hand. They had no idea I could use a gun. I do not advertise the fact. Furthermore, I see no need for trouble here. I believe nothing is at stake that you, Balch, Saddler and Henry Rossiter cannot arrange between you. If you go to war, you'll play right into the hands of whoever is stirring this up."

He was very quiet. For a moment he smoked, and then he asked, very gently, "And who might that be?"

"I do not know."

"And who could it be but one of us three? We are all there is."

The Madeira was good. I put my glass down and said, without really believing it, "Suppose it was an outsider? Someone safely away, who causes certain things to happen that arouse your suspicions?"

I waved my hand at the surroundings. "Several hundred thousand acres of range are at stake, Major." Suddenly, I changed the subject. "How is your gather progressing?"

He threw me a quick look. "So, so... Yours?"

"The same." I paused ever so briefly. "And your young stuff?"

He put his glass down hard. "Now what do you mean by that, young man? What do you know about my cattle?"

"Nothing at all, but I've a suspicion you are losing stock. I've a suspicion that you aren't finding much that is three years old or less."

He glared at me. "You're right, damn it! Now how did you know that?"

"Because it is the same with us, and the same with Balch and Saddler." I took up my glass. "We've found very little under four years old."

He put his glass down and wiped the back of his hand across his mouth. "It's damnable! Damnable, I say!" He gestured around him. "I live well, young man. I *like* to live well. But it costs money, damn it. It costs a lot of money, and I need every head of stock I can get. Believe me, young man. I'd say this to nobody else but you, but you're a gentleman, sir. I don't care what your job is, you're a gentleman, and you'll hold what I say in confidence."

He paused. "I *need* that breeding stock! I owe money. A lot of money. Folks believe me to be a rich man, and if the cattle I should have are out there, I am. But if they are not, and they do not seem to be, I'll lose all this. Every bit of it. And if you fail me and say I said that, I'll call you a liar, sir, and I'll call you out, gunfighter or no."

"You may be sure I'll not speak of it. Does your daughter know?"

"Ann? Of course not! Women have no head for business, sir. Nor should they have. Women have beauty, graciousness and style, and that is why we love them and why we work for them. Even a poor man, sir, wants those qualities in a woman, and his wife should have them in his eyes. Ann knows nothing of this, and shall know nothing."

"And if something happens to you? What then? How will she manage?"

Major Timberly waved a hand. "Nothing will happen." He got up suddenly. "Balch and Rossiter have lost young stock, too? That puts a different look on it. Unless..." he paused and turned to look at me, "unless one of them is stealing from himself, too, to appear innocent. My boy, if what we assume is true, those cattle have been stolen over a period of years, stolen very carefully so their disappearance would not be noted."

My thoughts were running upon what he had said about women not understanding business. He should have known my mother. Em Talon was a quarter of an inch under six feet, a tall, rawboned mountain woman. She had been handsome as a young woman, yet I doubt if she had ever been what one would call pretty... striking, perhaps.

Even while my father lived, she had been the one who operated the ranch. A shrewd judge of stock as well as of men, she was strongly a Sackett, which was her family name. She was a strong woman, a woman fit to walk beside a strong man, which Pa had been. Yet he was a builder, and only half a rancher.

Major Timberly and I talked long, and finally when it was time for bed, he said, "Young man, if you learn anything new, come quickly to me. If you have to take action to stop this rustling, do so, and I will back you."

"That's just it, sir. It must not be stopped."

"Not stopped? Are you daft?"

"No, sir. First we must find out what is being done with the cattle. I believe they are being held somewhere, in some hidden place, some distance off. If we put pressure on the rustlers now, they'll just get off with the herd and drive to Mexico. And that will be the end of it.

"Leave it to me, Major. I think I have an idea. If you wish to get in touch with me again, I'm at the line-cabin. If I'm not there, tell Fuentes."

"The Mexican?"

"He's the best hand on the Stirrup-Iron, Major, and a solid man."

"Of course. I meant no offense. I know Fuentes well, and he can go to work for me anytime he's of a mind to."

When I was at breakfast the following morning, the major did not appear, but Ann did.

She came in, looking bright and sunny in a starched gingham dress of blue and white with a kind of blue scarf at her throat.

"You and Pa talked a long time," she said brightly. "Did you ask him for my hand?"

"As a matter of fact," I said, "we talked about cattle. Didn't get around to you."

"You mean he didn't give you his little oration on women not knowing anything about business? I am surprised. He always enjoys that subject. He's a dear, but he's silly. I know more about the business of this ranch than he does, and have... since I was twelve. Ma told me I'd have to look after him."

I chuckled. "Does he know that?"

"Oh dear, no! He'd be very upset. But he's very bright about cattle and horses, Milo. He can make money, but he can also spend it... far too well. Even at that, we'd be doing well if it wasn't for the stock we've lost."

"Much?"

"Over half our young stuff... and some of the best six-year-olds are gone."

Over half? Balch and Rossiter had lost almost *all*. Was there a clue here? Actually, the major's stock was better than that of Stirrup-Iron or Balch and Saddler. He'd brought in a couple of excellent bulls, and was breeding more beef on his young stuff, so why only half or a bit more?

That needed some thinking, but when I rode out that morning I put the idea out of my mind. The first few miles led over a wide prairie where nobody could get within two miles of me without being seen. There were a few scattered cattle wearing the Stirrup-Iron, and I started them off ahead of me. But nearing the low rolling hills I grew cautious.

Such hills are deceptive, and they offer hiding places that do not seem to be there. I had cut wide to bring back a cow with a notion for the high country when I saw the tracks—several fresh tracks, clearly defined, of a fast-moving, smooth-stepping horse.

The tracks pointed toward the hills on my left, so my eyes swept the grassy crests but saw nothing that looked to be out of place. The steel-dust moved of his own volition to head a steer to the right, and I held my place there.

Suddenly, I let out a whoop and started the cattle running through the draw, yet once I had them started I swung the gray and went up the left slope at a run.

The gray topped out on the crest just as a bullet clipped past my ear, and then I saw a flurry of movement, somebody scrambling into a saddle, and a horse leaving at a dead run.

The gray was a runner, and it liked to run. Despite the quick scramble up the slope it was off and running without a word from me. I shucked my rifle, sighted on the bobbing figure ahead, and tried a shot.

I missed.

At the distance and at a bobbing target, it would have been a miracle had I not missed, but suddenly the rider whipped his horse over and vanished!

The rider was now two hundred yards off, and by the time I reached the place and saw the narrow slide that led into a wooded valley below, he was through the gap and gone. I went down it, and then pulled up.

Before me stretched a good half mile of thick brush ending in some broken hills. There was a scent of dust in the air, nothing more. The man I pursued might be in there anywhere, might be waiting for me to come on and be killed. Nonetheless, this was as close as I'd come and—

Tracks... The earth was dusty but I found a partial one and, taking that direction, picked up another. In a moment I was in the dense thicket, dodging prickly pear and mesquite.

Another track, a broken mesquite twig, leaves just coming back into place after something had pushed through them. I followed carefully, keeping a sharp lookout to left and right. Yet an hour of search brought me nothing.

Whoever had fired at me had gotten away again. I had a hunch my luck was running out. After all, how many times can a man miss?

Granted, he'd not had many good chances, but luck had saved my bacon, and such luck does not last. The odds were against me.

Dropping down in the arroyo, I rode on after my cattle, which had drifted on through a small, scattered thicket and were now beginning to spread out to graze. Once more I made my gather and started on, picking up two more head as I moved.

Fuentes was gone when I came in, but Danny Rolf was there.

He was seated at the table with a cup of coffee in his hand, yet I had the sudden impression that he had not been there long.

He looked up sharply, guiltily, I thought. Then he put his cup down. "Howdy," he said. "Wondered where you was."

FIFTEEN

Taking my cup, I went to the coffeepot and filled it. My eyes caught a bit of mud, still damp, near the hearth. I looked at it, suddenly every sense alert.

Mud? Where around here was there mud? I glanced out the door toward the water trough. It had not overflowed, and the earth around it was dry.

Straightening up, I took a swallow of coffee, taking the opportunity to look past the cup at Danny Rolf's boots.

Mud.

Dropping into a chair across the table, I glanced out the door again. His horse was tied on the far side of the corral, a curious thing in itself. The sort of thing a man might do who wanted to approach the cabin unseen, yet not to actually sneak up to it.

"Any luck?"

"Huh?" He was startled, obviously worried by something else. "Luck? Oh, no. Found a few head, but they're gettin' flighty. Hard to round up now, they've been drove so much."

He looked at my hat. "You're sure gettin' a good hat ruined. Better buy you a new one."

"I was thinking of that, but it's a far piece to where I can get one. Not many places this side of San Antone."

He looked at me suddenly. "San Antone? That's the wrong direction. Why, there's places north of us...I don't think they're so far off."

Neither of us said much, each busy with his own thoughts.

114

Danny's clothes were dusty—except for those boots. He'd been working or riding... But where?

"Danny," I said, "we've got to go easy. Lay off the Balch and Saddler outfit."

"What's that mean?" He shot me a straight, hard look.

"They've been losing stock, too. There may be somebody else who wants trouble between us so he can pick up the pieces."

"Ah, I don't believe it," he scoffed. "What are they hiring gunfighters for? You know damn well Balch would ride roughshod over anybody got in his way. And as for that son of his—"

"Take it easy. We don't have a thing to go on, Danny. Just dislike and suspicion."

"You ain't been around long. You just wait and see." He paused. "You been workin' south of here?"

"Some... Mostly east."

"Joe Hinge said you're needed over on the other side. He's fixin' to start cleanin' out our cattle from the Balch and Saddler stuff. If you're really good with that gun, that'll be the place for you."

"It needn't come to shooting."

He looked at me slowly, carefully. "That Ingerman, he shapes up pretty mean. An' Jory Benton... I hear he's gunnin' for you."

He seemed to be trying to irritate me, so I just grinned at him and said, "Ingerman is tough... I don't know about Benton, but Ingerman is a fighter. He's tough and he's dangerous, and any time you go to the mat with him, you'd better be set for an all-out battle. He takes fighting wages, and he means to earn them."

"Scared?"

"No, Danny, I'm not, but I'm careful. I don't go off half-cocked. When a man pulls a gun on another man, he'd better have a reason, a mighty good one that he's mighty sure of. A gun isn't a toy. It's nothing to be worn for show or to be flashed around, showing off. When you put a hand on a gun you can die."

"You sound like you're scared."

"No. I sound like what I am, a cautious man who doesn't want to kill a man unless the reason demands it. When a man picks up a gun he picks up responsibility. He has a dangerous weapon, and he'd better have coolness and discretion."

"I don't know what that means."

"He'd better have judgment, Danny. That other man who

wears a gun also has a family, a home; he has hopes, dreams, ambitions. If you're human, you must think of that. Nobody in his right mind takes a human life lightly."

He got up, stretching a little. The mud on his boots was drying. He had gotten it somewhere not too far from here, but where? There were other waterholes...the springs Fuentes had showed me and a couple we'd found, but they were over east. Of course, there was also the creek over there.

"Seen Ol' Brindle?" I asked him suddenly.

"Brindle? No. Hope I never do."

"Better stay away from the creek," I said casually. "That's where I saw him last."

"What creek?" he demanded belligerently. "Who says I been around any creek?" He stared at me suspiciously, his face flushed and guilty.

"Nobody, Danny. I was just telling you that's where Brindle is. Joe Hinge doesn't want any of us getting busted up by him."

He walked toward the door. "I better be gettin' back." He lingered as if there were something else on his mind, and finally he said, "That girl whose box you bought. You sweet on her?"

"Lisa? No. She just seemed to be all alone, and I didn't know anybody very much, so I bid on her box."

"You spent a lot of money," he accused. "Where'd you get that kind of money?"

"Saved it. I'm no boozer, Danny, and I'm a careful man with a dollar. I like clothes and I like horses, and I save money to spend on them."

"You fetched a lot of attention to her," he said. "You brought trouble to her, I'm thinkin'."

"I doubt it, but if I did it was unintentional."

He still lingered. "Where at did she say she lived?"

"She didn't tell me."

He thought I was lying. I could see it in his face, and I had a hunch, suddenly, that Danny had been doing his own thinking about her. Ann Timberly was out of his class, and so was China Benn. Barby Ann was thinking only of Roger Balch, and Danny was young, and he was dreaming his own dreams, and here was a girl who might fit right into them. If he had taken a dislike to me, which was possible, she might be the reason.

"If she didn't tell me, it's because she didn't want me to know. It was my feeling she didn't want anybody to know. I think she's got a reason for keeping herself unknown."

"You sayin' there's something wrong about her?" He stared at me, hard-eyed and eager to push it further.

"No, Danny. She seemed a nice girl, only she was scared about something. She did tell me that nobody knew she was there and she had to get right back."

We talked a little longer to no purpose, and he went out and rode away. I walked to where his horse had been tied. There were several lumps of dried mud that had fallen from his horse's hooves.

If he had come far, that mud would have been gone before this. The mud had been picked up somewhere not too far off... But where?

I was stirring up the fire for cooking when Fuentes came in. He stripped the gear from his horse, noticed the tracks Danny had left and glanced toward the cabin.

Standing in the door, I said, "It was Danny. Had something on his mind, but he didn't say what. Said he saw Hinge. He wants us to come in. He's going to work west of here, up on the cap-rock. He's afraid there'll be trouble."

After a moment, I said, "I don't think there will be. I think Balch will stand aside."

"What about Roger?"

Well, what about him? I thought about Roger, and those two guns of his, and the itch he had to prove himself bigger than he was. I'd ridden with a number of short men, one time and another, and some of them the best workers I'd ever come across... Good men. It wasn't simply that he was short that was driving Roger. There was some inner poison in the man, something dangerous that was driving him on.

Fuentes changed the subject. "Found some screwworms to-day. We had better check every head we bring in."

"Danny wants to work this part of the range."

Fuentes looked around at me. "Did he say why?"

"No, but I've got an idea it's Lisa. That girl at the box supper."

Fuentes grinned. "Why not? He's young, she's pretty."

All true enough but somehow the idea worried me. Danny was young and impressionable, and Lisa had been frightened of what she had done. She had slipped away secretly to go to the box supper, and that implied that somebody at her home did not want her to go?

A mother? A father? Or was it somebody else? For some other reason?

It was not logical that a family could be in this country long and be completely unknown. So... chances were, they had not been here long.

They were living off the beaten track, which didn't mean too much because nearly everything out here lived far apart.

Still, there was considerable riding around. I thought about her clothes. They had been good enough—simple, and a bit worn here and there but clean, ironed, and prepared for wearing by a knowing hand.

Even if Lisa had only been here a short time, it was obvious she did not want to be found... For her own reasons? Or because of that someone who did not want her away from home?

"Tony," I paused, "I don't want to leave here."

He shrugged. "Joe needs us. He expects trouble with Balch."

"There will be none."

"You think, amigo, that because of your talk, he will say nothing?"

"Yes, I do... But lord knows, I can be wrong."

We packed up what gear we had around the place and saddled up with fresh horses, yet I still did not wish to go. What I wanted was time to ride further south, further east. There were a lot of canyons in the Edwards Plateau country, a lot of places where cattle could be hidden.

Suddenly, I began to wonder. How many head had been stolen? I asked Fuentes.

"Five hundred... Maybe twice that many. After all, whoever is stealing is taking from all three ranches, and has been taking for maybe three years. "

"He's got to think about Indians."

"Sí... Maybe he doesn't have to think about them, amigo. Maybe they are friends, you think?"

"Or he's found some hiding place where they won't look."

Fuentes shook his head. "The Apache won't look? An Apache would look into the gates of hell, amigo. So would a Kiowa or a Comanche."

We rode on, not talking. Organized roundups were a new thing in this neck of the woods. Usually a man, with two or three neighbors, would make their gather, sort out the brands and start a trail drive. When they got to the end of the track, they would sell the cattle they had, keeping an account of any brands from their part of the country, and when they got home they'd straighten up.

Unbranded stuff was usually branded according to the brand its mother was wearing—if there was a mother around. And if the rancher was honest. Otherwise, any strays were apt to collect his own brand, and often enough there were a good many cattle that wore no brand at all... mavericks... to be branded in any way that pleased the roundup crew or the man in charge.

Years ago, down in east Texas, a man named Maverick had traded for a bunch of cattle, and never bothered to either count or brand them. Then when an unbranded cow critter was seen on the range, somebody would be sure to say, "Oh, that's one of Maverick's!" Hence, the name for unbranded stock.

All was quiet at the ranch when we rode in. We had brought few cattle, as we wished to move right along, and those few we turned in with the lot on the flat.

Joe Hinge was in the bunkhouse when we walked in. He looked up, his surprise obvious. "Wasn't expectin' you fellers. What happened?"

"Didn't you tell Danny to have us come down? He said you were ready to move west after those cattle."

"Well, I am... just about. But I surely didn't send Danny for you, nor nobody else. I figured the first of the week—"

Well, I looked at Fuentes, and he at me. "Danny said you wanted us," Fuentes commented. "He must have misunderstood you."

Ben Roper came in. "Seen anything more of Ol' Brindle?"

"He's over there. You want him, you can have him. He's got a few friends scattered around in that brush just about as mean and ornery as he is."

Irritated, I walked to the door. What was Danny up to? I heard Fuentes make some comment about it to Hinge, but my thoughts worried at the problem like a dog over a bone. He had given us... or so it seemed... misinformation, so he could have the field to himself. I had wanted a few days more over there.

Well, I swore a little, thinking of the ride I'd been planning over to the east and south. I wanted to find those missing cattle, and I had a hunch. Now it would be days, perhaps weeks, before I got over there again.

Ben Roper came out, rolling a cigarette. "What's up?"

I told him.

"Ain't like Danny," he said. "That's a pretty good lad. Good hand...works hard. Maybe you're right about the girl. He's been talkin' about her ever since the dance." He grinned at me. "No tellin' what a young bull will do when he's got somethin' on his mind."

He lit the cigarette. "Anyway, you'll get some good grub. Barby Ann's upset, too, and when she's upset, she cooks."

He looked at the glowing end of the cigarette. "That there Roger Balch was by...Stopped a while at the house. She's been upset ever since."

"How far is it to San Antone?" I said, changing the subject.

"Ain't never been there from here," he said doubtfully. "Maybe a hundred mile. Could be more." He glanced at me. "You goin' to light a shuck? Hell, man, we need you!"

"Just thinking."

Squatting on my heels, I took up a bit of rock and drew a rough outline of the cap-rock in the sand, as I thought it was...over west of us.

San Antone was the nearest big town, but it was a long way off...several days' ride.

Between here and there was a lot of rough country, and some plains—rolling hills and the like. There were streams, enough for good water even if a man didn't know where other waterholes lay. But a drive of young stuff over that route...stuff as young as some of it was...was unlikely. A man would be apt to lose half his gather, one way or another.

Wherever those cattle were, it was between here and there, and I'd bet it wasn't more than twenty miles off, somewhere down there in the Kiowa country. He would need water...Young stuff will drink a lot while growing...And he'd need somebody just to hold those calves...unless he had a lot of water and mighty rich graze.

I looked at what I'd drawn, but it wasn't enough. It told me nothing. There were several blank spaces I had to fill in. I needed to talk to somebody who knew the country, somebody who wouldn't be curious as to why I wanted to know. Better still, somebody from whom I could bleed the information without him even being aware I was trying.

Straightening up, I hitched up my gunbelt and was turning back toward the bunkhouse when there was a call from the house.

"Looks like you're wanted," Ben Roper said.

Barby Ann was on the steps, and I walked toward her. Ben went on into the bunkhouse.

She looked white and strained. Her eyes were unnaturally bright and her hands trembled a little. "Talon," she said, "do you want to make five hundred dollars?"

Startled, I stared at her.

"I said five hundred dollars," she repeated. "That's more than you'd make in a year, even at fighting wages for Balch and Saddler."

"That's a lot of money," I agreed. "How do I do it?"

She stared at me, her lips tightening. At that moment she looked anything but pretty. "You kill a man," she said. "You kill Roger Balch."

SIXTEEN

Well, I just stood there. Barby Ann didn't look to be the same woman. Her skin was drawn tight, and there was such hatred in her face as I'd rarely seen on any man's, and never on a woman's.

"Kill him," she said, "and I'll give you five hundred dollars!"

"You've got me wrong," I said. "I don't kill for hire."

"You're a gunfighter! We all know you're a gunfighter. You've killed men before!" she protested.

"I've used a gun in my own defense, and in defense of property. I never hired my gun and never will. You've got the wrong man. Anyway," I said, more gently, "you're mad now, but you don't want him dead. You wouldn't want to kill a man."

"Like hell, I wouldn't!" Her eyes were pinpointed with fury. "I'd like to see him dead right here on the floor! I'd stomp in his face!"

"I'm sorry, ma'am."

"Damn you! Damn you for a yellow-bellied coward! You're afraid of him! Afraid! It's just like he says, every damn one of you is scared of him!"

"I don't think so, ma'am. None of us have any reason to jump Roger Balch. I don't think anybody likes him too well, but that's no reason to kill him."

"You're scared!" she repeated contemptuously. "You're all scared!"

"You'll have to excuse me, ma'am." I backed away. "I'm no killer."

She swore at me, then turned and went into the house. Fuentes came to the door of the bunkhouse as I went in. "What was that all about?" he asked, curiously.

I told him.

He looked at me thoughtfully, then shrugged. "I guess he told her he was through. Or that he was marrying Ann Timberly."

"Marrying *who?*" I turned on him.

"He's been courting her. Going to call, setting out with her...Everybody knows that. I guess Barby Ann found out and faced him with it."

Joe Hinge had been listening. "She'll get over it," he said, carelessly.

"I don't think so," I said, after a minute. "I think we'd better tie down for squalls. The way she feels now, if she can't get somebody to kill him, she'll do it herself."

Hauling my dufflebag from under my bunk, I got out a shirt that needed mending and started to stitch up a tear in it. Most cowhands have a needle and thread somewhere, but this was a buckskin shirt, and I was stitching it with rawhide.

Hinge watched me for a minute. "Hell," he said, "you do that like you was a tailor!"

"Me? I learned watching Ma," I said. "She was handy."

He looked at me thoughtfully. "Where you from, Talon? You never said."

It was a question rarely asked in western country. So I just said, "That's right, I never did."

He flushed a little, and started to rise and, not minding, I said, "Up north a ways...Colorado."

"Good country," he commented, and went outside.

Fuentes was stretched out on his bunk. Now he sat up and tugged on his boots. "I've got a bad feeling," he said. "I feel like a mossyhorn steer with a storm comin' up."

I looked at him, then forked out my knife and cut the rawhide, tucking in an end and drawing it tight. "Me, too," I agreed.

Ben Roper rode into the yard and stepped down, stripping the gear from his horse. Then he shook out a loop and roped a fresh one. "Now where d'you suppose he's goin'?" I asked Tony.

"He feels it, too," Fuentes said. "He's just gettin' ready."

Barby Ann came out from the house and called to Ben. "I

forgot. Harley wants one of you boys should spell him. He's got to ride over home."

Fuentes started to rise but I waved him back. "I'll do it."

Outside, I told Ben. "Long's you got that rope in your hands, fish out one for me. That gray gelding will do. I'll take over for Harley."

"You just come in," he protested.

"Who didn't?" I grinned at him. "I got to get out of that bunkhouse. I'm gettin' cabin fever."

He put a loop on the gray, who quieted down when he felt the rope. It was a good horse, one I'd never ridden but had seen around. I threw my saddle on him and cinched up.

Ben stood by, coiling his rope. He kept looking at me, and finally he said, "Joe tells me you had words with Barby Ann. That she wanted you to kill Roger Balch."

"Uh-huh."

"How much did she offer?"

"Five hundred."

"Whew!" he glanced at me. "She's really mad!"

"Mad enough to do it herself." I glanced around. Nobody was close to us. "I wonder if her pa knows?"

Ben Roper finished coiling the rope. "He don't miss much," he commented. "Seems like he would, but he knows everything, seems like."

Harley was waiting by the herd when I came down. "Took you long enough," he said.

"She just told me." I didn't like his attitude very much.

He just turned his mount and rode out of there, not toward the ranch, but south toward where his place was, I guess. I walked my horse around the herd, bunching them a little. They had fed well, and watered, and now they were settling down for the night, although it was just evening. A bit later one of the other boys would be out to help, but the cattle were quiet enough, liking the holding ground. Usually of a morning they were drifted a mite to fresh grass, then brought in closer where the ranch and the hills helped to corral them.

As I rode around, I tried to spot the restless ones, the troublemakers. There's always a few ready to jump and run, or to cut up a mite.

Sitting a horse on night-herd can give a man a chance to dream. It was just dusk, the sun out of the sky, but night had not blacked things out. Here and there a star hung up there, advance agent for all those yet to come. Later on, the cattle might become restless, but now with the quiet of evening on them, they were laying down or standing, just chewing their cuds and letting time pass. Even the few calves born since we had them on the holding ground had stopped jumping about.

Turning the gray, I rode partway up the slope of the hill where I could see the entire herd. I curled one leg around the saddle horn, shoved my hat back on my head and went to contemplating.

First it was Ann... She was quite a girl, when you came right down to it, lots of fire there, but stamina, too. She'd stepped right in when I was hurt.

Aside from stiffness and a care how I wore my belt, my wound was much better. I'd lost blood, but the place had scabbed over, and unless I got to wrestling some steer it would stay that way. I tired fast, and would until I got my strength back, but in this wide-open plains country the air was fresh and clean and wounds healed fast.

From Ann my thoughts went to China Benn... We had danced together, and there for a moment all seemed right with the world.

My thoughts veered to the box social, and Lisa. Now I'd no romantic notion about her, yet the mystery of who she was, and where she went to, worried me.

She was in a hurry to get home, which spoke of a strict father or a husband... although she'd denied there was a husband.

When it was full dark, Ben Roper rode out. "Get some coffee," he advised. "You've got a long night ahead."

"All right," I said, but I sat my horse. "You know the country south of here?"

"A mite. South and east, that is. We used to ride over to San Antone now and again. If there's four, five in a bunch, it's safe enough. Although Rossiter told me there'd been news of Apaches raiding down thataway."

"Any settlers?"

He shook his head. "Not unless they keep themselves hid.

Oh, there's some German folks, moved over from around Fred-
ericksburg... But they just run a few cows down that way from
time to time."

"Has Danny showed up?"

"He's up at the line-cabin, I reckon." He glanced at me. "You
ready to go up against Ingerman an' them?"

"There won t be any trouble."

Ben Roper turned his hat in his hands, then replaced it on
his head. I'd noticed this was a way he had when he was thinking.
"All right," he said, doubtfully, "but I'll be there and I'll be
armed."

"Ben? You're a good man, Ben. There's nobody I'd rather have
behind me. I think this time they will try for an easy way out and
save face, but we've got to be ready for trouble from Jory. If they're
as smart as I hope, they'll have him somewhere else. He's got a
quick trigger, and he's anxious to prove he's a big boy now."

"That's the way I see it." Ben turned his horse. "Get your
coffee," he said. And I turned my horse and cantered back to the
ranch.

All was quiet at the ranch. A few stars hung in the the sky,
others were appearing. There was a light in the bunkhouse, and
two rooms were lighted in the ranchhouse. Turning my horse into
the corral, I roped and saddled my night horse and tied him at the
corral, then walked to the bunkhouse.

Joe Hinge was reading a newspaper, Fuentes was asleep.
"Danny show up?" I asked.

"At the line-cabin, I reckon," Hinge said. "How're the cattle?"

"Quiet. Ben's out there."

From a pair of spare saddlebags I took cartridges and filled a
few empty loops. Hinge put his paper down and took off the glasses
he used for reading.

"You ain't expecting trouble over west?"

"I had a talk with Balch. If we take it light and easy, I think
they will. It'll be touchy... especially with Jory Benton."

"Three, four days should do it."

"Joe? You've been around here a spell. What's off southeast
of here?"

"San Antonio," he smiled a little, "but that's some way... more'n
a hundred mile, I reckon."

"I meant in that Kiowa country."

"That's what's there. Kiowas, Comanches, often enough Apaches. It's a raiding trail when they ride up from Mexico or from the Panhandle. Comanches have themselves a hideout in the Panhandle somewhere. I've heard tell of it."

"I meant closer by."

"Nothin' I know of. Few good waterholes yonder, but folks fight shy of them because of Kiowas."

For a moment I stood there, wondering about Danny and thinking of Lisa... Now where the hell did she come from? And where did she go?

It was darker when I went outside. My horse turned to look at me, but I walked up to the house and went in.

The kitchen was lighted by one coal-oil lamp, and the table was set for breakfast with a blue and white checkered cloth. I got the coffeepot and a cup and went to the table. Several doughnuts were on the sideboard and I latched onto a couple of them, then straddled a chair and started to look at that tablecloth, but I was not seeing it. I was seeing the country southwest of here toward the Edwards Plateau country. There were a lot of canyons and brakes in there, room enough to hide several armies, and rough country with plenty of water if a body knew where to look... and nobody riding that way because of Kiowas.

Was there some tie-up between Lisa and whoever was stealing those cattle? I didn't like to think it, but it could be. And who had shot at me? Someone I knew? Or someone totally unknown to any of us?

Slowly my thoughts sifted the names and faces through the sieve of recollection. But it came up with nothing.

I heard a faint stir from the adjoining room, and a shadow loomed in the door. It was Rossiter.

"Joe?" His tone was questioning.

"It's Talon," I said. "Ben just relieved me for coffee."

"Ah!" He walked to the table, putting out a hand, feeling for the corner. "I hear you've had some trouble."

"Nothing I can't handle," I replied, with more confidence than I felt. "I've been shot at, but he can't always get away."

"How about you? He can't always miss, either."

"If that happens, there's always Barnabas," I said, "and the Sackett boys."

"*Sackett!* What have you to do with them?"

"Didn't you know? Ma was a Sackett. She was a mountain woman, living in Tennessee until Pa found her there."

"Well, I'll be damned! I should have guessed it. No," he was suddenly thoughtful, "I never knew." He drummed on the table with his fingers as I sipped coffee. "You mean that whole outfit would come if you needed them?"

"I reckon. Only we figure each of us can handle what comes our way. It's only when a man is really outnumbered that the clan gathers...or when one of us is dry-gulched. Whoever is trying to kill me doesn't realize what would happen if he did. There's only one of me, but you get seven or eight Sacketts and Talons in the country and they'll find whoever did it."

"If there's anything to find."

The doughnuts were good, and so was the coffee, yet Rossiter sat there after eating, obviously with something on his mind.

"Have you talked to Barby Ann?"

"Now and again," I said.

"She's a fine girl...a fine girl. Right now she's very upset about something, but she won't tell me what it is." He turned his face toward me. "Is it something between you two?"

"No, sir, it isn't."

"You could do worse. She's a fine girl, Talon, and there isn't a better cook or baker in the country. She'll make some man a fine wife."

Now I was getting uneasy. I didn't like the sound of what he seemed to be leading up to. I grabbed the last doughnut and took a bite, then a swallow of coffee. I got up hastily. "Ben's waitin' out there. I'd better go."

"All right," he sounded irritated, "but you think on it."

I took another swallow of coffee and went out the door, but paused a moment on the stoop to eat the last of that doughnut. As I stood there in the dark I heard Barby Ann's voice, and it sounded just like her face had looked that other day.

"Pa? What you trying to do? Marry me off to that no-good cowhand?"

"Nothing of the kind. I thought—"

"Well, don't think about it. When I marry I'll choose my own man. In fact, you might as well know. I already have."

"Have *what?* Married?"

"No, Pa. I've picked my man. I'm going to marry Roger Balch."

"Roger *Balch*?" His voice was a shade louder. "I thought his pa was figurin' on him marrying that Timberly girl."

Her voice was cold, a shade ugly. "That will change, Pa. Believe me, that will change."

"Roger Balch?" His tone was thoughtful. "Why, Barby, I hadn't given that a thought. Roger Balch... of all things!"

Back at the herd I watched Ben Roper ride off with my thanks, and then I started around the bunch. Most of them were laying down, settled down to rest until their midnight stretch.

Yet my thoughts kept going back to that talk I'd overheard. Not that anybody had said anything wrong, but it was the tone I detected... or thought I detected... in their voices.

I'd have sworn that Roger Balch had told her he was through with her, and that was the reason she had wanted me to kill him. Now she had changed her mind and was going to marry him.

Now just what did that mean?

Riding night-herd when things are quiet is a mighty easy time for thinking. It's almighty still out there and the cows are companions enough. You just set your horse, letting the natural habit of your mind listen and notice anything wrong with the herd, and then your thoughts go where they will.

Barby Ann, mad clean through, wanted me to kill Roger Balch. Yet now she told her father she was going to marry him?

A cover-up? Or a change of mind? Or... and the thought chilled me... had she thought of death for somebody else?

Like Ann Timberly...

SEVENTEEN

Joe Hinge sat his horse and looked at us. There were Ben Roper, Tony Fuentes and me, all mounted and ready to go, and it not daybreak yet.

"Take it easy," Joe advised. "Don't run no cattle. Roust out what you find of Stirrup-Iron or Spur and get them back here. Steer clear of Jory Benton or any of that outfit. He'll be on the prod, maybe. Talon thinks they'll lay off, and we got to hope he's right, but don't you boys scatter out more'n you have to. Three quick shots, and you come together."

"Where?"

"Right where we first met up with Talon the first time. Right there. But if you have to, hole up and make a fight of it. You boys are all grown men, and you know what you have to do. Do it easy as you can an' get out. We don't want trouble if we can help it. First place, it don't make no sense. Second place, we're out-numbered and out-gunned."

He paused. "Not that we can't fight. We can. I rode with Jeb Stuart. Fuentes grew up fightin' and Ben, here, he was in the Sixth Cavalry. If need be, we can do our share."

I glanced at Ben. "Sixth Cavalry? Ever run into a long-geared Tennessee boy named William Tell Sackett?"

He laughed. "I should smile. Right out of the mountains and didn't know from nothin', but he sure could shoot!"

"He's a cousin of mine."

130

Ben Roper glanced at me. "I'll be damned. You're cousin to Tell? I figured Talon for a French name."

"It is. My ma was a Sackett."

We rode out, not talking. We had a few miles to go before we reached the Balch and Saddler range, but their riders could be anywhere about and we hoped to see them first.

It was short-grass country, with scattered patches of mesquite. We spotted a few cattle, most of them Balch and Saddler.

We were coming up a cliff from the lowlands when we saw three riders coming toward us. One of them was Ingerman, another was Jory Benton, and the third was Roger Balch.

"Ride easy now!" Hinge warned. Then he added, angrily, "Just our luck to have that young hothead along!"

We pulled up and let them come to us. I reined my horse off to one side a mite, and Fuentes did the same.

Roger was in the lead. "Where the hell d' you think you're goin'?" he demanded.

"Roundin' up cattle," Hinge said. "We're after anything with a Stirrup-Iron or a Spur brand."

"You were told there were none around!" Roger said. "Now back off and get out of here!"

"A few weeks back," I said quietly, "I saw Stirrup-Iron and Spur cattle up yonder. Those are the ones we want, and nothing else."

He turned on me. "You're Talon, I take it. I've heard of you." He looked again. "At the social! You were the one bought the box!"

"I've been around," I said.

"All right," he said, "now move. Or we move you!"

"If I were you," I said quietly, "I'd talk to my pa first. Last time I talked to him, he didn't have any objections to us rounding up cattle."

"Get off!" he said. Then the gist of my comment seemed to reach him. "You talked to Pa? When was this?"

"Few days back, over east of here. Seemed like we understood each other. Had a right friendly talk. Somehow I don't think he'd like trouble where there need be none."

Jory Benton broke in, roughly. "Hell, Rog, let me take him! What's all this talk for? I thought you said we were going to run them off?"

Hinge spoke quietly. "There's no need for trouble here. All

we want is to drive our cattle off your range, just as your boys will want to drive some of yours off ours."

"Unless you want to make an even swap," Roper suggested. "You keep what you've got of ours, and we'll keep what we've got of yours."

"The hell with that!" Roger declared. "How do we know how many head you've got?"

"The same way we know how many you've got," Roper said.

Jory Benton was edging off to one side. There was a gnawing tension in him, a kind of driving eagerness to prove himself. "You told 'em to go, Rog," he said suddenly. "Let's make 'em!"

Roger Balch was uncertain. The mention of his father having a talk with me disturbed him. Arrogant he might be, and trouble-hunting he might be, but none of the trouble he hunted was with his father.

What might have happened I don't know. My own pistol was resting easy in its holster and my rifle was in its scabbard. I was dividing my attention between Jory Benton and Roger, when suddenly Ingerman spoke. "Hold it up. Here comes Balch."

My eyes never left Benton, but I could hear horses approaching... more than one.

Balch rode up, two riders with him. "Pa? This man says you and him had an understanding. That he can gather cattle."

Balch glanced at me. "What else did he tell you?"

"Nothin' else."

Balch reined his horse around. "Gather your cattle," he said to me, "but don't mess around. I don't want my stuff all spooked."

"Thanks," I said, and rode right past Benton.

"Another time," he said.

"Anytime," I replied.

The wind was picking up and turning cool. We rode on, found some Stirrup-Iron stock and began working the mesquite to round out the cattle.

We scattered, working carefully through a couple of square miles of rough, broken country. We saw many Balch and Saddler cattle, of course, but by nightfall we had thirty-seven head of Spur and nine of Stirrup-Iron. We bunched them in a canyon and built us a fire. By that time it was downright cold, a real Texas norther blowing.

For three days of cold, miserable weather we worked that corner of the range, collars turned up, bandanas over our faces except for Joe, whose hat had no chin strap. He tied his bandana over his hat to keep it from blowing away.

There was a good bit of mesquite wood in that canyon, and toward each nightfall we'd gather more to keep the fire going. Long ago somebody had grubbed out nearly an acre, probably figuring on building a house, and the roots lay piled nearby.

On the third day, Balch came riding with Ingerman. He looked over our cattle. "I'm going to cut them," he said.

I was standing at the fire, warming my hands. "Have at it," I said.

He needed little time to scan that herd. He rode through it several times and around it, then came up to the fire. "There's coffee," I said. "We're running short of grub."

"Send you some?" he offered.

"No, we've about got it. We'll drive 'em out come daylight."

"You made you a good gather." He glanced up at me. "No young stuff."

"No." I was squatting by the fire. "Balch, I'm going to take a few days off and do some snooping around, southeast of here."

"You'll lose your hair. I lost a rider down thataway maybe a year back...a good man, too. Feller named Tom Witt. Rode off here, huntin' strays, he said. I never seen him again but his horse showed up, blood all over the saddle. It rained about then and we found no trail."

"Balch," I said, "you've got you some gunhands. Ingerman is good...one of the best...but somebody needs to ride herd on Benton."

"Rog will do it."

I took a swallow of coffee and made no comment. He looked at me as if expecting something, but I'd nothing to say. "You lay off, Talon. Just lay off. Benton's a good boy even if he is a little anxious."

The dregs of my coffee I tossed on the ground. Then I stood up. "Well, he carries a gun. When a man straps one on, he accepts responsibility for his actions. All I want you to understand is that his trouble is Benton trouble, and it need not be Balch trouble."

"He rides for me."

"Then put a rein on him," I said, a little more sharply. "If you hadn't come right then, somebody would be dead by now. Maybe several somebodies. You've got a son, and a man carries a lot of pride in a son."

"Rog can take care of himself." Balch looked up at me. "Don't tangle with him, Talon. He'll tear you apart. He's small, but he's fast and he's strong."

"All right," I said.

He got to his feet and mounted up. Then he turned, started to say something, and rode away. He was a hard man, a very hard man, but a lonely one. He was a man who believed the world had built a wall around him, and he was eternally battering at it to make breaches, never understanding that the wall was of his own building.

We moved our cattle out, come daybreak, having close to two hundred head, mostly Spur.

It was spitting cold rain when we came up to the high ground. It looked level as a floor, but I knew it wasn't, for there were canyons cut into the earth, some of them two hundred feet deep. There would be cattle in some of them.

Hinge was no fool. "Talon, you an' Fuentes work the nearest canyons, start 'em down-country, or if there's a way, bring 'em here. Ben an' me will stay by." And then he added, "Might be an attempt to stampede the stock, so we want to be on hand."

It was something I had not considered, but Roger Balch or Jory Benton might do just that. Purely as an annoyance, if nothing else.

We rode out over the plain until the nearest canyon split the earth wide open ahead of us. There was no warning. We were riding and suddenly there it was—a crack several hundred yards across. In the bottom there was green grass, some mesquite, even a cottonwood or two. And there were cattle.

Scouting the rim, we found a steep slide that stock had been using. With my horse almost on his haunches, we slid down and moved toward the cattle.

There was Indian writing on some of the rocks, and I was wishing for time to look around. Fuentes glanced at the writing, then at me.

"Old," he said. "Very old."

"You read that stuff?"

He shrugged. "A little." He glanced at me. "My grandmother was Comanche, but this was not their writing. It is older, much older."

He spotted a big Stirrup-Iron steer and started him moving. The steer didn't want to go, putting his head down at me. He had forward-pointing horns, looking sharp as needles, but I rode right at him, and after a moment he broke and turned away, switching his tail in irritation. There was a nice little pocket of our stuff here, and by the time we'd come out at the canyon mouth some three miles below, we had thirty-odd head, mostly big stuff, well-fleshed.

We opened out on a flat scattered with mesquite. There were a few cattle, and with Fuentes holding and moving what we had, I rode off to check the brands. This was Balch and Saddler stuff, with a few of the major's. I cut out a four-year-old and started it toward the herd, my horse working nicely. It was a good cutting horse with a lot of cow savvy, which made the job easier. Riding that horse, the most I had to do was sit up there and look proud.

Yet I didn't like it. We were now a good five miles from Hinge and Roper, and we should be working together.

Pushing a few head, I rejoined our bunch. "You know how to get up there?" I asked.

He pointed toward what looked like a long unbroken wall of the mesa. "See that white point of rock? Back of that. It's an easy way up."

We started the bunch, and while he kept them moving, I rode wide, checking on brands, finding none of our stock. Suddenly, half-hidden by a clump of mesquite, I came on a small fire. A thin trail of smoke was lifting but the coals were black, only a few charred ends showing a thin tracery of glowing red.

Nearby, the earth was torn up and I knew the signs. Somebody had thrown and branded a steer. There was a spattering of blood from the castration, and the earth had been chewed up by kicking hoofs.

I was turning away from the fire when I glimpsed something else—a place where a rifle with two prongs on its butt plate had been standing, tipped against a fork of a mesquite.

Tony was not far off, and I gave him a call. He cantered over. I showed him what there was, including the mark left by the rifle.

"I want to see that brand, Tony," I told him.

He nodded, and we left the herd standing while we rode swiftly around, checking every brand for a fresh one. No such brand appeared. Tony reined in alongside me. Taking off his sombrero, he shook the weight of water from it. "This one is smart, Milo. He drove it away...maybe miles from where it was branded."

I'd been thinking the same thing, and had been watching for tracks, but saw none.

We started on with the cattle. Was the man who branded that critter a rustler? A cowhand slapping his boss's brand on a maverick? It was no youngster, but a full-grown animal that he had cut and branded...A bull that was making trouble?

More than anything, I wanted to go looking. But Hinge and Roper were up on the mesa holding cattle, and we had more to drive to them so reluctantly I turned away. Meanwhile I tried to remember if I'd seen anybody with that kind of a rifle.

There were a sight of different gun types around in those days, and I could recall four or five I'd seen with those points on the butt plate, set so's they'd kind of fit against the shoulder. A Sharps of one model was fixed that way, and there was a Ballard, too. And some of the James Brown Kentucky rifles.

"You know a man with a rifle like that?" I asked Tony.

Fuentes shook his head. "Not that I recall, amigo. I have seen such rifles, but not here."

We were turning our cattle to climb the mesa when we heard a shot.

It was sharp and clear in the afternoon air, a single, flat-hard report, and an echo, racketing against the rock walls.

Leaving the herd, I jumped my horse past it and scrambled for the rim. As I topped out, I saw our herd scattered a little, heard a pound of hoofs and saw a horse racing away in the distance, a wild whoop trailing back.

A second shot, close by, and I saw Joe Hinge sprawled on the ground, saw him trying to rise, then slip back down.

Roper, rifle in hand, came running. I took one glance after the fleeing rider, then raced up to the cattle and dropped from the saddle.

Joe Hinge looked up at me. "Jory Benton! Damn it, I never was fast with a gun!"

EIGHTEEN

"**B**en? What happened?"

He stared at me, his face flushed with anger and shame, "Why, damn it! I went over the rocks, yonder. Wasn't aimin' to be gone more'n a minute, but that dirty coyote must've been holed up somewhere, watchin'."

Ben shook his head. "Soon's I was out of sight he come up. I heard the sound of his horse and figured it was you or Fuentes. Next thing there was shootin'. Only thing I heard him say was, 'If they're buffaloed, I'm not! I'll show 'em!' And then the shot."

"Was it Benton?"

"It was his voice. I didn't get back in time to see more'n his back, but he was ridin' that blaze-faced sorrel he rode when we saw him before. I took a shot, but he was too far off and movin' too fast."

Fuentes was on his knees beside Hinge, plugging the hole and trying to make him easier. Fuentes was a good hand with a wound—I saw that right away.

"Ben, we need a wagon. You want to go for it?"

"Yeah." Roper turned toward his horse, standing a few yards off. "Damn it, I had no business leavin' him. Hell, I—"

"Forget it, Ben. Hinge is a grown man. He's the boss here. Nobody needed to stand guard over him."

"I'll kill him!" Roper said vehemently.

"Don't butt up against him, Ben. It isn't worth it. Jory's fast... If

137

you do go after him, remember this. He's too fast for his own good... He doesn't take time. If it comes to a shooting between you, make your first shot count. I've seen his kind, and with them the fast draw is everything. Seven times out of ten his first bullet goes right into the dust in front of his target. Just make sure he doesn't get a second shot."

"The hell with him!"

"Leave him to time, Ben. His kind never lasts long. Now how about the wagon?"

When Ben was gone, we moved Joe to a place slightly below the level of the prairie. Then, with slabs from the edge of the mesa, I built a screen to wall off the wind. We covered him with his saddle blanket, and then we waited.

"One damn hothead," Fuentes said irritably. "He'll get some good men killed, blowing off like that."

"Let's make sure it isn't Joe," I said, scanning the horizon.

Unless I was mistaken, Jory Benton would ride right on back and make his brag about what he'd done. That he had beaten Joe Hinge to the draw and killed him... Well, Joe was going to live! He had to live! Yet it was a long way to the ranch—and a long way back with a wagon. I swore bitterly.

Yet I had an idea what would happen. Jory would go back and tell his story. If Balch was smart, he would fire Benton on the spot. But there was another chance that some of his men would be for cleaning house, finishing what they had started before we had a chance to retaliate. For that reason, I had stayed with Hinge and Fuentes rather than going for the wagon myself.

Going to my horse, I shucked my Winchester. Tony glanced at me, but offered no comment. Nor was any needed. He knew as well as I what might happen, and I think Ben Roper did too.

Gathering a few sticks, I prepared a fire for the night, glancing from time to time over the rim at the canyon below. If we were just down there...

Any place but this mesa top, with small concealment and no shelter.

Joe opened his eyes and looked around, then started to rise. "Take it easy, Joe," Fuentes said. "You caught a bad one."

"Will I make it?"

"You're damn right!" I said flatly. "Just take it easy." Then I said, "Joe? Think you're up to being moved? We've sent for a wagon, but I mean now...down into the canyon?"

He looked at me. "You think they'll come back? It was Jory shot me. Damn it, boys, he never gave me a chance. Just rode up and said if they wouldn't do it, he would, and then he drew on me."

We waited for him to continue. "Hell, I can shoot, but I never was no gunman! He just shot me down, and then Ben topped out over yonder and Benton taken off, yelling. I never figured on him shootin'. He come ridin' up—" His voice trailed off weakly and he closed his eyes. Then they opened. "You got a drink of water? I'm bone-dry."

Fuentes picked up his canteen. He held it while Joe drank. Then Joe slowly closed his eyes. After a moment, he opened them. "I'm up to movin', boys. I don't like this here no better'n you do."

There was water down there, fuel, and some shelter could be rigged if it started to rain. And down there we could at least heat up a place for him, but keeping a fire up on the mesa in the wind wouldn't be easy.

We brought up his horse and lifted him into the saddle. Joe was a typical cowpoke. He had spent more years up on the hurricane deck of a bronc than he had afoot, so he latched onto the old apple with both hands while we led the horse down the cliff.

Glancing at him, I saw his face had gone white. But his lips were drawn thin and tight and he made no sound. There was nothing but hooves against rock and the creak of the saddles as we went down, Fuentes leading, me coming right along behind.

Once on the ground near the cottonwoods I'd seen, and among the willows, we got busy and made a bed for him out of willow boughs, leaves and such-like. Knowing there would be no buckboard wagon there much before morning, we rigged up a lean-to above him. We staked out the horses, and gathered fuel for a fire.

Hinge was mighty quiet, sometimes asleep, maybe unconscious, and sometimes wandering in his talk. He kept mentioning a "Mary" I'd never heard him speak of when he was himself.

"Be gone a while," I said, "come daylight. I'm going to gather our stock and drift it down this way and give it a start toward home."

"Sí." Fuentes had been turning the idea around in his own

head. I was sure of that. "If the buckboard comes we can bring them in."

Fuentes slept and I kept watch, giving Hinge a drink now and again, easing his position a mite, sponging off his forehead or his lips with a bandana.

Hinge was a good man, too good a man to go out this way because of some hotheaded young no-account. Mentally, I traced Ben Roper's route as he rode toward the ranch, trying to pace him, trying to figure out when he would arrive and how long it would take him to return. We had our fire in a sort of hollow where there were some rocks, and we let it die to coals but kept it warm. It would be a comfort to Joe if he happened to awaken.

At midnight, I stirred Fuentes with a boot. He opened his eyes at once.

"I'll sleep," I said. "Call me about three."

"*Bueno*," he agreed. "Do you think, amigo, that they will come?"

I shrugged. "Let's just say they will. I don't know. But if we figure it that way we'll be ready."

For several minutes I lay awake, listening. There was a frog somewhere nearby in the creek or near it, and there was an owl in one of the cottonwoods.

A hand on my shoulder awakened me. "All is quiet. Joe is asleep."

I shook out my boots in case they had collected any spare spiders, lizards or snakes, and then pulled them on, stamping them into place. Fuentes lay down and I went to the sick man. He lay with his head turned on one side, breathing loudly. His lips looked cracked and dry.

I walked to the fire and added a few sticks. Sitting down in darkness with my back to a huge old cottonwood, I tried to sort the situation out.

Balch was not stealing, nor were we. I doubted if the major was . . . but what about Saddler? I had never trusted the man, never liked him, yet that was no reason to believe him a thief.

An unknown? And was the unknown some connection of Lisa's?

What to do?

First, try to find where Lisa came from, locate her, study the situation, possibly eliminate her as a possibility.

Perhaps the next thing would be to scout the Edwards Plateau country.

From time to time I got to my feet and prowled about, listening. I stopped by the horses, speaking softly to each one. The night was very still, and very dark.

My thoughts went to Ann Timberly, and to China Benn. It was rare to find two such beautiful girls in one area. Yet, on second thought, that wasn't unusual in Texas, where beautiful girls just seem to happen in the most unexpected places.

Moving back to the small fire, I added a few sticks, then went back to the shadows at the edge of camp, keeping my eyes away from the fire for better night vision. A wind stirred the leaves, one branch creaked as it rubbed against another, and far off under the willows something fell, making a faint plop as it struck the damp ground.

Uneasily, I listened. Suddenly I shifted position, not wanting to stand too long in one place. I did not like the feel of the night. It was wet and still...but something seemed to be waiting out there.

I thought of the unseen, unknown marksman who had shot at me. What if he came now, when I was tied to this place and the care of a wounded man?

Something sounded, something far off...A drum of hoof beats...A rider in the night.

Who...on such a night?

Again the wind stirred the leaves. A rider was coming. Moving back to the edge of darkness and firelight, I spoke softly:

"Tony?"

He was instantly awake. There was a faint light on his face from the fire, and I saw his eyes open.

"A rider...coming this way."

His bed was empty. As suddenly as that, he was in the shadows and I caught the gleam of firelight on a rifle barrel. He moved like a cat, that Mexican did.

The rider was coming up through patches of mesquite, and I could almost hear the changes of course as the horse moved around and among them—but coming on, unerringly. This was no casual rider, it was someone coming *here*, to this place.

Suddenly the horse was nearer, his pace slowed, but the horse still came on. A voice called from the darkness.

"Milo?"

"Come on in!" I called back.

It was Ann Timberly.

NINETEEN

She stared at me, shocked. "But... but I heard you were wounded!"

"Not me. Joe Hinge caught one. Jory Benton shot him."

"Where is he?" She swung down before I could reach out a hand to help her, bringing her saddlebags with her. Before I could reply, her eyes found him and she crossed quickly to his side and opened his shirt.

"I'll need some hot water, and some more light."

"We've nothing to heat it in," I protested.

She gave me a disgusted look. "Tony has a canteen. Hang it over the fire and it will heat fast enough. And don't look at me like that. I've treated wounds before. You seem to forget that I grew up in an army camp!"

"I didn't know." Tony was stripping the covering from his canteen, and rigging a forked stick he could prop it over the fire with. I broke sticks, built up the flame.

"How'd you get here?" I asked.

"On a horse, stupid. They're bringing a rig, but I knew it would take too long. So I just came on ahead to see what I could do."

She was working as she talked, cleaning the wound as best she could, using some kind of antiseptic on a cloth, after bathing it with water.

Nobody had any illusions. She might know a good deal about gunshot wounds, as well as other kinds, but doctors themselves knew mighty little, and there were no hospitals anywhere near.

143

Survival usually meant reasonable rest and a tough constitution—
and mostly the latter. Yet I'd seen men survive impossible injuries
time and again.

Tony had taken her horse, walked him around a little and was
rubbing him down. That horse had been running, all-out and too
long. Seeing her there bending over the fire, I could only shake
my head in wonder. She hadn't hesitated, but had come as fast as
a horse would carry her.

I asked about that. "Switched horses twice," she said, "at the
Stirrup-Iron and at the Indian camp."

My hair stiffened on the back of my neck. "*Indian* camp?
Where?"

"About twenty miles east. A bunch of Kiowas."

"You got a horse from *Kiowas?*"

"Why not? I needed one. I just rode into their camp and told
them a man had been hurt and I needed a horse, that I carried
medicine in my bags. They never asked another question, just
switched horses and saddles for me and watched me ride off."

"Well, I'll be damned! Of all the gall!"

"Well, what could I do? I needed the horse and they had a
lot of them, so I just rode right in."

"They had their women with them?"

"No, they didn't. It was a war party." She looked up at me
and grinned. "I startled them, I guess, and they just gave me the
horse without any argument... Maybe it was the medicine bag."

"More likely it was your nerve. There's nothing an Indian
respects more, and they may have thought some special kind of
magic rode with you."

I looked at Fuentes, and he merely shrugged and shook his
head. What could you do with a girl like that?

Nevertheless, we both felt relieved. Neither of us knew too
much about wounds, although Fuentes was better than I. We had
nothing with us to treat such a wound, and I knew nothing of the
plants of the area that an Indian might have used.

After a while, she came out to where I stood. There was a
faint gray light in the east, and we stood together, watching the
dark rims of the hills etch themselves more sharply against the
growing light.

"I thought it was you," she said. "I was frightened."

"I'm glad you came. But you shouldn't have, you know. You just lucked out with those Indians. If they'd seen you first, the story would be different now."

"Jory shot him?" she asked.

So I told her how it was, and just what had happened. "Now that you're here, Fuentes and me will ride up on the mesa and bunch those cattle again. They won't have strayed far."

"What will happen now?"

Considering that question had got me nowhere, and I'd done a lot of considering since Jory fired that shot. We could only wait and see.

"I don't know," I replied.

It could be a shooting war, and I knew how that went. It could begin with scattered gunfights, and then it could turn into dry-gulching and no man would be safe—not even passing strangers, who might be shot simply because if they were not on the shooter's side they must be on the other.

A thought occurred to me that I'd not considered before. "I rode in from the northwest," I said, "an' had no reason to think about it. But where's your supply point? This is a long way from anywhere."

"San Antonio," she replied. "We get together. Your outfit, ours and Balch and Saddler. Each of us sends two or three wagons and each sends drivers and a couple of outriders. Sometimes the soldiers from Fort Concho meet us and ride along to protect us."

"But if you didn't go to San Antone?"

"Then there isn't much. Oh, there's a stage station that has some supplies for sale, a place called Ben Ficklin's, this side of the fort about four miles. There's a place across the river from the fort called Over-the-River. There's a supply point there, several saloons, and a few of those houses that men go to. The boys tell me it's very, very rough."

If somebody was to the south of us, Lisa's people, whoever they were, must be getting supplies at one of those two places. It was possible—but hardly likely—they would go to San Antonio alone, through Kiowa and Apache country. Yet even a ride to Ben Ficklin's or Over-the-River would be rough. But suddenly I knew it was a ride I had to make.

Come good daylight, Tony and me, we cut loose from camp

and headed for the high ground. A few of our cattle had already found their way down to the creek for water, but we couldn't wait on the others.

They were scattered some, but we swung wide and began bunching them. By now, most of them were used to being driven and we were going toward water. Here and there, some bunch-quitter would try to cut off by himself just to be ornery, but we cut them back into the herd and drifted the cattle down off the mesa and scattered them along the creek to get tanked up on water.

It was close to sundown before we had them down there, and Tony rode in close to me, hooked a leg around the pommel and dug out the makings. He tilted his sombrero back and said, "She likes you?"

"Who?"

He looked disgusted. "Ann Timberly... The señorita."

"Her? I doubt it."

"She does. I know it. If you want to know about romance, ask me. I have been in love... oh, dozens of times!"

"In love?"

"Of course. Women are to be loved and I could not permit it that they linger and long for some gay caballero to come along. It is my duty, you see."

"Tough," I said. "I can see how it pains you."

"Of course. But we Mexicans were made for suffering. Our hearts accept it. A Mexican is happiest when he is sad... sad over the señorita, whoever she may be. It is always better to be bro-kenhearted, amigo. To be brokenhearted and sing about it—rather than win the girl and have to support her. I cannot think of loving just one. How could I be so cruel to the others, amigo? They deserve my attention, and then..."

"Then?"

"I ride away, amigo. I ride into the sunset, and the girl, she longs for me... for a while. Then she finds someone else. That someone is a fool. He stays with her, and she becomes without illusion, and always she remembers me... who was wise enough to ride away before she realized I was no hero, but only another man. So I am always in her eyes a hero, you see?"

I snorted, watching a four-year-old with markings not unlike Ol' Brindle himself.

"We are but men, amigo. We are not gods, but any man can

be a god or a hero to a woman if he does not stay too long. Then she sees he is but a man, who gets up in the morning and puts his pants on, one leg at a time like any other man. She sees him sour and unshaved, she sees him bleary from weariness or too much drink. But me? Ah, amigo! She remembers me! Always shaved! Always clean! Always riding the pretty horse, twirling his mustaches."

"That's what *she* remembers," I said. "What about you?"

"That is just it. I have the memory also, a memory of a beautiful girl whom I left before she could become dull. To me she is always young, gay, lovely, high-spirited."

"No memory will keep you warm on a cold night, or have the coffee hot when you come in from the rain," I said.

"Of course. You are right, amigo. And so I suffer, I suffer, indeed. But consider the hearts I have brightened! Consider the dreams!"

"Did you ever brighten any hearts around Ben Ficklin's?"

When he looked at me again, he was no longer showing his white teeth. "Ben Ficklin's? You have been there?"

"No... I wish to know about it... And Over-the-River, too."

"Over-the-River can be rough, amigo. Only now they are beginning to call it San Angela, after DeWitt's sister-in-law, who is a nun."

"I'm studyin' on taking a ride down that way, to Over-the-River and Ben Ficklin's. Seems it might be a good idea to know who comes there, and what happens around about."

"Soldiers from Concho, mostly. Maybe a few drifters."

We cut out a couple of Balch and Saddler steers that wanted to join our bunch, and moved our stock toward the camp. When we came in sight, we saw the buckboard, horses unharnessed, and Ben Roper standing by the fire chewing on a biscuit. Nearby, Barby Ann was talking to Ann.

Barby Ann gave me a sharp glance, no warmth in her eyes, then ignored me. Roper glanced at me and shrugged.

"How's the gather at the ranch?" I asked.

"Middlin'. We brung in a bunch, and we're fixin' to brand what we've got when you all come in to help."

"We'll be shorthanded to do much," I said. "Joe won't be around for a while, so there's just you, me, Fuentes and Danny."

Roper glanced at me, a sidelong look from the corners of his

eyes. "You ain't heard? Danny never come back." He paused a
moment. "I rode up to the line-shack to bring back any stock he'd
gathered, and he wasn't there. Hearth was cold . . . No fire for days,
and the horses hadn't been fed."

He kicked a toe into the sand. "I picked up a trail. He was
ridin' that grulla he fancies. Follered him south maybe seven or
eight mile, then I come back. Looked to me like he knew where
he was goin', or thought he did."

Suddenly Roper swore. "I don't like it, Talon. I think he got
what Joe Hinge almost got. I think somebody killed him."

TWENTY

When morning came again, with sunlight on the hard-packed earth, there was no change in Joe's condition. He had been hit hard, he had lost blood, and the exhausting ride in the buckboard had not helped. Yet his constitution was rugged, and such men do not die easily.

We needed no foreman to tell us our duties. There were cattle to be moved to fresh grass, then watched over during the day, and the herd had grown in size. One man could no longer keep them in hand. Although during the early hours, when there was plenty of grass with the dew upon it, and when they'd had their fill of water, there was small need to worry.

Danny had not returned during the night, and we looked at the empty bunk, but no comment was made. Each of us at one time or another had found such empty bunks in the morning; sometimes a horse returned with a bloody saddle, sometimes nothing.

It was a hard life we lived and a hard land in which we lived, and there was no time for mourning when work had to be done.

There would be one man less to do the work. And one man less at the table, one horse less to be saddled in the morning.

Ben Roper was coiling his lariat when I walked to the corral and dabbed a loop on the almost white buckskin I'd come to like. He glanced at me as I led the horse through the gate.

"You think he's tomcattin' around that Lisa girl?"

Both hands resting on the buckskin's back, I thought about

that. "Not now," I said, "although that's likely what took him off south. Maybe he knew where she was, maybe he just went hunting. But I think he found more than he expected."

"Fool kid," Ben said, irritably.

"Well," I said, "we've all put in our time at being fools. He had no corner on it, and he was lonesome for a girl. The last time he was in the cabin," I continued, "he had fresh mud on his boots, and there was mud dropped from his horse's hoofs. Made me a mite suspicious." That was all I wanted to say.

Ben considered that. "Could be picked up in a lot of places. Lacy Creek, maybe... or over east. The Colorado is too far east."

"The Colorado?"

He nodded. "We've got one here in Texas, too."

"The stolen cattle," I said, "seemed headed southeast. Do you suppose he got wind of something?"

He shrugged. "He might have gone off huntin' that gal and stumbled into something."

"You know anybody with a rifle that has kind of prongs on the butt plate?"

Ben considered that, then shook his head. "I seen 'em on one kind of a Sharps, and some of the Kentucky rifles had 'em. Yeah, I know." He began saddling up. "I've seen those marks, too."

"Ben, we've got to bait the rustler. He's hunting young stuff. Let's leave some where he can get it, then follow him."

"Maybe," Roper was doubtful. "There's just you, me and Fuentes now, and work enough for six—even if it doesn't come to a shootin' war."

"Barby Ann will make a hand. I mean, she'll pitch in and help, but we'll need more."

With our horses saddled, we went back to the bunkhouse. Joe had been moved to the ranch house, where Barby Ann could see to him when we boys were out.

I fed a couple of cartridges into my Winchester and carried it to the saddle. I slung the saddlebags, then put the Winchester into the boot. We were stalling. All of us were stalling. There was work to do and we knew it, but we were just sort of waiting around for something to happen.

Finally, I straddled my bronc and rode out where the cattle were. Fuentes lifted a hand and turned back to the ranch house for breakfast. There were too many cattle for one rider, but they were busy with the fresh graze for the time being. I rode around a mite, tucking in a few strays that were taking a notion to wander. Then I rode up on the high ground for a look around.

Far off to the west, there was just a blue haze hiding the caprock, and from up high I could see the dim shape of some low hills against the horizon... maybe twenty miles away.

There was a thin green line where Lacy Creek was, and where Ol' Brindle seemed to hang out. It was better country for sheep than for cattle, and coming from mountain country I was less prejudiced against sheep than most cowmen.

Bert Harley should be back. Yet I saw no sign of movement out there. It was a vast sweep of country. Far to the east was a line that might be a branch of the Concho... I didn't know this country anywhere near well enough, and had to guess at what I didn't know... always a dangerous thing.

Ben rode up to me. "Rossiter figures we should start branding when we can. He wants to get the herd out of the country before they're scattered to hell an' gone."

"All right." I pointed toward a shoulder of hill on the southern skyline. "What's that?"

"Flattop, I reckon. Air's clear this morning."

"You ever been to Harley's place?"

"No. As a matter of fact, Bert's never invited no visitors. Stays to hisself. You know him. He's a good man but he's got kind of an ingrown disposition and he just shuts people out. I don't even rightly know where his place is. This here country's only had people in it four or five years, you know, and nobody knows it well."

Ben continued. "Marcy explored through here, but I don't rightly know where he went. North of here, I expect. Folks have been kind of moving gradually thisaway, but many have been killed by Indians and some just gave up after a couple of dry years and moved on."

He stopped to scan the horizon. "There's usually said to be six ranches in the basin, as we call it. That's the major's outfit, Balch and Saddler, Spur, Stirrup-Iron, Bert Harley's place, and off to the southeast there's a Mexican outfit... Lopez. We never see much of them. They mind their own affairs and most of their graze is south of them."

Ben paused. "I never seen Lopez. He was here before any of us, but from all I hear, he's a good man."

He drifted off, cutting a couple of bunch-quitters back into the herd.

Branding that lot of cattle was a big job for three men, even if Barby Ann helped. It would be slow, and it would mean a lot of work. For myself, while never shirking any job, I'd no wish to tackle that one.

Bert Harley showed up about the middle of the morning, and I headed off for the ranch. Fuentes was there. He'd been up to the line-cabin.

"Amigo? That shirt you wore when you were shot at? The red-checked one?"

"What about it?"

"Did you bring it back with you? Back here?"

"As a matter of fact, I washed it out one day and when it was dried, I folded it and left it under the pillow on my bunk. Why do you ask?"

"I thought that was what you'd done. Seen it there a time or two... But now it's gone."

Well, I looked at him, wondering what he was getting at, and all of a sudden it came to me. "You think Danny borrowed my shirt?"

"Look..." he held out a dirty blue shirt that was surely Danny's. "He was going courting, no? He saw your shirt, figured you'd not care, and swapped his dirty shirt for your clean one, all red and white checked."

Ben Roper had come up, listening. "You think somebody figured he was you?"

"Well, I was on a hot trail. I don't know which horse I was riding that day, but I believe it was a gray. If he wore my shirt and was riding a grulla... at a little distance?"

That was all that was said at the time.

We started the branding at daylight. Fuentes was the best man on a rope, so Ben and I swapped the throwing and branding. It was slow work with just the three of us, but Tony never missed a throw and we worked the day through. It was hot, dusty work, and most of the stuff we were branding was bigger, older and a whole lot meaner than was usual.

It was coming up to noon when Fuentes suddenly called out. "Riders coming!"

Ben turned around, glanced toward the trail, then walked to his horse and slid his Winchester from the boot. I just stood waiting. Branding or no, I had my smoker on, expecting trouble.

It was Balch. Ingerman was nowhere in sight, but Vansen and Klaus were with him.

Balch drew up close by and looked over at me. "If you're branding, I want a rep right with you."

"Fine," I said. "We're branding, so get him over here."

"I'll leave Vansen," he said.

"Like hell," I said. "You'll leave a cattleman, not a gunman."

"I'll leave whoever I damn well please!" Balch said roughly.

It was hot and dusty and I was tired. Only a moment before, we'd finished throwing and branding a five-year-old maverick that had given us trouble, and I was in no mood for nonsense.

"Balch, anybody who comes over here had better be a cattle-man. And if he is, he's going to lend a hand when we need him. We haven't any time for free-loaders. Every head we've got in this bunch belongs to Stirrup-Iron or Spur, but your cattleman is free to look 'em over whenever you like. But I'd rather you'd stay yourself. I want a man who knows cattle and who knows brands."

"You think I don't?" Vansen said belligerently.

"These are cattle," I said roughly, "not playing cards or bot-tles."

His lips tightened, and for a moment I thought he was going to ride me down, but Balch put out a hand to stop him.

"Hunting trouble, Talon?" he asked coolly.

"We've had trouble," I replied shortly. "Benton shot Joe Hinge, or didn't you know? If there's to be any riders from your outfit around here, you handle the job yourself or send somebody who is only a cattleman, not a gunman."

Vansen swung down and unfastened his gunbelt. "You said no gunman. All right, my guns are off. Want to take off yours?"

I glanced at Roper. He had a Winchester in his hands. "All right," I said. I took off my gunbelt and handed it to Fuentes, and Vansen came in swinging.

They didn't call him Knuckles for nothing. He was supposed to be a fistfighter. There'd been bunkhouse talk that he had whipped a lot of men. I don't know where he found them.

He swung his first punch when my back was half-turned, but

I heard his boot grate on gravel as he moved, and threw up an arm. He had swung a right for my face with my right side toward him, and my arm partially blocked his punch. Then I backhanded him with a doubled fist that staggered him. Turning around just as he was getting his feet under him, I beat him to the punch with a left to the face, ducked under a pawing swing and hit him in the belly with a right.

His wind went out with a grunt, and I took a step back, nearer Fuentes and my gun, which was slung from his saddle horn within easy reach.

"You better take your boy home," I said to Balch. "He's no fighter."

Vansen's breath back, he lunged at me and I stepped in, hitting him with a short right to the chin. He dropped to his knees in the dust, then to his face.

"Better get him a new name, too," I said. "Better call him Wide-Open Vansen from now on."

Balch's face was stiff with anger. For a moment, I thought he was going to get off his horse and tackle me himself, and that would be no bargain. Whatever else Balch was, my guess was that he was a fighter... And I'd already been warned that he was better with a gun than any of his would-be gunmen.

"I'll send a cattleman," he said coldly.

"You send him, and he's welcome. We're working cows here." I paused. "Another thing... Is Jory Benton still working for you?"

"No... he's not. That shootin' was his own idea. If he's still around, that's his idea, too."

Taking my gunbelt, I buckled it on. They had turned to go, waiting only for Vansen to crawl into the saddle, but I said, "Balch?"

He turned, his eyes still ugly with anger.

"Balch, you're no damned fool. Don't let us fly off the handle and do something we'll both be sorry for. What I said before, I still believe. Somebody is stealing your cattle and ours, and that somebody would like nothing better than to see us in a shooting war. It takes no kind of a brain to pull a trigger, but if we come out of this with anything, it will be because we're too smart to start shooting."

He turned his back on me and rode off, but I knew he was shrewd, and what I had said would stay in his mind.

As they rode away, Ben Roper turned to look at me and shook his head. "I didn't know you could fight," he said. "When you hit him with that right, I thought you'd killed him."

"Come on," I said, "let's brand some cows."

Nobody else came around, and we worked cattle for the next three days without interruption. It was hard, hot, rough work, but none of us had ever known much else, and we leaned into it to get the job done. As we branded stock they were driven over into a separate little valley nearby, where they could be held and watched over by Harley.

Each morning we were up and away from the ranch house before daybreak. And each night, when we'd packed our supper away, we wasted little time. Mostly we were too tired for playing cards or even talking. The cattle we were handling were rarely calves, but big, raw stuff that had somehow run wild on the range without branding.

Then we took a day off... it was Sunday... and just loafed. Only my loafing was of a different kind.

"I'm taking a ride," I told Barby Ann.

She just looked at me. Never, since I'd refused to accept five hundred dollars to kill Roger Balch, had she spoken to me except to reply to a question.

Fuentes was there, and Ben Roper.

"There's work to do, and I know it," I said, "and I doubt if I'll be home by daybreak."

"Where are you going?"

"I'm going to find Danny," I said.

We were shorthanded and there were cattle to hold, but the thing was eating on me, worrying me. If he was dead, as he probably was, that would be one thing. But suppose he was hurt? Lying out there somewhere, slowly dying?

Danny meant nothing to me, except that he was another human being and we rode for the same brand. But I knew the others had been thinking of it also.

Throwing the saddle on my own dun, I rode out of there when the sun was high. Topping out on the ridge, I pulled my hat brim down to shield my eyes from the sun, and scanned the country.

There had been rain, and the trail would be wiped out. Yet

he had been riding a grulla and wearing my red and white checked shirt.

And he had probably been looking for Lisa, who was somewhere south and east... Or so we believed.

South and east was Kiowa country, Comanche country, and the land where the Lipans rode.

Even the supply wagons from the ranches crossed it only with a heavily-armed escort. And into that country I was riding... alone.

TWENTY-ONE

I rode alone into a land of infinite distance. Far, far away stretched the horizon, where the edge of the plains met the sky. Yet having ridden such distances before, I knew there was no edge, no end, but only a farther horizon, a more mysterious distance.

There were antelope there, occasional groups of buffalo left from the vast herds that for a few years had covered the land, constantly moving like a vast black sea.

My dun rode with ears pricked toward the distance, for he was as much the vagabond and saddle tramp as I, always looking beyond where he was, always eager for the new trail, the new climb, the new descent.

I followed no trail, for the rain had left none. I rode my own way, letting my mind seek out, letting the horse detect. For the dun had been a wild mustang, and they are as keen to scent a trail as any hound, and as wary as any wolf. Somewhere to the south and east, cattle had been taken, and although their tracks were gone, their droppings were not.

More than that, land lies only in certain ways, and a traveling man or a driven herd holds to the possibilities. Rarely, for example, will a man top out on a peak unless looking over the land, and a herd of cattle will never do so. Cattle, like buffalo, seek the easiest route, and are as skilled as any surveyor in finding it.

The herd would go around the hills, over the low passes, down the easy draws. Hence, to a degree, I must follow there. The trouble was these were also the ways the Indian would go—until he got within striking range of his goal. Although once in a while

157

an Indian would top out on a ridge to look around the country.

This was a land of mirage, and even as a mirage would occasionally appear to let one see beyond the horizon, man himself could be revealed in the same way. If a man were accustomed to mirages, he could often detect a good deal from them. And none knew them better than the Indians who rode this wild land north of Mexico.

The Lopez peaks were off to the southeast, and I kept them there, using them as a guide to hold direction. Right ahead of me was a creek and when I reached it, I rode down into the bottom and stopped under some pecan trees, to listen.

There was no wind stirring beyond enough to move the leaves now and again. I could hear the rustle of water, for the creek was running better since the rains. Turning east, I rode along studying for tracks, but drawing up now and again to listen and look around. It was almighty quiet.

There were antelope and deer tracks, and some of javelinas, those wild boars that I'd not seen this far north and west before. They might have been there a long time, for this was new country to me.

There were some cow tracks and, sure enough, there was a big hoofprint, fairly recent, made by Ol' Brindle. I'd learned to distinguish his track from others.

Somewhere those stolen cattle had been driven across this creek, of that I was sure. The rain might have wiped out other tracks, but where they went through the mud there'd still be tracks. It was likely that Danny Rolf had crossed along here somewhere, scouting for Lisa. And she herself had probably crossed, unless... unless her direction had been a blind. And when I'd left her at the creek, she might have gone off to east or west.

West? Well... maybe, but not likely. The further west a body rode, the wilder it grew. And the least water was toward the west. It was more open, too, for a good many miles toward the Pecos it was dry... damned dry, in fact.

The odds said she had gone east or south... But what about Indians?

And where, I thought suddenly, was Bert Harley's place?

The stage stop known as Ben Ficklin's must be forty miles off, at least.

Harley's place was not likely to be more than ten miles from the Stirrup-Iron, so it should be somewhere along this creek, or in some draw leading to it. Well, that wasn't what I was looking for.

Suddenly, not fifty yards off... Ol' Brindle.

He had his head up, watching me. His head high, thataway, I could have stood up straight under his horns, he was that big. He was in mighty good shape, too.

For a moment, we just sat there looking at him, that dun and me. Then I reined my horse away with a casual wave of the hand. "Take it easy, boy," I said, "nobody's huntin' you." And I rode wide around him, his eyes on me all the way. When I was pretty nigh past him he turned suddenly, watching me like a cat.

The creek ran silently along near the way I followed, and I wove in and out among the pecan trees, occasional walnuts and oak, with mesquite mostly farther back from the water.

Suddenly, maybe a half mile from where I'd seen Ol' Brindle, I pulled up.

Tracks of cattle, quite a bunch of them, crossed the creek at this point heading south. The tracks were several days old, and there were vague impressions of still earlier drives, almost wiped out by rain and time. Starting forward, the dun shied suddenly and I saw a rattler crossing the trail. He stopped, head up, looking at me with no favor. He was five feet long if he was an inch, and half as thick as my wrist.

"Stay out of my way," I said, "and I'll stay out of yours." I reined the dun around and waded the creek. The water was just over his hocks. Following the cow tracks, I worked my way through the mesquite and out on the flat.

There, on the edge of the plains country that lay ahead, I drew up. The Lopez peaks were still east and south. More closely due south was another peak that might be even higher. They called them mountains here, but in Colorado they wouldn't rank as such. Nonetheless, this was rugged country.

The peak that was almost due south must be a good twenty-five miles away, but there was some green that might be trees along a creek not more than five or six miles off. The trouble was, once out on the plain I'd be visible to any watcher... There was low ground here and there, but not nearly as much as I wanted.

Scouting the banks of the creek again, I found no tracks of a shod horse. Whoever was driving those cattle must have been riding... Unless he was atop an Indian pony!

That was a thought.

I had thought he must have been riding on air, for there had been no tracks of a shod horse... or of any horse, when it came to that.

Puzzled, I worked over the ground again... No tracks of a horse, yet cattle rarely bunch up like that unless driven. Usually, given their own time they will walk single file.

Another thought came suddenly from nowhere. Six ranches, I'd been told, and I knew of no farms... Where, then, did China Benn come from?

The blacksmith from Balch and Saddler had brought her to the dance... Was she a relative of one of them? Somehow I'd had no such impression.

Thinking of China turned my thoughts to Ann Timberly. Now there was a girl! Not only lovely to look at, she was a girl with a mind of her own—swift, sure, always on the spot in trouble and never at a loss as to what to do. Even when it was taking a swing at me with a quirt! I chuckled, and the dun twitched his ears, surprised, I guess.

The cattle tracks were headed south, and I fell in behind. Once in a while there was a hoof print. But more than that, there was a sort of trail here, a way where cattle or something had gone many times before, and bunched-up cattle, at that.

Under the shoulder of a small bluff, some twenty feet high, I drew up in the shadow, wanting to think this out. From here on, I would be in enemy country, and not only cow-thief country.

South of me somewhere, likely close to the Lopez peaks was the Middle Concho. This was deadman's country, and I was a damned fool to be riding here.

Danny was undoubtedly dead or had left the country, and there was no sense in adding my bones to his on the plains of the Concho.

My dun started off of his own volition, wearied of standing. Yet we had gone no more than fifty yards when a wide draw cut into the one along which I rode. It came in from the northeast and I saw the tracks before I reached the opening.

Two riders...

Puzzled, I studied the trail.

One always ahead of the other—who followed a little offside and behind. The tracks were from last night, because I could see tiny insect trails in the sand where they had crossed and recrossed the tracks during the night.

Warily, I looked around...Nothing in sight. A few more tracks...I knew that long, even stride of the first horse: the unseen rider—and probably the marksman who had been trying for my scalp...The tracks were clear and definite in a few places, a horse freshly-shod not long since.

Following at a walk, I studied the tracks, tried to understand what it was about the situation that disturbed me. There were a number of places where two could have ridden side by side, but they had not.

Both horses were shod...it came to me with a sudden hunch. The second horse was being led!

It was pretty much of a guess, but it fitted the pattern. A led horse! I knew there was also a rider in the led horse's saddle from the way the horse had moved.

What I needed was a definite set of tracks for the second horse. I got them when they passed some damp sand near a seep...

My breath caught and I drew up sharply.

No mistake...Those were the tracks of Ann Timberly's horse.

These were days when men lived by tracks, and the average cowpoke, ranchman, Indian or lawman could read a man's track or a horse's track as easily as most eastern folks could read a signature. You saw tracks, and somehow they just filed themselves away in your memories for future reference.

I'd had occasion to follow Ann Timberly to her pa's ranch. And I knew the way that horse stepped, knew the tracks he left.

Ann Timberly riding a led horse behind the man I was sure was the stock thief.

She was forever riding the country, and she must have come upon him or his trail—and been caught when he saw her coming, and laid for her. That was a good deal of surmising, but the fact was: he had her.

For three to four years, this man had been stealing stock, preparing for something. And now he had been seen and recognized, and his whole plan could blow up in his face if Ann got away to tell of it.

Therefore, he dared not let her get away. He had to kill her.

Then why hadn't he? Because he didn't want the body found? No doubt. Killing a woman, particularly the major's daughter, would blow the lid off the countryside. Every rider who could straddle a horse would be out for the killer.

Take her out of the country and then kill her? That made some kind of sense. Of course, he might have other plans.

Now there was no nonsense about it. I had to stay with them. Moreover, I had to stay alive and save her life, and that would take some doing.

That trail had been made yesterday evening, perhaps near to dark. They had camped... I'd find their camp soon. They might still be there, but I doubted it. This gent would travel far and fast.

I shucked my Winchester.

Taking it easy, I walked my horse forward, lifted it into a canter, and moved along the shallow draw, alert for trouble.

Maybe I'd come upon their camp. Right now I was seven or eight miles from the creek where I'd seen the tracks of Ol' Brindle, and twelve to fifteen miles from the line-cabin.

Topping out on the plain, I followed the tracks at a gallop, went into another shallow draw—and suddenly got smart. I stepped off my horse and put one flat stone atop another, then another alongside to indicate direction. If something happened to me, and the major and his boys started looking, they might need to know where I'd gone.

Dipping down into another draw among the mesquite, I smelled smoke. Rifle in my hands, I walked my horse through the mesquite until I could see the smoke... only a faint trail of it from a dying fire near some big old pecans.

A small fire... I could see where the horses had been tied, and where she had slept between two trees. He had slept some fifteen to twenty feet away, near the horses. Where she had bedded down... and I could see her heel prints and the marks left by her spurs... there were dry leaves all around. He had also taken the precaution to break small, dry branches and scatter them all about where he left her. So if she got free during the night, she couldn't make a move without making noise.

Cagey... he was very, very cagey. But I'd known that all along. Whoever the man was, he was a plainsman, a man who knew his way around wild country.

He had made coffee... there were some coffee grounds near the fire... And the dew was mostly gone from the grass before they had moved out.

They'd made a late start, but that didn't help much because the day was almost gone before I found their camp. Yet I rode on, wanting to use all the daylight I had. And before it was full dark, I'd covered a good five miles and was moving due south.

Now there was mighty little I knew about this country. But sitting around bunkhouses there's talk, and some of the boys had been down into this country a time or two. Where I now was, if I had figured right, was Kiowa Creek, and a few miles further along it flowed into the middle Concho.

This man seemed to be in no hurry. First, he was sure he wasn't followed. Second, this was his country and he knew it well. And, also, I had an idea he was studying on what to do.

When Ann Timberly had come up on him, the bottom fell out of his set-up. For nigh onto four years, he'd had it all his own way. He'd been stealing cattle and hiding them out. There'd been no roundup, so it was a while before anybody realized what was happening.

Now, on the verge of success at last, this girl had discovered him. Maybe he was no killer... at least not a killer of women. Maybe he was taking his time, trying to study a way out.

The stars were out when I pulled up and stepped down from the dun. There was a patch of meadow, some big old pecans and walnuts, and a good deal of brush of one kind or another. I let the dun roll, led him to water, then picketed him on the grass. Between a couple of big old deadfalls, I bedded down.

Sitting there, listening to my horse eating grass, I ate a couple of biscuits and some cold meat I'd brought from the Stirrup-Iron. The last thing I wanted was to sit, but by now Ann and the man who had her prisoner had probably arrived where they were going... Yet one thing puzzled me.

There'd been no more cattle tracks.

Trailing Ann and her captor, I'd completely forgotten the cattle, and somewhere the trails had diverged. Yet that was not the problem now.

With a poncho and a saddleblanket, I made out to sleep some. It was no more than I'd had to sleep with many a night before so, tired as I was, I slept. And ready as I was to ride on, I opened my eyes with the morning stars in the sky.

Bringing my horse in, I watered him, saddled up and wished I had some coffee. Light was just breaking when we started on, the dun and me. And I carried my Winchester in my hands, and spare cartridges in my pockets.

It was all green and lovely around me now. Their trail was only a track or two, a broken green twig, grass scarred by a hoof...

Suddenly the trail turned sharply away from the creek, went a couple of hundred yards off, then swung around in a big circle to the creek again...

Why?

Reining in, I looked back.

There was an old trail following along the creek bank that had been regularly used, so why the sudden swing out from it? A trap? Or what?

Riding back around the loop, I peered into the trees and brush, trying to see what was there, and I saw nothing. Back at the creek where they had turned off, I walked my horse slowly along the old trail. Suddenly, the dun shied.

It was Danny Rolf.

His body lay there, maybe a dozen feet off the trail, and he'd been shot in the back. The bullet looked to have cut his spine, but there was another shot into his head, just to make sure.

He wore only one boot... the other probably pulled off when he fell from his horse and his foot twisted in the stirrup.

Poor Danny! A lonesome boy, looking for a girl, and now this... Dead in the trail, dry-gulched.

Something about the way the body lay bothered me. And studying the tracks, I saw what it was.

When Danny was shot he was *coming back!*

He had been to where he was going, and he had started home... And the rider who was Ann's captor had known the body was there, and had circled so Ann would not see it.

He, then, was the killer.

TWENTY-TWO

Moving over into the shadow of the trees, I studied the situation. Whatever doubts there might have been before, there could be none now. The unknown man with the rifle had killed once, and he would kill again. Yet as he had brought Ann this far, he might be having doubts. To kill a man was one thing, a woman another.

Moreover, he was wily and wary. In this seemingly bland and innocent country, there were dozens of possible lurking places for a rifleman, and anytime I moved into the open, my life was in danger. Yet so was the life of Ann.

Ahead of me, if what the boys at the ranch had said was true, this Kiowa Creek flowed into the Middle Concho. There was a fork up ahead, and the killer might have gone either way. Yet I did not believe he thought himself followed. He had passed along this creek yesterday, and by now had probably reached his destination.

I swore bitterly. How did I get into these situations? The fact that I was good with guns was mostly accidental. I had been born with a certain coordination, a steady hand and a cool head, and the circumstances of my living had given them opportunity to develop. I knew I was fast with a gun, but it meant no more to me than being good at checkers or poker. It would have been much more useful to be good with a rope, and I was only fair.

Now I was facing up to a shooting fight when all I wanted to do was work cattle and see the country. I'd heard of men who supposedly looked for adventure, but to me that was a lot of nonsense. Adventure was nothing but a romantic name for trouble, and nobody over eighteen in his right mind looked for it. Most of what people called adventure happened in the ordinary course of the day's work.

The chances were, the killer had taken Ann on to wherever he was going, and they should be there by now. There was no time to think of Ann now . . . she was where she was and she was either dead or momentarily safe.

What I had to think about was me. If I didn't get through to where she was, we might both be dead. I could ride right out of here and summon the major and his men, but by that time it might be too late for Ann.

I was no hero, and did not want to be one. I wanted to look through my horse's ears at a lot of new country, to bed down at night with the sound of leaves or running water, to get up in the morning to the smell of woodsmoke and bacon frying. Yet what could I do?

You don't follow a man's trail across a lot of country without learning something about him, and I liked nothing I had learned about this one.

What did I know? He was cool, careful and painstaking. He had succeeded in stealing at least a thousand head of cattle, probably twice that many—*and* over a period of three to four years— without being seen or even suspected.

He had managed to create suspicion among the basin ranchers, so they suspected each other and not an outsider. He had moved around in what seemed to be a wide-open country, without anyone knowing he was around.

. . . Unless he was around all the time and therefore unsuspected.

That thought gripped me. If so . . . Who?

Moreover, he had shown no urge to kill anyone until I came along and seemed to be closing in on him.

Danny had probably been shot by mistake because of the red shirt.

But wait a minute . . . Hadn't somebody mentioned another cowhand who rode off to the southeast and never came back?

The chances were, the killer did not kill unless it looked like his plan was about to be exposed. He had several years' work at stake and, just on the verge of success, things started to go wrong.

I had tracked him. Danny had come into his own country. And then Ann Timberly, forever riding the range, had come upon him somehow.

One by one I turned the suspects over in my mind. Rossiter was naturally the first I thought of, because he was a shrewd man, dangerous, and known to me as a cow thief. Nor did I believe he was as blind as he let on. Nevertheless, he could not long be away from the ranch without folks worrying, because of his blindness.

Roger Balch? A tough little man who wished to be known as such, driving to prove himself, but neither cautious nor shrewd.

It could be Roger Balch. It could be Saddler.

Harley? He came and went to his place, wherever it was. He handled a rifle like it was part of him, and he was cool enough, cautious enough, cold enough. He would, I was sure, kill a man as quickly as a chicken.

Fuentes? He had been with me too much. Fuentes wasn't a killer.

Somewhere in my memory, there lurked a face, a face I couldn't quite recall, someone I had seen, someone I remembered. Somehow, from somewhere. But that was all.

That face was a shadow, elusive, indistinct, something at which the fingers of my memory grasped, only to come away empty.

Yet it was there, haunting, shadowy... The odd thing was, I had the fleeting impression it was something from my own past.

Only minutes had passed since I'd seen Danny's body. The wind stirred the leaves, the water rustled faintly in Kiowa Creek. Like it or not, I was going to have to go forward.

And I didn't like it. In such a case, the waiting rifleman has every advantage. All he has to do is sight in on a spot he knows you have to pass and just wait until you ride right into his sights. When he sees you coming, he can take up the slack on his trigger. And when he squeezes off his shot, you're a dead man or damned lucky... and I didn't feel lucky.

Nevertheless, Ann was up ahead, and there was no way I could get around that.

Using every bit of cover I could, varying my pattern of travel when possible, I rode parallel with Kiowa Creek. Once, in a thick stand of hackberry and pecan, I watered my horse and took time to scan the country.

Right ahead of me was that other arroyo that came into a

junction with Kiowa Creek to form the Middle Concho. That was
the one Ben Roper had once said they called Tepee Draw. I spotted
a trail climbing out of the draw pointing toward the mountain and,
returning for my horse, I rode down to where Kiowa Creek and
Tepee Draw joined.

A fresh horse trail went up the bank and I started up, then
reined in sharply. Not a hundred yards away was a corral, a cabin,
and smoke from the chimmey!

Turning my horse, I slid back down the bank and back into
the thickest stand of hackberry and pecan I could find. There were
some big mesquite trees there, also.

Shucking my Winchester, I loose-tied my horse and found a
place in the brush where I could climb up for a look at the cabin.
Nothing about the climb looked good. It was a natural for rattlers,
who like shade from the sun, but after taking a careful look around,
I crawled up. And there, under the roots of one of the biggest
mesquite trees I'd ever seen, I studied the layout.

It was a fair-sized cabin for that country, with two pole corrals
and a lean-to shed. There was water running into a trough from a
spring. I could see it dropping—and almost hear it. There were
a half dozen head of horses in the corral, and one of them was a
little black I'd seen Ann riding. Another was Danny Rolf's grulla.

Aside from the movement of smoke and the horses, all was
quiet.

What surprised me was that I found no cattle anywhere around.
Signs were there aplenty, but not one hoof of stock did I see.

It was very still, and the sun was hot. Probably the coolest
place around was right where I was, against that bank, among the
roots of that big mesquite and under its shade. Occasionally, a faint
breeze stirred the leaves. A big black fly buzzed annoyingly about
my face, but I feared to brush it away for I had no idea who was in
the cabin. And even where I lay, a quick movement might be seen.

A woman came to the door and threw out a pan of water,
shading her eyes to look around. Then she went back inside. I felt
certain it was Lisa, but it was more by hunch than recognition, for
her face had been turned only briefly my way.

If it was her, I surely didn't blame her for riding up to that
box supper, nor for being scared at being away. More than likely
he, whoever "he" was, had been off driving stolen cattle to wherever they'd been taken.

Suddenly, the woman came out again. And now there was no mistake.

It was Lisa.

Leading a horse from the corral, she saddled up, then she hazed the grulla into a corner and got a rope on it, then Ann's black. Mounting up, leading the two horses, she started for the trail. In so doing, she would pass not fifty feet from where I was hidden.

Sliding back, I worked around to the edge of the trail. And as she started down, I stepped out.

"Lisa?"

Her horse shied violently, and she jumped. Her face went a shade whiter, and then she was staring at me, all eyes. "What are you doing here?"

"I'm looking for the girl who rode that horse."

"Girl?" Her tone was shrill, with a note of panic. "This is no girl's horse."

"It is, Lisa. That horse belongs to Ann Timberly. The girl I danced with at the box supper."

"But it can't be!" she protested. "The brand —"

"HF Connected is one of the brands Timberly runs," I said, "and when she left home, Ann was riding that horse."

Her face was deadly pale. "Oh, my God!" There was horror in her eyes. "I don't believe it! I don't believe it!"

"The other horse belonged to Danny Rolf, who rides for the Stirrup-Iron," I said. "At least, it was a horse he rode. He rode down here hunting you, I believe."

"I know it. He came to the house, but I sent him away. I told him to go away and never come back."

"And he went?"

"Well," she hesitated, "he argued. He didn't want to go. He said he'd ridden all day, hunting me. Said he just wanted to talk a little. I was scared. I *had* to get him away, I *had* to." She paused. "Finally, he went."

"He didn't get very far, Lisa. Only a few miles."

She stared at me. "What do you mean?"

"He was shot, Lisa. Killed. Shot in the back and then shot again by somebody who stood over him and wanted to make sure he was dead. And now that same person has captured Ann... and I don't know whether she's dead yet or not."

"I didn't know," she pleaded. "I didn't know. I knew he was bad, but—"

"Who is he, Lisa?"

She stared at me. "He's my brother."

Her face looked frozen with fear.

"Lisa, where is he? Where is your brother? Where's Ann?"

"I don't know. I don't believe he has her. I don't..." her voice broke off. "...Maybe ...There's an old adobe down on the Concho. He's never let me go there."

"Why?"

"He...he met the Kiowas there...Maybe others. I don't know. He traded horses with them sometimes, and sometimes he gave them cattle."

"Where were you aiming to take those horses?"

"Over on Tepee Draw. He told me to turn them loose over there, and to start them south. I should have done it last night, but I was tired, and—"

"Where is he now? Where's your brother, Ann?"

"He's gone. He drove some cattle south. And when he does that, he's always gone all day."

"Lisa, if you'll take my advice, just take those horses out, turn them loose, and keep right on going. Don't ever come back."

"I can't do what you ask. He'd kill me. He told me that if I ever tried to run away, he'd kill me." She stared at me. "He...he's been good to me. He's kind and gentle and never raises his voice around home. We always have enough to eat, and he's never gone very long. But I was afraid... He came back one day with another rifle and a pistol. I never knew where they came from and I think he gave them to the Kiowas. After that, I was scared."

"You didn't know he was around when Danny was killed?"

"Oh, no!" Her expression changed just a little. "I don't know that Danny *has* been killed. Only that you say so."

"He's been killed. Take my advice and get out. I'm going to look for Ann."

She stared at me. "Are you in love with her?"

"In love?" I shook my head. "I never thought of it. Maybe I am. I only know she's a girl alone and in bad trouble—if she's alive."

"He wouldn't kill a woman. Not him. I don't believe he'd even

touch one. He's always been kind of afraid of women. Good women,
I mean. He certainly sees enough of the other kind."

"Where?"

"That place they call Over-the-River. He goes there."

"What's his name, Lisa?"

She shook her head. "Stay away from him... *Please!* His name
is John Baker... He's only my half-brother, but he's been good to
me. They call him Twin."

"Twin? Why?"

"He was a twin. His brother Stan was killed up north some
years back. They'd been stealing cattle. He never would tell me
who killed his brother. Or how, except that it was a woman."

"A *woman?*"

"They'd stolen some cattle from her, and she trailed them.
She had a couple of her boys. And that woman shot Stan. Killed
him."

Ma....

"Please, Milo, get away from here! Ride! Do anything. But
get away! He'll kill you. He's talked about it, lives for it. And he's
killed other men in gunfights. I know he has because he's told me.
And he always says, 'But just you wait! Them Talons! Just you
wait!'"

Henry Rossiter had engineered the steal, but we knew there'd
been four other men waiting to drive the cattle away... *four.*

Ma shot one, Henry Rossiter got away, and she turned two
men loose in the Red Desert in their underpants with no boots.
Somehow, in all the excitement, nobody ever gave any further
thought to the fourth man.

Twin Baker...

TWENTY-THREE

"Danny... He was a nice boy... Why, oh, why did Twin kill him?"

"He's been stealing our cattle, Lisa. He probably thought Danny had tracked him down. Or maybe he thought Danny was me... Danny was wearing a shirt of mine."

She was frightened... anguished. Her teeth gnawed at her lower lip until I thought it would draw blood.

"Get away, Lisa. Get away now. Go to Major Timberly and tell him all you know... Go now. Don't stop for anything, or Twin may kill you, too."

"He wouldn't do that. I know he wouldn't."

"You know nothing of the kind. I said you should get away, and you must." I paused, suddenly curious. "How long have you been here, Lisa?"

"In this place? Oh... five months. Almost six. My father died and I came to Twin. He was in San Antonio on business. He had an address there, and I had no other relatives. He was very kind, and he brought me here.

"I loved it... at first. Then it was so lonely, and he'd never let me go anywhere or ride out, unless I went south. Then one day, when I was riding south, I met a drifter... He'd been working up north—said he hated to leave because they were having a box supper at Rock Springs Schoolhouse."

She paused. "He rode on, but I kept thinking about what he

172

said. Then Twin left for San Antonio... He said he'd be gone for several days, so I decided to go."

"I'm glad you did. Now get your things and get away. If anything has happened to Ann... Have you told me the truth, Lisa? You know nothing about her?"

"Honest! I know nothing... Except he did pack some food to take away, and there is that old cabin."

She started off, and I spoke quickly. "One more thing, Lisa. Where does he keep the cattle?"

She hesitated, then shook her head quickly. "I won't tell you. Anyway, I don't know they were stolen. He says they are his. He told me he would be one of the biggest cattlemen in Texas soon."

"All right, Lisa. But ride! Don't wait any longer!"

First I had to know that Ann was not up there in their cabin. Lisa offered no argument when I took the lead ropes on the horses from her. She just stared at me, her eyes wide and empty.

I rode up to the door and stepped down. The house was empty. A large kitchen-living room, two bedrooms—painfully neat.

In his bedroom, Twin's clothes were hung neatly, his boots polished. There were a couple of store-bought suits in the closet, some white shirts, and there were three rifles. All in excellent shape, all fine weapons.

Mounting the dun, I led the other horses to the corral. No saddles.

I turned up the Middle Concho. My eyes searched for tracks. He was less careful of his trail up here. Apparently, this was a place where no one ever came. It was off the beaten path. So there were tracks, and I followed them at a gallop. Suddenly they veered and went up a draw.

On the bank of the draw, under some pecan and hackberry trees, I saw an old adobe. There was a pole corral nearby, obviously little used. Grass had grown up around the place, and the roof of the adobe was sagging. Already the outside walls showed the effects of wind and rain. It must have been very old.

Drawing up in the shadow of a tree, I studied the house. Then I looked all around. I was very uneasy, for I had a hunch Twin Baker might not be as far away as would seem to be the case. He might be inside the adobe there, or he might be waiting up behind those rocks across the Concho.

Stepping down, I trailed the reins and took my rifle. On second thought, I loose-tied my horse for a quick escape—if need be.

Somehow, Twin was tied in with the Kiowas...Suppose they were watching? I'd no wish to tackle a bunch of renegade Indians.

Finally, I took a chance and walked directly across to the house. The door was closed, a hasp in the lock.

I spoke softly. "Anybody there?"

"Milo?" It was Ann's voice, the first time I'd ever heard a tremble in it.

Lifting the hasp, I opened the door.

She was tied to a chair, the chair tipped slightly back so that if she struggled at all, even moved, the chair would fall back with her head in the fire.

She might then wriggle free of the chair, but scarcely without catching her hair on fire.

Swiftly, keeping my face toward the door, I cut her free. She stood up, almost fell, then tried to soothe her wrists and arms where the tightly-drawn ropes had left deep marks.

"He said if I screamed, the Kiowas would come. He said he might trade me to them for a horse...He hadn't yet decided, he said."

"Do you know him?"

"I'd never seen him before. Not his face, at least. He came up behind me and warned me that if I moved, he'd kill me. And I think he would have done it. It was very dark when we got here, and he did not take the blindfold off until we were in here and I was tied. Then he went away."

Her saddle was in the corner. "Ann? I'm going to have to ask you to carry your own saddle, and to saddle your own horse. I must have my hands free."

"All right."

We went quickly out, and I carried my rifle at the ready, poised for a quick shot.

Nothing happened.

She saddled her horse and mounted. Her rifle had been on her saddle but he had left no ammunition. Fortunately, it was a .44 calibre. She loaded it with ammunition from my saddlebags.

As she did so, I took a quick look around. No man left so little sign of his presence as this Twin Baker. The only thing...and it might be nothing...had been a little dried mud near the hearth, not unlike the mud that Danny had left in the line-cabin.

Of course, there were places aplenty along the Concho and up the draws where a man might get mud on his boots.

Whatever was to be done now must be done with Ann in a safe place. But, my mother having raised no foolish children, I did not go back the way I had come. In Indian country, that could be the last mistake one made. Even Lisa might have had a change of heart and be waiting back there with a Winchester. For me.

I am not a trusting soul. All of us, me included, are sadly, weakly human. We can all make mistakes. We can all be sentimental about a brother or sister, even when you know they are doing wrong. We can also be greedy, and I preferred not to tempt anybody too much.

What we did was take off up that draw—which pointed almost due north—then top out on the plains and continue north, staying in the open as much as possible. Live Oak Creek was on our right. Some scattered trees and brush lined it, so I kept wide of the creek with a ready rifle for trouble.

Nobody needed to tell me that Twin Baker was as good as they come with a gun. His shooting, often under adverse conditions, had been good, mighty good. That I was alive was due to a series of accidents, none of them due to my brains or skill. By this time, he must be exasperated and ready to try anything.

We rode steadily north. It was a good thirty-five miles to the Timberly ranch and Ann's horse was fresh. My dun had done some traveling but I had the grulla for good measure. So we set a good pace, moving right away from there.

Meantime, I'd had a sudden hunch, and one that might be good for nothing at all. Ann was quiet. She was undoubtedly worn to a frazzle, with the riding and the worry over what was to become of her. Now she was just going through the motions. I knew she wanted to be home and resting... So did I.

What worried me was that it had been too easy. We just didn't stand to have that much good luck.

If Twin Baker came up on me, I had to win the fight that was sure to take place. I *had* to win. Because otherwise, Ann would be right back where she had been.

Something else worried me, too. He had some kind of a tie-up with the Kiowas, or a renegade bunch of them, and if they spotted us they'd be scalp-hunting.

That hunch I had was no more than a hunch, but suddenly

I'd begun wondering about that man who had been with Balch and Saddler the first day I'd seen them—the man who had looked familiar, but whom I couldn't find a name for.

Since then, I had seen him nowhere around, and he had not been at the box supper. Could be, I'd remembered him from a glance or two when Ma and us had first came up on those rustlers. So he might be Twin Baker.

The chance was a slim one, and I couldn't see that it helped any. So maybe I had seen him? What then?

When Ann and I had ten miles behind us, I spotted a waterhole off to one side. It was likely just a place that had gathered rainwater from the latest storm, but it was a help. We walked the horses over and let them drink. Meanwhile, I switched saddles from the dun to the grulla. If I was going to have to run, I wanted it to be on a fresh horse, although as Ma had said, the dun would go until it dropped.

"Milo?" Ann's voice was tremulous. "Do you think he will follow us?"

There was no sense in lying to her, and I'd never been given to protecting womenfolks from shocks. Mostly, they stand up to them as well as a man, and it's better for them to be prepared for what may come.

"He's got to, Ann. He's got four years of stealing behind him, and a rope if he's caught. But mostly he doesn't want to spoil everything now he's so close to having what he wants. He's got to find us and kill us, but he doesn't have much more time. I just hope he doesn't get back and find out what's happened until we're safe out of the country."

"Will Lisa tell him?"

"I don't know. She may run, like I advised, but the chances are she won't. She's got no place to go, and usually a person will accept a known risk rather than blaze off into the unknown. She thinks she knows him, and she trusts in that."

With the horses watered, we started on. Now we let them walk, saving them for a run if need be, and letting them get used to having a bellyful of water.

I glanced at the sun... Time was running out. But if darkness came, we might not be found. Not that I had much faith in that.

Where were the cattle? Twin Baker had driven them off to the south, somewhere, and when he made such a drive he was usually, Lisa said, gone all day. Cattle would move at two and a half to three miles an hour, and he would ride back a little faster. Figure fifteen miles, and maybe less.

My eyes never stopped, yet I could see nothing but the wide plain with scattered yucca or bear grass, occasional buffalo bones and no sign at all of Indians.

Ann came up alongside me. "Milo? Who are you?"

The question amused me. "Me? Here I am. This is all I am. I'm a sort of drifting cowboy, moving from ranch to ranch, sometimes riding shotgun on stages... Anything to make a living."

"Have you no ambition? Is that all you wish to be?"

"Well, I sort of think about a ranch of my own, time to time. Not cattle so much as horses."

"Father says you are a gentleman."

"Well, I hope I am. I never gave much thought to it."

"He says you have breeding, that no matter what you seem to be, you came from a cultured background."

"Don't reckon that counts for much out here. When a man rides out in the morning, all they expect of him is that he can do his job—that he can ride, rope a little, and handle stock. A longhorn doesn't care much whether you know who Beethoven was, or Dante."

"But *you* know who they were."

"My brother sets store by such things, and so did Pa. Maybe I take more after Ma. She knew cattle, horses and men. She could read men like a gambler reads cards, and she could shoot."

Ann was looking at me.

"Ma sang some. Didn't have much of a voice, but she knew a lot of old Scotch, English and Irish songs she'd learned back in those Tennessee hills she came from. When she was a girl she had no more than eight to ten books. She grew up on *Pilgrim's Progress* and the writings of Sir Walter Scott. She rocked me to sleep singing 'Old Bangum and the Boar,' 'Bold Robin Hood' and 'Brennan on the Moor.' And Pa, he could speak three or four tongues. He used to quote Shakespeare, Molière and Racine at us sometimes. He told us wild tales about the first Talon to land in America. He was a pirate or something and sailed clean around the world to get here."

I paused. "A mighty hard old man, by all accounts. Had a claw for a right hand, a claw he'd made himself after he lost his hand.

Came to Canada and built himself a home up on the mountains in the Gaspé... A place where he could see a wide stretch of sea... Lived his life out there, they say."

"Milo?" She was looking at something.

I had seen them, too. Riders... three of them, all carrying rifles.

"Ride easy now," I warned her. "Sometimes talk is enough... or a bit of tobacco."

"I've never seen you smoke!"

"I don't, but Indians do. So I carry a sack of tobacco, just for luck. Use it on insect bites sometimes."

We rode slowly forward, and then suddenly Ann said, "Milo... the man on the gray horse! That's Tom Blake, one of our men!" She stood in her stirrups, waving.

Instantly, they started toward us. They were wary of me, although two of them had ridden to the box supper with the major and Ann.

When we met, Blake wanted to know where Ann had been. After I had explained, Blake looked at me carefully. "You know this Twin Baker?"

"Only by name and what Lisa told me. But I've an idea he's been around, under one name or another."

Then we rode toward the major's ranch.

When we rode up to the ranch-house door, the major came out. When he saw Ann, he rushed toward her. "Ann? Are you all right?"

"Yes. I am. Thanks to Milo." Briefly, she explained. The major's face stiffened.

"We'll go get him," he said flatly. "Tom, get the boys together. Full marching order, three days rations. We'll get him, and we'll get those cattle, every damned one of them!"

He turned to one of the other men who had come up. "Will, ride over to Balch. Tell him what's happened, and tell him to come on over here with some men."

"I'll ride back to my outfit," I said. "Remember, if that girl's there... she's done no harm. But we'd better move fast, because Twin Baker will."

Swinging my horse around, I lit out for the Stirrup-Iron, riding the grulla and leading the dun.

They were all there in the ranch yard when I rode in. Henry

Rossiter, Barby Ann, Fuentes, Roper and Harley. From the look of them, I knew something was wrong.

"You got back just in time!" Rossiter said. "We're ridin' after Balch! Last night they run off the whole damn herd! More than a thousand head of cattle! Gone, just like that!"

"Balch had nothing to do with it." I rode between Rossiter and the others. "When was the last time you saw Twin Baker?"

TWENTY-FOUR

Had I struck him across the face with my hat, the shock could
have been no greater. He took half a step forward, his features
drawn and old, staring up at me from blind, groping eyes.

"Twin? Twin Baker?" His voice shook. "Did you say Twin
Baker?"

"When did you last see him, Rossiter?"

He shook his head, as if to clear it of shock. "It's been years
...*years*. I thought... Well, I thought they were dead, both of
them."

"Ma killed one of them, Rossiter. She killed Stan Baker when
she got her cattle back. But it's the other one I'm talking
about... John, I think his name was, but they call him Twin."

"We got to get Balch," he stammered. "He stole our herd."

"I don't think it was Balch," I said. "Twin Baker got your herd,
like he's been getting all the rest of the young stuff around here."

"You're lyin'!" he protested. "Twin's dead. He's been dead.
Both those boys... John an' Stan. They're both dead."

"What's this all about?" Roper demanded. "Who's Twin Baker?"

"He's a cow thief. He's the man who's been running cattle off
this range for several years. He's been easing them off the range
a few head at a time, keeping out of sight all the while. He's been
stealing young stuff from every outfit in the basin... And he killed
Danny Rolf."

"What?" Ben Roper said.

180

"Danny's dead . . . Dry-gulched, then shot in the back of the head at close range. To make sure. Maybe it was because he was wearing my checked shirt and Twin mistook him for me. But more likely it was because Danny found Baker's hideout."

"I thought he had gone girlin'," Roper muttered.

"He had . . . Lisa is Twin Baker's half-sister. She's down there . . . Or was. I advised her to get out before he killed her, too."

"John?" Rossiter said. "Twin?"

We looked at Rossiter, then at each other. He wasn't paying us no mind. He was just blindly staring off across the yard toward the hills.

So I told them about finding Danny's body, about trailing him with Ann, of talking to Lisa, taking Ann home. "The major is getting a bunch together to go after the cattle, and after Twin Baker—if he can be found," I said.

"He's a gunfighter," I commented. "Lisa said he's killed several men, and that he wanted me." I looked around at them. "My mother killed Stan Baker, his twin, when they were trying to rustle some of our stock."

Barby Ann was staring at me. "*Your* stock?" She spoke contemptuously. "How much stock would a saddle tramp have?"

Rossiter shook his head irritably, and spoke without thinking. "Barby Ann, Talon's got more cattle than all of us in the basin put together. He lives in a house . . . Why, you could put the major's house in his livin' room!"

Now that wasn't true. They were all staring at me now. Only Fuentes was smiling a little.

"I don't believe it!" Barby Ann snapped. She'd never liked me much, but then she'd had no corner on that. I didn't think much of her, either. "He's filled you full of nonsense!"

"We'd better go if we're going," I said. "But one man had better stay here." I looked over at Harley. "How about you?"

"Joe Hinge is up. He can use a gun. Let him stay. I never did like rustlers."

Rossiter stood there, a huge frame of a man, only a shell of the magnificent young man he'd been when he rode for us on the Empty. Now he was sagging, broken.

"Here they come!" Harley said suddenly. "The major, Balch . . . the lot of them!"

"Talon?" Rossiter's tone was pleading. "Don't let them hang him!"

Puzzled, I stared at the blind man. "I wouldn't like to see any man hang, Rossiter. But Twin Baker deserves it if ever a man did. He killed Danny, and he would probably have killed Ann Timberly. And he's stolen enough cattle to put you all out of business."

"Talon, you can stop them. Don't let them hang him."

Balch rode up, Roger beside him. There was no sign of Saddler, but Major Timberly was there. Ingerman was with Balch, and so were several other riders, their faces familiar.

"Balch," I said suddenly. "Recall the first time we met? Over near the cap-rock?"

"I remember."

"There was a man with you...Who was he? He wasn't one of your boys."

"Oh, him? He wasn't from around here. He was a cattle buyer, tryin' to get a line on beef for the comin' year. He was fixing to buy several thousand head."

"Did he?"

"Ain't seen him since. He was a pleasant fella. Stayed two, three days. Rode out with Roger a couple of times."

"He said he was from Kansas City," Roger offered. "And he seemed to know the town. But he talked of New Orleans, too. Why? What's he got to do with anything?"

"I think he was Twin Baker," I said. "I think he was our rustler."

Balch stared, his face growing dark with angry blood. "That's a lot of poppycock!" he declared irritably. "He was nobody from around here."

"Maybe," I said.

"Time's a-wastin'," Roger said. "Let's ride!"

"All right." I started for my horse.

Rossiter came down off the steps. He put out a hand. "Talon! I got no right to ask it, but don't let them hang Twin Baker."

"What difference does it make to you?" I asked. "He stole your cattle, too."

"I don't want to see any man hang," Rossiter protested. "It ain't right."

"You comin' or not?" Balch asked.

"Get going," I said. "I'll not be far behind."

Angrily, Balch swung his horse. The major beside him, they rode out—a dozen very tough men.

"They could jail him," Rossiter protested. "They could hold him for trial. A man deserves a trial."

"Like the trial he gave Danny?"

At the corral I shook out a loop and walked toward that almost white horse with the black mane, tail and legs. I liked that horse, and I would need a stayer for a tough ride. I didn't think the ride would end on the Middle Concho. Twin Baker was no fool, and he would be hard to catch.

Leading the horse out, I got my saddle on him. Rossiter started toward me but Barby Ann was trying to turn him back.

"Pa? What's the matter with you? Have you gone crazy? What do you care about a no-account cow thief? Or that saddle tramp you seem to think is such a big man?"

He pulled away from her, tearing his sleeve in the process. He came after me in a stumbling run, and when I led the horse toward the bunkhouse, he followed.

"When you were a boy," he babbled, "we talked, you an' me. You was a good boy. I told you stories. Sometimes we rode together—"

"And then what happened?" I said bitterly.

"You don't understand!" he protested. "You folks had everything! You had a big ranch, you had horses, cattle, a fine house...I had nothing. Folks were always saying how good-lookin' I was. I rode fine horses. I wore good clothes. But I had nothing...nothing!"

I was listening. "Pa worked for it. He came into that country when there were only Indians, and he made peace with some, fought others. He built that ranch, he and Ma, built it with their own hands. They worked a lifetime doing it. And we boys helped, when we could."

Rossiter's face was haggard now. "But that takes *time*, boy! *Time!* I didn't want to be a rich old man. I wanted to be a rich *young* man. I deserved it. Why should you folks have so much and me nothing? All I did was take a few cattle...Just a few head!"

He put his hand on my shoulder. "Talon, for God's sake!"

"Rossiter," I said patiently, "I suspect everybody wants to have it all when they're young, but it just doesn't work that way. Pa worked, too. Worked hard. Maybe a man shouldn't have it when he's young. It robs him of something, gives him all he can have when he's too young to know what he's got. I don't know... Maybe I'm a damned fool, but that's the way it seems to me."

I looked at Rossiter. "Now you go back inside. There's nothing to worry about."

Barby Ann had come closer. She was standing there staring at her father as at a stranger. She had changed, somehow, these past few days. Maybe it was the rejection by Roger Balch. Maybe it was something that had been there all the time and we were only now seeing. "Forget it, Rossiter. I don't think we'll ever catch him. He's too smart."

"He is, isn't he?" Rossiter said eagerly. Suddenly, his expression became thoughtful. "Why, sure! He's got a good start. He won't try to keep that last herd, and they'll be so busy getting it back they won't get on to the others. That will split their party. My boys will have to take over that herd and start it back. Balch and the major won't have more than eight men with them... why, that's smart! That's thinking!"

They were words of desperation.

I got my saddlebags and threw them over the saddle, then my blanket roll. I had an idea this was going to take a long time, and I was a man who believed in preparing for all possibilities.

Rossiter, I thought, was crazy. I had not realized it until now, but he must be off his head. Nothing he said was making sense, and it was obvious that Barby Ann felt the same way.

"Pa?" she said. "Pa, you'd better come back to the house."

"He will do all right, that boy will! Have an outfit bigger'n yours someday, Talon."

"Rossiter, don't fool yourself. Twin Baker will wind up at the end of a rope, or killed in a gun battle. I don't know what you think he is but he's shown himself a thief and a murderer, and hanging's too good for him."

He stopped and stared at me, then shook his head. "You don't understand," he protested.

My horse was restless to go, as I was. Barby Ann said, "Pa? Let's go up to the house."

He pulled his arm away from her. He put his hand on my shoulder. "Talon, get him away from them. Don't let them hang him. You're a good man... a good man. I know you're a good man. Don't let them hang him."

Rossiter spat. "That Balch! He'll want a hangin'. I know he'll want it. And the major... he's just like all them army men. Discipline! He'll be for a hanging, too. You've got to stop them, Talon."

I put a foot into the stirrup and swung to the saddle, turning the horse away from him. "You're pleading for him? When he stole your cattle, too?"

"He didn't know they was mine. He couldn't have known." Rossiter shook his head admiringly. "Slick, though. Real slick." He peered up at me, squinting his eyes. "You don't think they'll catch him? You said that. You don't think they will?"

"Rossiter, you'd better go to the house. You need some rest. We'll find him, and if your cattle are still around to recover, we'll recover them."

He turned away from me, his head shaking a little. At the moment, I could feel only sorrow for the man. I'd never liked him. Even as a boy, when I'd often talked with him, I'd never liked him. There was always something shallow and artificial about him, something that was all show, all front with nothing behind it. Now the physical magnificence was gone, and all that remained was a shell.

Since joining his crew I'd only seen him inside, in the half-light of the house. And there had been a shadow of strength remaining. At least, there'd seemed to be. But under the sun, the deterioration was evident.

"Go!" Barby Ann said irritably. "Get out of here! It was a sorry day for us when you came here to work. It's you who's done this to him... *You*."

I just looked at her and shrugged. "When we bring the cattle back, I'll quit. You can have my time ready. I'm sorry you feel as you do."

Rossiter turned from us. "John?" he muttered. "John...."

He turned suddenly to me. "Don't let them hang him! *Don't!*"

"Damn it, Rossiter! The man's a thief! He stole your cattle, he stole from everybody in the basin, and he tried to stir up a shooting war. Why the hell should you care what happens to him?"

He stared at me from his blind eyes. "Care? *Care?* Why shouldn't I care? *He's my son!*"

TWENTY-FIVE

My horse could walk as fast as many horses could trot, and he moved right out, heading south away from the ranch. Yet I had no idea of overtaking the posse. I'd never been one to travel in a crowd, and I had noticed that too often the wrong men wind up as the leaders of groups or mobs.

It was a rough thirty-five miles and a bit more from the ranch to the cabin on the Concho, and I made a beeline for it.

Shortly before night fell, I stepped down near the head of Kiowa Creek and, without unsaddling, built myself a fire and made coffee and bacon. When I'd eaten, I loaded up frying pan and coffeepot, drinking the last of the coffee from the pot itself, and I took off toward a hollow in the prairie maybe a half mile from the creek. I'd spotted this place before, and there was a seep that didn't quite make it to the surface but did green up the grass. There I staked my horse, rolled up in my blankets and, with my horse for lookout, slept like a baby until the last stars lingered in the sky.

Moving out, I held to low ground well west of Kiowa country, and I came out of the timber on Tepee Draw on the south side of the cabin.

There was no smoke, no sign of life.

For several minutes I sat the buckskin, watching the house. It had every appearance of being deserted, and there was a plain enough trail heading off toward the southeast. Chancing it, I rode up.

The cabin was empty. Most of the food had been cleared out. Only a few shabby clothes remained, and a few cast-off utensils. There was some coffee on the fire that was still warm. Stirring up the coals, I heated it again and drank from a broken-handled cup while pacing from window to window.

I went outside. After watering my horse, I went back to the house. Everything that was worth anything had been cleaned out.

Mounting up, I followed the trail southeast past the mountain, and after a few miles I reached Spring Creek.

One rider was ahead of me, riding easy. The trail was several hours hold. It was that long-striding horse again.

Twin Baker!

Southeast of here lay the San Saba and the Llano River country, and I knew almost nothing about it except from bunkhouse or saloon talk.

The next day, shortly after sunup, I rode down into Poor Hollow.

There was a crude brush and pole corral there, big enough to hold a few head for a short stay. And from the droppings, cattle had been kept there recently—as well as several times in the past.

At one side, under some trees, I found a small circle of stones where repeated fires had built quite a bed of ash. The ashes were cold, but the tracks looked no more than two to three days old.

Squatting under a big old pecan tree, I studied the corral, yet my mind was ranging back over the country. Twin Baker had evidently stolen the cattle in relatively small bunches, then drifted them by various routes to this or other holding corrals where he left them, while going back for more.

There was water from the creek and enough grass to keep a small bunch. When he returned with another lot, he'd probably drive them further south and east.

Moving out of Poor Hollow toward a prong of the San Saba, I made camp under some trees. I fixed a small bait of grub where the smoke would rise through the leaves and dissipate itself among them, leaving no rising column to be seen. It was on fairly high ground with a good view all around. My back to a tree, I studied the layout.

I saw a huge old buffalo bull with two young cows, a scattering of antelope, and a few random buzzards. Otherwise, nothing but distance and dancing heat waves. Nevertheless, I had an eerie, unpleasant feeling at odds with the beauty of the land. I had the feeling that I was heading right into a trap.

Someplace, Baker had to have a base, a place with water, and good grazing, where cattle might be held for some time. After a rest I drifted on, taking my time. This country was more rugged, and there was a good bit of cedar.

Twice I camped. Twice I came up to holding grounds where cattle had been corraled for a time, mostly young stuff, judging by the tracks and the droppings.

It was lonely country. Several times I saw an Indian sign, but it was old. There were several sets of tracks, mostly made by that long-stepping horse, but now I began to come on other tracks, lone riders or sometimes two or three in a bunch. All of them headed east.

Come daybreak, I was up on the hurricane deck of my bronc again, and looking down the trail... And it was a trail. Yet this was what I liked, riding far in a wide, lovely country with distance all around. At every break in the hill, there was a new vista, yet the apparent emptiness of the country could fool you. And wherever a man looked, there were hidden folds of the hills that could hide an army... or an Indian war party looking for scalps and glory.

Suddenly, there opened ahead of me a lovely green valley and some buildings. From a hill, I'd seen some adobe ruins off to the north and east of where I was... mostly east. That was the San Saba Presidio, an attempt by the Spanish in early times to settle and administer this country. Comanches did them in, wiping out the last few priests who didn't get away ahead of time.

The buildings I now saw must be south of the old Presidio. There were only four or five, a town if you wanted to call it that— a store, a saloon, a few cabins. Some empty, some occupied. There were some corrals.

The saloon was a long low adobe building. There was a bar in it, and a lean, savage-looking man with an almost bald head. Suspenders were holding up his pants. He wore a slightly soiled undershirt, and his brows were a straight bar across his head above his eyes.

"What are ya having?" He stared at me with glassy blue eyes.

"Beer, if you've got it."

"We got it an' it's cold, right out of the springhouse." He reached for the bottle, put it on the bar. "Driftin'?"

"Sort of. I've got a liking for new country."

"Me, too. This ain't my place. I just agreed to set in for the boss. He had to go down to San Antone for a spell. Stomach botherin' him, he said, and it could be."

"Can you feed a man here?"

"If you like Mexican food. We got a gal here who can really put on the beans. We got beans, rice and beef. In the early morning we'll have eggs... The woman's got chickens."

He laughed. "Second batch she's had. Weasel got the whole bunch here a while back. Some folks say that man is the only one who just kills to be killing... Those folks never saw a hen house after a weasel has been in it. He'll kill one or two, drink their blood, and then just kill all the rest. Seems to go kind of wild, crazylike."

I agreed.

"Mountain lion will do the same thing. Kill two, three deer, sometimes, eat a little off one of them and bury it in brush, then go off."

I tasted the beer. It was good, much better than I'd expected. I gestured toward the north. "Isn't that the old Presidio up yonder?"

"Sure is. Ain't much account except for holdin' cattle. Buildings and the walls make a fine corral... hold a mighty big herd, comes to that." He looked at me again. "You headin' for San Antone?"

"Sort of. But I'd latch onto a cow outfit if there was one needin' a hand. I'd rather drive cattle, if it comes to that. I'd rather just sit up there on my bronc an' let the world slide by. I got a good cuttin' horse yonder, and he knows more about cows than I do, so I just set up there and let him do the work."

"Not many outfits this far west. Away over on the North Concho, I hear there's some. Never been that far west, myself," he said.

"You said they sometimes held herds in the Presidio? Any cattle up there now?"

He shook his head. "Been some a few days back... Just a small bunch, though. Maybe a hundered and fifty head. Two men drivin' them."

He chuckled, suddenly.

When I looked a question, he smiled and shook his head. "Beats a man how some folks get together. They come in here for a beer, just like you. One of them a real quiet man. Still face... good-lookin' feller, but mighty quiet. Never missed anything, though. Other feller, he was younger... Kind of a flashy sort, swaggers it around, and you can just see he's proud of that big gun on his hip. Never saw such two different fellers together before."

"Didn't the quiet one have a gun?" I asked.

"Surely did. But you know something? You had to look two or three times to see it. I mean it was right out there in plain sight, but he wore it like he'd been born with it and it was hardly so's you'd notice it."

He paused. "That younger feller, he wore two guns, one stuck behind his belt on the left side with his vest hangin' over it a mite... But the way he wore those two guns you'd a thought he had six. Just seemed to stick out with guns all over."

"High forehead? High wave of hair thrown back? Striped pants, maybe?" I asked.

"That's him. You know him?"

"Seen him around. Name's Jory Benton. Hires his gun some-times."

The bartender shook his head. "He never hired it to that other man. Never in this world. That other feller, he don't need any gun hands. I seen his kind before."

"A hundred and fifty head, you say? If they're trail-broke, two men could handle them, so they wouldn't need me," I said.

"They're trail-broke, all right. He had one old cow, splashes of red an' white. She was the leader and the rest of them just trailed along behind... young stuff... three, four years old. Some year-lin's."

Taking my beer, I walked to a table near the window. The bartender brought his bottle along and sat down opposite me. "I'm holed up here until spring," he said. "Got me a dugout yonder. There's beef around, and a good many turkeys. Come spring I'll head for San Antone. I'm a teamster," he added.

We saw a man come out from a house across the way. The bartender indicated him with a nod of his head. "Now there's somethin' odd. That feller... He's been around here two, three days, just a-settin'. Never comes over here. Never talks to nobody but his partner. I got a feelin' they're waitin' for somebody."

He was a tall, lean, easy-moving man, with a stub of cigar in his teeth and a beat-up black hat on his head. He wore a tied-down gun and a Bowie knife and he was looking at my horse. When he turned his head and said something over his shoulder, another man came out of the house. This second man was fat and short, with unshaved jowls and a shirt open at the neck, with a dirty neckerchief tied there.

Both men looked carefully around.

"Amigo," I said to the bartender, "if I were you I'd get back of my bar and lie on the floor."

He stared at me. "Look here..." He hesitated. Then he asked, "They comin' for you?"

I smiled at him. "Well now, I wouldn't rightly know. But that tall gent is called Laredo, and folks do say he's right handy with a six-gun. The fat one could be Sonora Davis. Either one of them would shoot you for fun... Except they usually only have fun when they get paid for it."

"They lookin' for you?"

I smiled again. "They haven't said, have they? Maybe I'd better go see."

Getting up, I slipped the thong from my six-shooter. "I never did like to keep folks waiting. If they respect you enough to make an appointment, the least you can do is not keep them sitting around. You keep that beer for me, will you?"

There was no door, just the open space for one. I stepped into the doorway and walked outside.

Stopping in the shade of the awning, I looked at them in the sunlight near their door.

It was very still, and the sun was hot. A black bee buzzed lazily about, and a small lizard paused on a rock near the awning post, his little sides moving as he gasped for air.

"Hello, Laredo," I said, loud enough for him to hear. "It's a long way from the Hole."

He squinted his eyes under his hat brim, staring at me.

"Last time I saw you," I said, "you were holding four nines against my full house."

"Talon? Milo Talon? Is that you?" Laredo asked.

"Who'd you expect? Santa Claus?"

We were sixty feet apart, at least. His partner started to shift off to the right. "Sonora," I said, "I wouldn't do that. Might give me some idea you boys were waitin' for me. I wouldn't like to think that."

Laredo shifted his cigar stub in his teeth. "We had no idea it would be you. We were just waitin' for a rider on a Stirrup-Iron Horse."

I jerked my head to indicate my horse. "There he is. I'm the rider."

Laredo was good with a gun, and so was Davis, but Laredo was the better of the two. Yet I could sense uncertainty in him. He didn't like surprises, and he had been expecting some random cowhand, not somebody he knew.

"I hope he paid you enough, Laredo," I said quietly.

"Well, we didn't figure on you. He just said a snoopy cowhand was followin' along behind him. Hell, if he'd known it was you, he'd have done it himself."

"He knew. I'm sure he knew," I said.

There were two of them, and I wanted an edge. I didn't know whether I needed it or not, but I wanted it. They had taken money to kill, and they would not welsh on the job.

"We taken this money," Laredo said, "an' we got to do it."

"You could always give it back."

"We done spent most of it, Milo. We just ain't got it no more," said Laredo.

"Well, I could let you have a few bucks," I said quietly. "I could let you have... Let's see what I've got." I moved my right hand as if toward my pocket and when they went for their guns I was a split second ahead of them.

Sonora's gun was coming up when I shot him. Sonora was on the right. It is an easier move from right to left, so I took him first.

Laredo had been fast... too fast for his own good. And he neglected to take that split instant of time that can make a good shot better.

His thumb slid off the hammer as his gun was coming up, and the bullet spat sand a dozen feet in front of me. Mine hit the target.

Long ago, an old gunfighter had told me, "Make the first shot count. You may never get another."

I wasn't going to need another.

Laredo fell against the side of the house and his gun went off into the dust at his feet. His shoulder against the wall, his knees buckled and he slid down to the hard-packed earth.

For a moment, I stood very still, just waiting. It was warm, and there was the acrid smell of gun smoke. Somewhere up the street, if you could call it that, a door slammed. A woman stood in the street, shading her eyes toward us.

Slowly I crossed to my horse, thumbing cartridges into my gun. When I holstered it, I stepped into the saddle.

The bartender was in the door, looking at me. "What'll I do?" he pleaded. "I mean, what—"

"Bury them," I said. "There'll be money in their pockets, and it will buy you an easy winter...Take it. Keep their outfits. Bury them, and put some markers on their graves."

I pointed at each in turn. "His name was Laredo Larkin, and his was Sonora Davis."

"Where they from?"

"I don't know," I said, "but they got where they were going. They've been riding down the road to this place for a long, long time."

Then I rode out of there.

Laredo and Davis. Was I riding the same road as them?

TWENTY-SIX

The trail of the stolen cattle turned south toward the Llano River country. The worst of it was, I'd ridden out of town without getting anything to eat, and my belly was beginning to think my throat was cut. So when I saw an adobe house up ahead, I rode up to it and swung down.

A slender young woman came to the door, shading her eyes at me. I also saw a man come to the door of the barn to watch me.

"I'd like to buy something to eat," I said. "Or grub I can take with me."

"'Light an' set," she said. "I'll put something on."

The man walked up from the barn, a thin young man with a quick, shy smile. "Howdy! Passin' through?"

"That's my name," I said, grinning. "Seems to me that's about all I do. Pass through. Been here long?"

"Nobody's been here long. I come in when the war was over. Found this place, fixed up the old 'dobe and the corrals. Got a few head of cattle on the range, and then I went back to West Virginia for Essie, there."

"Well, you've got water, grass an' time. Seems like you won't need much else."

He glanced at me again. "Surprised you didn't eat in town. That Mexican woman's a good cook."

"There was a shooting up there, so I lit out. No tellin' when there might be more."

194

"A shootin'? What happened?" he asked.

"Looked to me like a couple of gunhands had been waitin' for a man. He rode into town and they had at him and came up short."

"He got them? Both of them?"

"Looked that way. I just straddled my bronc and lit out," I said.

We walked to the trough, where I let the horse drink, then tied him on some grass while I went inside. We sat down, and the man removed his hat, wiping his brow and then the sweatband of his hat.

"Hot," he said. "I've been down in the bottom putting up some hay."

Essie came in and put plates on the table. She shot me a quick, curious glance. News was scarce in this country, and visitors were few. I knew what was expected of me. They wanted to know what was happening... anywhere at all.

So I told them all about the box supper at Rock Springs Schoolhouse, about the cattle thefts up in the Concho country, and repeated what I'd said about the recent shooting.

Essie put a pot of coffee on the table, then beans, beef and some fried potatoes—the first I'd had in some time. "He grows them," she said, proudly, indicating her husband. "He's a good farmer."

"Seen some cattle been driven through here. Some of yours?" I asked casually.

He shook his head quickly. "No. No, they aren't. They come through here from time to time... Never stop." He glanced at his wife. "That is, they never done so until this last time... There was a stranger along then, flashy looking man. I didn't take to him much."

Essie's face was flushed, but I avoided looking at her.

The man continued. "He stopped off, started talking to Essie. I guess he took her for a lone woman, so I came up, and he kind of edged around her, and I seen him take the loop off his gun."

"A man with a high forehead?" I asked.

"Yes, sir. He did have. Kind of wavy hair. Anyway, I was afraid of trouble, but that other man came back and spoke real sharp to him, and this first man, he rode off. When he looked back he said, 'You wait, honey. I'll be ridin' this way again.' I heard that other man say 'Like hell you will! I done too much to keep this trail smooth. I don't figure to have it messed up by—' Then his voice kind of trailed off, but I heard the other man speak. Believe me, they were none too friendly when they left."

"The one who talked to you," I said to Essie, "is a gunman named Jory Benton."

"A gunman?" Her face paled. "Then if—"

"Yes," I said bluntly. "He might have killed your husband. He wouldn't hesitate to do just that. He shot a friend of mine up north of here."

They exchanged glances.

"Those cattle," I asked casually, while refilling my cup, "does he take them to his ranch?"

"Wouldn't call it a ranch, exactly. He's got him a place down on the Llano... Runs maybe a thousand head... or more. All young stuff." He hesitated. "Mister, I don't know you, and maybe I shouldn't be tellin' you all this, but that there outfit doesn't size up right to me."

"How so?" I asked.

"Time an' again they drift cattle through here. They never bothered me, nor me them, until that last feller came along who bothered Essie. Hadn't been for him, I might have kept my mouth shut. I got no call to suspicion them except that it don't seem likely a man would have so many calves without cows, always driftin' along the same route."

"How many men does he have?"

The young man shrugged. "Can't say. Most often he's driftin' only a few, an' he's alone. Sometimes it's after dark, and I can't make them out. Time or two, when I was scoutin' for game down south of here, I cut their trail. One time I looked across the Llano and saw the cattle. Seemed to me there were two or three men down there, but I was afraid they'd see me and I wanted no trouble, so I lit out."

"South of here, you say?" I asked.

"Almost due south. The Llano takes kind of a bend this way. There's quite a canyon there, and he's running his cattle in south of there. Good grass, plenty of water, and lots of oak, elm, mesquite and some pecans. It's a right nice locality."

When I'd finished eating, I went out and brought up my horse, tightened the cinch and stepped into the saddle. "Friend," I suggested, "you could make yourself a couple of dollars if you want to take a ride."

"A ride to where?"

Now I knew that cash money was a hard thing to come by in these places, and any two-bit rancher like this was sure to be hard up.

"Up north of here along the Middle Concho... Likely they're south of there by now, and you could meet them half way. There's a party of riders... a Major Timberly and a man named Balch will be leading, I think. Tell them Talon sent you, and that the cattle are on the Llano."

"Those are stolen cattle?" he asked.

"They are. But you just ride, and don't tell anybody why or wherefore. The man you had trouble with was Jory Benton, and the man bossing the move is Twin Baker... and he's five or six times tougher and meaner than Benton. Don't cross them.

"They'll see my tracks if I miss them and they come back this way. So don't lie. Tell them I was here, that I ate here and just pulled out. I didn't talk or ask questions. I just ate. You understand?"

He agreed.

My trail was southeast, through rough, broken country with a scattering of cedar and oak. Nor was it the kind of country a man likes to travel if he's worried about being dry-gulched; the country was perfectly laid out for it.

Like I said before, my mother raised no foolish children that I knew of, so I switched trails every few minutes. That horse must have thought I'd gone pure loco. Suddenly, I turned him and started due east toward the head of Five Mile Creek. Then south, then west.

I scouted every bit of country before I rode across it, studying the lay of the land and trying to set no pattern so that a man might trap me up ahead. I'd ride toward a bunch of hills, then suddenly turn off along their base. I'd start up the hills on a diagonal, then reverse and go up the opposite way. Whenever I rode into trees or rocks, I'd double back when I had concealment and cut off at an angle. It took time, but I wasn't fighting time. The main idea was to get there alive and in action.

Not that I had any very good idea of what I was going to do when I arrived. That part I hadn't thought out too well. I decided to just let things happen.

Mainly I wanted them not to drive off the cattle.

Nightfall found me under some bluffs near the head of Little Bluff Creek. It was a place where a big boulder had deflected the talus falling off the rim to either side, leaving a little hollow maybe thirty yards across. And the slope below was scattered with white rocks.

There was a cedar growing near the boulder, low and thick, and some mesquite nearby. I scouted it as I rode past. Then, stopping in a thick patch of trees and brush, I built myself a small fire, made coffee and fried some bacon. When I'd eaten and sopped of the bacon gravy with one of the biscuits Essie had packed for me, I dowsed my fire, pulling the sticks away and scattering dirt over the ashes. Then leading my horse, I walked back several hundred yards to the hollow below the boulder.

Stripping my rig from the horse, I let him roll, watered him and picketed him on the grass below the boulder. Then I unrolled my bed, took off my boots and stretched out. And believe me, I was tired.

If I had it figured right, the Llano was about eight or nine miles due south, and the holding ground for the cattle right beyond that river. That young rancher I'd sent north after Balch and Timberly had laid it out pretty good for me, and Baker was running his cattle in a sort of triangle between the Llano and the James, and just east of Blue Mountain... but trying to hold them between Blue Mountain and the Llano.

The moon was up when next I opened my eyes. Everything was white and pretty. I could see that black-legged horse cropping grass out there, but I couldn't see his legs at all, only his body, looking like one of those white rocks.

I turned over and started to go to sleep again, and then my eyes came wide open. Why, I was a damned fool. If they came sneaking up on me...them or the Kiowas...I'd never have a chance. They'd spot my bed right out there in the open and fill it full of lead.

Well, I slid out of that bed like a greased eel through wet

fingers. I rolled a couple of rocks into my bed, bunched the bedding around it and went back into the deeper shadows under that big boulder. And with the saddle blanket around my shoulders, I leaned back and dozed again, rifle to hand and my gunbelt on.

Dozing against that rock, suddenly I heard my mustang blow like a horse will sometimes do when startled. My eyes opened on three men walking up on my camp.

One whispered, "You two take him. I'll get his horse."

Flame blasted from the barrels of two rifles and there was a roar of sound—the harsh, staccato barking of the rifles.

They stood there, those two dark figures, within twenty feet of my bed, and they worked the levers on their rifles until they shot themselves out of ammunition. I had my Winchester in my hands, pointed in their direction, and I was maybe forty feet from them.

That ugly roar of sound was to ring in my ears for many a day, as they poured lead into what they thought was me, shooting and shooting again.

I heard the horse snort, and a voice called out, "You get him?"

There was a rude grunt and the other man said, "What the hell do you think?"

The moonlight was bright.

I stood up—one nice, easy movement—taking a pebble from the ground as I did so. They had half turned, but some slight rustle or shadow of movement must have caught the ear of one of them because he looked toward me. Backed up against that big boulder as I was, he could have seen nothing or, at best, only a part of something. With my left hand, I tossed my pebble off to the right, and they both turned sharply.

"You bought the ticket," I said quietly. "Now take the ride."

My Winchester stabbed flame and knocked one man staggering, reaching for his pistol. The other turned sharply off to his left, diving for cover as he drew, but I was always a good wing shot, and my bullet caught him on the fly and he went plunging straight forward on his face.

The echoes of my shots chased each other under the eaves of the cliffs, then lost themselves along the wall.

There was then a moment of absolute, unbelievable silence, and then a voice: "Boys?... Boys?"

I said nothing. Somewhere out there in the night, and I could have put a bullet through the sound, was Jory Benton. The trouble was, he had my horse, and I'd no desire to kill a good horse in trying for a bad man.

So I waited . . . and after a moment there was a drum of hooves. And I was alone with two dead men and a moon that was almost gone from the sky.

I was alone, and I was afoot, and when daylight came I would be hunted down.

A faint breeze stirred the leaves, moaning a little in the cedar, rustling in the mesquite.

I thumbed shells into my Winchester.

TWENTY-SEVEN

Of course, Benton had taken his men's horses, also. I had to be certain, but I was sure from the sounds that he had taken them.

Rolling the rocks from my bed, I shook it out and rolled it up. Shot full of holes, it was still better than nothing, and the nights were cold.

One other thing I did. I went to where the men I'd shot had fallen...

Only one remained!

So one of them was still alive, able to move, able perhaps to shoot. I stripped the cartridge belt from the remaining man and slung it across my shoulders, after a brief check to make sure he was using .44s as I was.

His six-gun was there, so I tucked it behind my belt, and both rifles lay nearby. Evidently, the wounded man had been more eager to get away than to think of fighting, and had failed to take his rifle.

Carrying both of them, I walked away, keeping to the deeper shadows, wary of a bullet.

When I was off a hundred yards or so, I pointed myself south and started to walk. There were men beyond the Llano, as well as cattle, and where there were men, there would be horses, including mine.

When I had walked about four miles or so—I figured it took me about an hour and a half, and that would come to close to four miles—I found myself in the bottom of another creek. Maybe it was Big Bluff. I could only guess, knowing the country only by hearsay.

It was dark under the trees and, finding a place off to one side, I kicked around a little to persuade any possible snakes that I wasn't good company. Then I unrolled my bed and stretched out, and would you believe it? I slept.

The first light was filtering its way through the leaves when my eyes opened. For a moment I lay there between two big logs, listening. There were birds twittering and squeaking in the trees, and there was a rustle, as some small animal or maybe a lizard moved through the leaves. And there was the faint sound of water running.

Sitting up, I looked carefully around. Great old trees were all around, some mossy old logs, and a few fallen branches—a blow-down of three or four trees, and not much else. First off I checked the spare rifles. One was empty, the other had three shells, which I pocketed. Finding a hollow tree, I stashed the rifles there, then checked the loads on my rifle and the extra pistol.

Shouldering my bed, I crossed the creek, stopped at a spring that trickled into the creek and drank, then drank again. Following it upstream, I left it and headed for the breaks along the Llano.

By the time the sun was well into the sky, I was looking down on as pretty a little camp as I'd ever seen, tucked away in the trees with several square miles of the finest grazing in Texas laid out there in front of it. Now grass is an uncertain thing. Some years it can be good, and some years it wouldn't keep a grasshopper alive. This was a good year, and in spite of the cattle down there it was holding up.

There were a couple of lean-tos facing each other maybe a dozen yards apart. There was a fire going, with a kettle hanging over it, and a coffeepot in the coals. There were a couple of pairs of undershirts and drawers hanging over a line that ran tree to tree. And there was a man stretched out on the ground, hands behind his head and a hat over his face, napping in the morning sun.

Two saddled horses were nearby, and my horse unsaddled. My own saddle was back where I'd left it, half hidden under the edge of that big boulder where I'd started my sleep. When the time came, I could pick it up again.

For a spell, I just lay there. Another man—too far off to tell who—came from a lean-to and began stropping a razor. Evidently, there was a piece of mirror on a corner post of the lean-to, because he stood there, shaving. It was a sore temptation to dust them up a little with my Winchester, but I put the idea aside.

Studying the herd, I could see several hundred head of cattle. And although it was too far to see for sure, they appeared to be in good shape.

Now that I was here, I had no idea what to do. Before anything else, I must recover my horse—or another one—and prepare to guide the posse in when it arrived.

Easing back off the hill, I worked my way down a gully to the Llano. It was wide at this point, but not deep. Working my way down to the bank, I studied the situation with care. To attempt to get a horse by daylight would be asking for trouble that I did not want, so my best bet was to lie quiet and see what developed. I was hidden in thick brush near a huge old fallen tree, and although I could see almost nothing of the camp, I could hear voices.

Only occasionally could I clearly make out a word. Straining my ears, I heard the man who was shaving... At least I guessed it was him, because it sounded like a man talking while he was shaving a jowl.

"...tonio...deal. Figure we should drive...Guadalupe River."

There was a muttered response that I could not clearly hear, then some further argument.

"...don't like it." The voice came through louder and stronger. "He ain't alone, I tell you! You know Balch? Well, I do! He's meaner than hell, an' if he gets you he'll go no further than the nearest tree! I say we sell out and get out!"

There was more muttering. As their emotions became stronger, their voices rose. "What became of Laredo? You seen him? Have you seen Sonora? All we were supposed to do was drive some cows. Now look at it!"

There was a faint sound from upstream and, craning my neck, I saw a man stagger to the edge of the stream, fall, then saw him drinking, lapping at the water like a dog.

Lifting his head, he called out, a hoarse, choking cry.

"What the hell was *that?*" one of the men said. And then I heard running.

They came out on the bank of the stream, maybe fifty yards

up from where I was hidden. They stopped, stared, then splashed across the stream to the wounded man. This was probably one of the men I'd shot the previous night.

They knelt beside him. I came swiftly to my feet, and eased down the bank into the water. Moving with great care to make no sound, I moved across the Llano.

Their backs were to me, both kneeling beside the wounded man. In a moment they'd be helping him up, trying to get him back to the camp.

Up the bank I crept. At the edge of the camp I stopped, taking a swift look around... Nobody was in sight. Running swiftly, I crossed the camp to the saddled horses. My horse was tied to the pole corral and I took his lead rope and one of the saddled horses, then turned the other loose and shied him off.

He ran off a few steps and stopped, looking back. I could not see the stream and could hear no sound. Leading the two horses, I walked across the camp.

There was a skillet with bacon on one side of the fire, keeping warm for somebody. I took up several slices and ate them, then picked up the pot and drank the hot coffee right from the edge of the pot.

Stepping into the saddle on the roan, leading my own horse, I went back toward the Llano. Glancing upstream, I saw that the men had disappeared from the bank. So I rode my horses across and headed north to where I'd cached my saddle.

It was no plan of mine to steal the man's horse, and least of all his saddle. Shoot a man I might, but stealing his saddle was another thing entirely. When I came back to the boulder where my own rig was, I dismounted, saddled my own horse and turned the roan loose.

Good crossings of the Llano were few, for the cliffs along each side were high and the country rugged. From the highest ground I could find, I looked north. But there was no sign of Balch or the major.

Riding west along the Llano, I found a place further upstream where I could cross over. Mounting the south bank, I worked my way back through scattered cedar and oak toward the cattle. I came upon a few scattered ones, and started to bunch them to move toward the main holding ground southwest of their camp.

The man I'd shot the night before had seemed to be shot in

the leg or hip, from the way they were handling him. It was possible he could still ride.

Suddenly, I wondered.

Where was Twin Baker?

He had not been in the camp. There had been some discussion of San Antonio, and Lisa had said he often went there. Was he there now?

Keeping to the brush, trees and rocks, I worked nearer to the holding ground. As Baker seemed to have bunched and stolen the cattle by himself, these were probably just hired hands, outlaws he had picked up to help with the final drive.

Whatever had been his original plan, apparently that plan had now changed, due to the events of the past few days. The discovery of his thefts, the escape of Ann Timberly, and my pursuit—of which he was certainly aware.

Laredo and Davis had been sent to stop me, at least until Baker could get the cattle moved... Did he know they had failed?

It was all uncertain. And the fact that Twin Baker was not visible did not mean he was nowhere around. At any moment, he might have me locked in the sight of that rifle... And he could shoot!

Where were Balch and the others? Had they all turned back? Was I alone in my effort to recover the cattle?

The more I looked at it, the less I liked it.

Had Rossiter sent for his men to return? Had Twin Baker known he was stealing from his own father, among others?

From her reactions, it was obvious that Barby Ann had no knowledge that Twin Baker was her brother—or that she even had a brother. She had been aghast and confused by her father's erratic words, unable to guess what he was talking about.

Uneasily, I began to wonder if I was not alone out here. And fated to be left alone!

In the shadow of a bluff, I drew up. From where I sat my horse, I could see out over the plain where the cattle grazed, and I was not the only one bunching cattle. Other riders were out there, working swiftly, bunching the cattle, with the apparent intention of moving them off toward the southeast.

They were working the breaks on the north and west, working carefully but swiftly, and moving them not southeast, as I expected, but due east.

The small lot of cattle I'd started moved out on the plain and a rider turned toward them, then suddenly slowed his pace. I chuckled grimly.

He'd seen those cattle. Then suddenly he'd begun to wonder who had started them. Now he was approaching, but much more carefully. I held my horse, watching. He swung in behind the cattle, glancing over his shoulder as he did so. But I made no move, just watched. Reassured, he moved the cattle toward the drifting herd.

Glancing north again, I searched the sky for dust, hoping for the posse's arrival. I saw nothing.

I swore, slowly, bitterly.

My eyes looked toward the river and saw the wind move the leaves. I looked beyond the bobbing horns of the cattle, beyond the horsemen, weaving their arabesques as they circled and turned, gathering the cattle.

Maybe there was more of Pa and Barnabas in me than I thought. For when I looked upon the beauty and upon the distance, I could only think how short was a man's life, with all the things to be done, the words to be spoken, the many miles to ride.

Those men were gathering stolen cattle, and I waited, trying to think of a way to recover them. The distance between us was so very, very small.

The law is a thin line, a line that divides those who would live by rules with men from those who would live against them. And it is easy to overstep and be upon the other side. Yet I'd known many a man in the west who had made that step, only to see the folly of his ways and step back.

In a land of hard men living rough lives, they found it easy to understand such missteps and to forgive.

There were the others, like Henry Rossiter, who wanted the rewards without the labor, who, to get them, would take from others what they had worked hard to gain. It was the mindless selfishness of those who had not come to understand that all civilization was simply a living together, so that all could live better.

Why I did such a damn fool thing, I'll never know. But suddenly I rode out from my shadow and into the sunlight of the plain. There'd come a time when I'd lie awake and sweat with the realization of what I'd done, but it came to me to do it, and I did. I rode right out there, and one of the riders close to me turned to stare.

The others...and there were three others now...kind of drew up and looked. But they were scattered out from one another, and too far off to make out faces.

When I rode up to him, I saw a stocky man with a barrel chest and a square, tough face.

"Point 'em north," I said. "We're takin' 'em back."

"What? Who the hell are you?"

"Milo Talon's the name, but that doesn't matter. The only thing that matters is that we point these cattle north and start them for the Concho, where they were stolen."

He stared at me. What I was doing made no sense to me, so how could it make sense to him? He was puzzled and worried. He glanced toward the others, then toward the shadows of the bluffs I'd come from, like he was expecting more riders.

"No, I am alone. The posse is still a few miles off and they won't get here for a while, so you boys get a break. That posse is in a hangin' mood, and I'm giving you boys your chance. You know who Balch is...Well, he's with that posse.

"To get any money out of these cattle you've got to drive them and then sell them, and you can't drive them fast and you can't sell them anywhere near fast enough."

The man looked stupefied.

"Looks to me like you've got a plain, simple choice. You help me drive these cattle north and you can ride off scot-free. But give me an argument and all of you hang."

The other riders were coming around the herd toward us.

"How do we know there's any posse?" asked the man.

I grinned at him. "You got my word for it, chum. If you don't like my word, you've got some shooting to do. If I win, you're dead. If I lose, you've still got a mighty mean posse to deal with...Either way, you lose the cattle. You just can't drive this big a herd with any speed, and you can't hide it."

"What the hell's goin' on?" The speaker was an older man, his mustache stained with tobacco juice. "Who's this hombre?"

I grinned at him. "Name's Milo Talon. I was just suggesting you boys could make your stars shine brighter in the heavens was you to drive this herd north to meet the posse."

"Posse? What posse?"

"A very hard-skulled gent named Balch, and with him, Major Timberly and some other riders. These are their cattle, and Balch is a man with a one-track mind when it comes to rustlers. He thinks in terms of r's... Rustlers and ropes."

A redheaded cowhand chuckled. "There's another r got those beat all hollow... *Run!*"

"Try it," I suggested, "and you just might make it. On the other hand, you might lose... and that's quite a loss. You win, or you get your necks stretched. Was I you, I'd not like the odds."

"You got you a point there," the redhead agreed.

"I've got another one, which I was pointing out to your friend here. There's no way you can drive a herd fast enough to get away from a posse... So you've lost the herd, anyway. Do it my way and you'll still lose the cattle, but the posse will shake you by the hand and thank you. Then you ride off, free as a jaybird."

"Milo Talon, huh?" The older man spat. "Well, Milo, I don't know you from Adam, but you make a kind of sense."

The redhead shook his head, grinning. "He's got too much nerve to shoot, ridin' down here to talk the four of us out of a herd of cows. Mister, you got more gall than one of these here lightnin'-rod salesmen I hear about. You surely have."

"Look, boys," I said, "conversation is all right. You boys surely do carry on with the words, but meanwhile that posse gets closer. Now I want this herd pointed north before they see you, else my arguments may come to nothing."

"What'll we tell Twin?" asked the older man.

"To hell with him!" the redhead said. "He offered us fifty bucks apiece to drive these cattle to San Antone. My neck's worth more'n fifty bucks to me. Come on, boys! Let's move 'em out!"

They swung around, turning the cattle, stringing them out toward the crossing of the Llano.

Me, I mopped the sweat off my face with a bandana. As long as I had a Sackett for a mother, I was glad I had a smooth-talking Frenchman for a pa. He always told me that words were better than gunpowder, and now I could see what he meant.

We strung out the herd and pointed them north, and I rode up to take the point.

TWENTY-EIGHT

Two hours north of the Llano, we raised a dust cloud on the horizon and, shortly after, the posse topped a rise and started down the slope toward us.

The redheaded puncher pulled up short. "I just remembered! I got a dyin' grandmother somewhere's east of Beeville! I'm takin' out!"

"You run now, and they'll start shooting," I said. "Hold your horses, boys. Let me handle this!"

"Last time somebody said that he was reachin' for a hangin' rope," said the redhead. "All right, mister, you do the talkin', an' I pray to God you use the right words!"

Balch and the major were in the lead, and right behind them was Ann. Riding beside her was Roger Balch.

I rode out to meet them. "Here's your cattle, or most of them. These boys offered to help with the drive until we met you."

"Who are they?" Roger Balch demanded suspiciously. "I never saw any of them before!"

"They were just passin' through," I said glibly, "headin' for San Antone. They helped me make the gather and the drive."

"Thank you, men," Major Timberly said. "That was mighty nice of you!"

"Major, these boys were in quite a hurry, and I talked them into helping. Now if you could spare the price of a drink—" I suggested.

"Surely!" He took out a gold eagle. "Here, boys, have a couple on me. And thanks... Thanks very much!"

"Don't mind if we do," the older man said. He spat, glancing at me. "Sure is a pleasure to meet an honest man!"

"See you in San Antone!" I said cheerfully. "I'd rather see you hanging out there than here!"

They trotted their horses away, and we started the herd again.

Ann rode over, followed by Roger. "We were worried," she said, "really worried. Especially after we saw the buzzards."

"Buzzards?" My expression was innocent.

"Father found a dead man. He had been shot. It wasn't you."

"I noticed that," I commented, dryly.

"There's been some shooting in Menardville, too," she added.

"What d' you know? Is that up yonder near the Presidio? Nothing ever seems to happen where I'm riding. Looks like I missed out all along the line."

Ann glanced at me sharply, but Roger didn't notice. "That's what I told Ann," he said. "You couldn't have been involved, because your messenger said you'd talked about the shooting right after it happened."

Fuentes had ridden alongside. "Talked to an hombre at the saloon. Said he'd never seen anything like it. Like shootin' a brace of ducks, one right, one left. Picture-book shooting, he called it."

"What about Twin Baker?" Balch demanded.

"Gone. His sister said he often went to San Antonio, so that's probably where he is."

"At least we got the cattle back," Fuentes said.

"Roger said we would," Ann said proudly. "He told me not to worry. We'd get them all back, and without trouble."

"I like confidence in a man," I said.

"Father didn't want me to come," Ann admitted, "but Roger said it would be all right. He said such rustlers had little courage, and Twin Baker would probably be gone before we got there."

Seemed to me Roger was expressing himself an awful lot, and being quoted more than usual. Fuentes was noticing it, too. His eyes carried that faintly quizzical expression.

"It's the memories that count," Fuentes said. "And never stay long enough to let 'em see you just put your pants on one leg at a—"

"The hell with that," I said irritably.

*   *   *

When we rode into the yard at Stirrup-Iron, all was dark and still. One light showed from the ranch-house kitchen, and a horse spoke to us from the corral.

"S'pose there's any grub in there?" I suggested hopefully.

"We can look. Maybe that's why the light's burning," said Fuentes.

Fuentes and I turned our horses in at the corral and I dropped my bedroll and saddlebags down on the stoop.

There was a plate of cold meat on the table, some bread and butter, and a couple of thick slices of apple pie. The coffeepot was on the stove, so we got cups and saucers and sat down opposite each other in silence and gratitude.

"That hombre at the saloon," Fuentes said, "spoke to me of a man who was just sort of passing by... riding a horse with black legs."

"He should've kept his mouth shut."

"He spoke only to me," Fuentes said. "Were they waiting for you? Laredo and Sonora?"

"Twin Baker paid them to kill a rider on a Stirrup-Iron horse, no names mentioned."

"The saloon keeper said you knew one of them?"

"Played poker with him a time or two. He was no friend of mine. He and Sonora had taken money for the job. They'd spent some of it."

Fuentes pushed back from the table. "At the poker table with Laredo that time... Who won?"

"He did."

"You see? Nobody wins all the time, not with girls, guns or poker."

We walked outside under the stars, and Fuentes lit a cigar. "Nobody... Not even you."

I looked at him.

"This time it is you who can ride away. The girl will marry the other man but she will remember you, who came so gallantly from out of the distance and then rode, gallantly, into another distance."

"Are you trying to tell me something?"

"Ann Timberly. She will marry Roger Balch. Did you not see it?"

"Two big ranches, side by side. It figures."

"And you but a drifting cowhand. You did not mention your ranch, amigo?"

"I told nobody. Nor will I."

"It is the way of things. I think we should sleep now."

"Harley and Ben with the herd?" I asked.

"Of course," Fuentes replied.

"How'd you leave Joe? Still in the house?"

"Of course." Fuentes snapped his fingers. "Hah! I had forgotten. There was a note came for you. It is in my coat, hanging on my saddle, and in the morning I will get it for you."

"Get it for me now, will you, Tony?"

"Now? But of course!" He turned away and I walked to the bunkhouse and picked up my blanket roll. For a moment I stood there, feeling the night, knowing the stars. Then, very carefully, I pushed the door open with my left toe and thrust my blanket roll into the door.

A stab of flame punched a hole in the night, and the thunderous blast of a shotgun slammed against my ears. In that same instant my right hand drew, the gun came level, and I put three bullets where the fiery throat of flame had been.

Drawing back, gun in hand, I waited.

A long, slow moment of silence, then the thud of a dropped gun. Then there was a slow, ripping sound as of tearing cloth, and something heavy fell.

The night was still again.

"Amigo?" It was the voice of Fuentes, behind me.

"All right, amigo," I said.

He came forward and we stood in the darkness together, looking from the ranch house to the bunkhouse. We had blown out the kitchen light when leaving, and no new light appeared, nor any sound.

"I have some miles to go before I camp. I'll saddle the dun," I said.

"You knew he was there?" asked Fuentes.

"There was a rifle near the kitchen door with prongs on the butt-plate," I said. "That was his fatal mistake. Leaving it there. I figured he was waiting in the bunkhouse."

"That was why you sent me away to get the note?"

"It was my fight."

"*Muchas gracias*, amigo."

At the corral I saddled the dun.

"We ride together, amigo... *bueno?*" he asked.

"Why not?" I replied.

He smiled, and I could see his white teeth.

The ranch house door creaked open, and an old man called into the night.

"John?...John...Twin?"

There was no answer. And there would be no answer.

Fuentes and I rode out of the ranch yard.

When morning came, and the stage stop at Ben Ficklin's was not far away, Fuentes said, "The note, amigo?"

It was a woman's handwriting. I tore it open.

> *I enjoyed the dancing. There will be another social soon. Will you take me?*
>
> CHINA BENN

Maybe not on that day. But on another, at some time not very far off.